"*You don't want a friend,*"

Lizette accused him.

"No, I want a mature woman who knows her own needs and her own mind and isn't afraid to go after what she wants. But I'll take you instead. For now."

How could she be insulted when Chris's eyes were warm enough to set the deck on fire? Lizette leaned toward him and rested her hands on his shoulders. "You must be crazy."

"That's possible."

"Or a man who likes pain."

"Not a chance. Are you going to kiss me, woman, or are we both going to end this evening frustrated?"

She stretched and touched his mouth with hers. "Like that?"

"If I were J.J., that would be a perfect good-night kiss."

"If you were my son, you'd already be in bed by now."

"If the *E* in your name didn't stand for Elusive, *we'd* be in bed by now."

Dear Reader,

Each and every month, to satisfy your taste for substantial, memorable, emotion-packed stories of life and love, of dreams and possibilities, Silhouette brings you six extremely *Special Editions*.

This month, to mark our continually renewed commitment to bring you the very best and the brightest in contemporary romance writing, Silhouette *Special Edition* features a distinguished lineup of authors you've chosen as your favorites. Nora Roberts, Linda Howard, Tracy Sinclair, Curtiss Ann Matlock, Jo Ann Algermissen and Emilie Richards each deliver a powerful new romantic novel, along with a personal message to you, the reader.

Keep a sharp eye out for all six—you won't want to miss this dazzling constellation of romance stars. And stay with us in the months to come, because each and every month, Silhouette *Special Edition* is dedicated to becoming more special than ever.

From all the authors and editors of *Special Edition*, Warmest wishes,

Leslie Kazanjian
Senior Editor

EMILIE RICHARDS
A Classic Encounter

Silhouette Special Edition

Published by Silhouette Books New York

America's Publisher of Contemporary Romance

SILHOUETTE BOOKS
300 East 42nd St., New York, N.Y. 10017

Copyright © 1988 by Emilie Richards McGee

ISBN: 0-373-09456-6

First Silhouette Books printing May 1988

Printed in the U.S.A.

EMILIE RICHARDS

believes that opposites attract, and her marriage is vivid proof. "When we met," the author says, "the *only* thing my husband and I could agree on was that we were very much in love. Fortunately, we haven't changed our minds about that in all the years we've been together."

The couple lives in New Orleans with their four children, who span from toddler to teenager. Emilie has put her master's degree in family development to good use—raising her own brood, working for Head Start, counseling in a mental health clinic and serving in VISTA.

Though her first book was written in snatches with an infant on her lap, Emilie now writes five hours a day and "rejoices in the opportunity to create, to grow and to have such a good time."

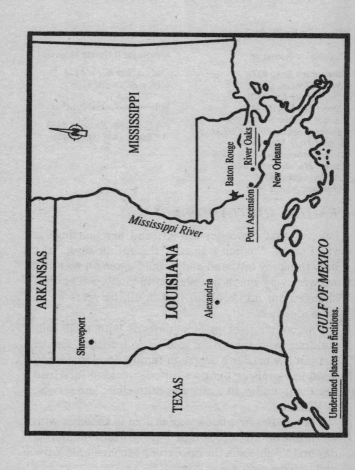

MISSISSIPPI

ARKANSAS

TEXAS

LOUISIANA

Shreveport

Alexandria

Mississippi River

Baton Rouge

River Oaks

New Orleans

Port Ascension

GULF OF MEXICO

Underlined places are fictitious.

Chapter One

Beneath the frilled net skirt of the shocking pink tutu was a pair of the hairiest legs Dr. Christopher Matthews had ever seen. But even the thick growth of curling black hair couldn't obscure the heavily muscled thighs or the taut calves tapering down to sturdy ankles and size-eleven feet encased in brand-new Adidas running shoes.

"How's it going, Tutu-man?" Chris asked, squatting to give the shoes a cursory examination. "Think we're going to have to put in orthotics?"

"Everything seems to be fine." The thoroughly masculine voice held just a note of humor. "Now if I could find shoes to match this shade of pink." He fluffed his skirt in demonstration.

Chris laughed and ran his fingers under the leather tongue of one shoe. "You might want to lace this a little tighter."

"Does this count as a house call?"

Still squatting, Chris looked up to grin at the dark-haired man. "This one's on me."

"In that case, why don't you check the other shoe? I'm not sure about the heel."

Obligingly Chris manipulated the padded heel tab of Tutu-man's right shoe. "It fits fine. If you have any problem with it, the medics will be giving out Band Aids."

"Thanks, Doc."

Chris stood and clapped him on the back. "Good luck."

Tutu-man melted into the crowd, and no one looked twice at him. This was, after all, New Orleans, and in New Orleans men in costume were as normal as corn in Kansas or traffic jams in Manhattan. It might not be the carnival season, but the Crescent City Classic, world-famous ten-kilometer footrace, was an event. And any event in the City That Care Forgot was an excuse for good-natured high jinks.

Chris wasn't in costume, but then, Chris wasn't a native New Orleanian. He was a transplanted Californian wearing the traditional casual racing uniform of white jogging shorts and a matching mesh singlet. His shoes were Nikes, once as white as his shorts, but now scuffed and dirty from miles of running through city streets. The red bandanna knotted around his forehead was there simply to keep sweat from dripping into his good-humored green eyes. But even if he wasn't in costume himself, he appreciated those who were.

In the dense crowd he spotted a man in a top hat and tails worn over electric-blue shorts. Balanced on the palm of one hand was a tray with two glasses perched on top of it. Farther away a buxom blond with the longest legs Chris had ever seen was appropriately garbed as a Playboy Bunny. The man by her side was a lecherous Lucifer.

Chris moved through the mob up and down Decatur Street, occasionally spotting someone he knew, more often just enjoying the prerace commotion. It was only April, and it was still early morning. Already, however, the pavement beneath his feet was absorbing the sun's rays. Soon the heat and the humidity would hold their own race to see which would keep the greatest number of runners from making the best times of their racing careers.

The brick shops trimmed with cast-iron balconies that lined Decatur were a festive natural barrier cordoning the race participants on the narrow street. Because of the normal stream of traffic it wasn't often that anyone in New Orleans could see the city from such a unique vantage point. Many of the twenty-five thousand plus who came to participate in the race each year did so just to stroll along and examine their city, beginning on Decatur in the French Quarter and continuing to Prytannia Street in the Garden District and beyond to Audubon Park.

Then there were others who couldn't have cared less about the stately live oaks lining the streets or the huge Greek Revival and Victorian houses that they would pass. They were there to run.

Chris was one of those. He wasn't scheduled to run in the *A* section, with the world-class runners who were there to compete for money and renown. But neither was he scheduled to join the walkers, or even those runners who planned to go the distance at a comfortable jog. He was scheduled to be in the *B* section, with the men and women who were going to run their personal best, the men and women who trained long, tough miles for months before this date just for the satisfaction of knowing they had cut a minute or two off their previous times.

"Hey, Doc!"

Chris knew he wasn't the only physician in the crowd, but his head swiveled just the same. He waved at a young man who had been in the clinic several months before with a dislocated shoulder suffered in a soccer pileup. He wasn't surprised to be seeing so many of his former patients. He was an orthopedic surgeon, a doctor of sports medicine, and although his patients came to him with a variety of injuries from a variety of sports, they generally had one thing in common. They loved using their bodies to their greatest potential, and they loved competition. Running might not be their first love, but it would be difficult for almost any of them to resist the lure of the Crescent City Classic.

Chris continued to maneuver his way along Decatur and enjoy the warmth of the sun on his bare head until he got to his own section. Section *B* had fewer runners in costume. Here, excitement permeated the air and everyone was busier. He watched the eclectic warm-up exercises with interest. Most of these runners knew what they were doing. There wouldn't be many muscles strained from neglect or ignorance in this group.

He admired the trim bodies of his competitors. Section *B* had no overweight, "I'm-a-candidate-for-a-coronary" runners. As a whole, this group looked fit and trim and serious. Almost without exception.

The exception, however, was so lovely that for a moment Chris wondered if she had been placed there among the dedicated runners as a reminder of all the wonderful things that could be achieved through perseverance and hard work. Certainly, Chris thought, if he knew this woman would be waiting for him at the finish line, he would race the wind and beat it with seconds to spare. She was all the incentive any man would need.

Incentive was all she was, however. She couldn't possibly be a serious runner. Even Tutu-man's costume was more appropriate than the knee-length, striped walking shorts and lace-collared, lavender knit shirt covering her gently curving body. He let his gaze wander down her shapely legs to end at lavender canvas shoes worn over pristine-white bobby socks. The shoes weren't designed for running; they weren't even designed for fast walking. They were designed for decoration, just like the woman wearing them.

She was truly a beauty. Her mane of long chocolate-brown curls was tied off her face with a lavender ribbon that was sure to disintegrate at the first drop of sweat. Her perfect ivory skin stretched over cheekbones any model might envy, and her lips were full and sensual, a pleasing paradox in a heart-shaped face that in every other way belonged to a traditional beauty queen.

But only a beauty queen would come to the Crescent City Classic wearing a thin gold chain around her neck, gold button earrings, two gold bangle bracelets on one wrist and a dainty gold watch on the other. She was a sensuous Miss

America and an advertisement for Fort Knox rolled into one. What she wasn't was a runner.

As Chris watched, the young woman bent to touch her toes and began to bounce up and down, her barely restrained curls rioting in protest. He winced, unable to tear his eyes away from the sight of such a lovely body in the process of being systematically destroyed. If she continued to bounce up and down like a basketball at a Globetrotters game she was going to pull every muscle she was trying to warm up. It was bad enough that she had somehow wandered into the *B* section to be trampled by thousands of zealous runners when the race began, but now she was decreasing her chances of survival by insuring that she wouldn't be fit to move when the starting cannon sounded.

Chris knew what a sports injury could mean. He'd worked with hundreds of agonized athletes to overcome their disabilities, and years before he'd suffered his own agonies of disappointment and pain. True, straining a muscle and being bumped and pummeled by runners breaking free of the crowds was nothing compared to broken bodies and shattered dreams. Still, if he could help... Chris grinned. Admit it, Doc, he admonished himself. His motives were one-fifth altruism and four-fifths interested male.

As he watched, the young woman straightened, then began to energetically bounce to one side. Chris winced again and threaded his way through the crowd in her direction. He was a physician, a healer, a servant of mankind—and womankind, too. If the Hippocratic oath didn't quite cover this situation, it was only because ancient Greece had never produced a woman as beautiful as this one.

Lizette St. Hilaire put her hands on her hips and leaned backward, bouncing as she did. She rarely warmed up before she ran. She rarely prepared in any way. Sometimes she didn't even think about it. One minute she'd be walking sedately along the dirt road that led into River Oaks' vast fields of sugarcane, contemplating the latest problems on her fifteen hundred acres. And then, the next thing she knew, she was running, her head thrown back, her hair bouncing frantically against her shoulders, her feet slapping the good earth as if to punish it for making life so difficult.

Lizette admired people whose schedules were so organized that they ran at precisely the same time every day. She couldn't even imagine what it must be like to get off work and go home to change into running gear and begin a long series of warm-up exercises that drained away the stresses of daily living. And then to be able to run as far and as fast and as freely as she wanted!

She bounced a little harder to shake the image of that much freedom out of her head. She was an adult, a mother, the owner of a historic plantation. She had been trained from childhood to do what was expected of her and to be proud of who she was and what she had. Neither the child Lizette Stanhope nor the adult Lizette St. Hilaire had ever had reason to feel sorry for herself. Now was not the time to begin.

Lizette straightened and found herself staring into the greenest eyes she had ever seen.

"I'm worried about you."

She blinked, and her hands dropped to her sides. The green eyes were set in a tanned face framed by golden hair so artfully streaked that only the sun could have done it. The face itself was all angles and strong, wide bones, except for the mouth, quirked now in a humorous grin. The mouth was wonderful, finely etched and just wide enough to accommodate the grin and the straight white teeth it exposed.

Lizette studied the man's chin before she spoke. She was a student of chins, chiefly because she had always hated the pointed one nature had cursed her with. This chin was no such curse. It was square, with just the hint of an indentation, not even enough to rate as a cleft. It was a first-class chin in a first-class face. The man was probably first-class, too.

But whether he was or wasn't really didn't matter. First-class or no class, Lizette St. Hilaire avoided men the way she avoided the giant black snakes that sunned themselves between the rows of sugarcane at River Oaks.

"Why are you worried?" she asked, stepping back a little to put his face in proper perspective. From what she could tell, his body was first-class, too. He was about six foot, a good six inches taller than she was, with shoulders that looked like they could hold up the world and a slim waist and flat stomach that probably testified to his appropriate placement in section *B*. The man was an athlete. She wished she could study his legs as she'd studied his chin. She wondered if men knew that most women were as interested in thighs and calves and ankles as they were.

"I think you may be in the wrong section."

The fact that she was in any section at all still amazed Lizette. She cocked her head at the man's words. "Think so?"

Chris nodded. He had been surprised to discover that up close the young woman was even prettier than he had originally believed. Her wealth of dark brown hair gleamed with russet highlights, and her eyes were a brown so light as to be gold—or a gold so dark as to be brown. He couldn't be sure which.

"In order to be in section *B*, you've got to be able to finish the race in around forty-five minutes," Chris began.

"That's what I've been told," Lizette agreed.

Chris tried a different tack. "Do you run much?"

"As much as I can, which is never enough."

"Have you ever run the Classic?"

Lizette's lips curved into a smile. "I've never run in a race before, period."

"Then you might want to think about going to the back. You might be more comfortable in section *E*. I'm afraid you'll be trampled up here." Chris wanted to sound concerned, but he was afraid he sounded like a pompous know-it-all instead. "Look," he tried again, "I'm a doctor, and I see people who are injured in races like this all the time. Maybe I'm just being too protective."

"Maybe." Her eyes lit with humor. "Tell me, how did you single me out as a potential tramplee?"

Chris relaxed. Obviously he hadn't offended her. He liked a woman who didn't bristle over the slightest thing. "You'll have to admit you're not dressed like everybody else."

Lizette looked down at her clothes. "It's the lavender, isn't it? Everybody else is in primary colors."

Chris laughed. "Everybody else is in running shorts and singlets or T-shirts. You look like you're planning a long day of shopping."

"But I've never been like everybody else," she said, only half-kidding.

"And those warm-ups you were doing," Chris went on. "They're guaranteed to immobilize you fast."

"Well, we can't have that, can we? Not if I'm going to make my best time."

"Do you know what your best time is?"

Lizette lifted one shoulder in a half shrug. "Not really. I guessed on the registration form."

Chris's answer was interrupted by the blare of the loud-speakers. He checked his watch. The race was about to begin. "When the cannon goes off the runners at the front move like lightning, and things heat up quickly back here," he warned.

"Is that when I get trampled?"

"You've got it."

"Then I'd better get ready to take off fast myself."

Chris realized he had done what he could. Miss America was going to have to find out for herself. He just hoped somebody behind them stopped to pick her up if she went down. "Well, I'll see you at the finish line."

"Holding a poster?" she asked, referring to the prize for the top five hundred runners of the day.

"Starting this far back? Not a chance."

"Where's your competitive spirit?" Lizette gave him a last smile, then turned to face the proper direction. She realized she was actually excited. Suddenly it mattered if she did well in the race. The Greek god physician who was so worried about her would never know her time, but now she had something to prove to herself. Running the Classic was going to be fun.

There were no fast starts. The starting cannon sounded, but was barely audible except to the runners at the front, who, by the time the sound had stopped resonating, were out of sight. Usually the Classic winner was already at Audubon Park before the walkers at the back of the crowd had even crossed the starting line.

Lizette felt the runners surge forward, and she began to jog, slowly at first, until the space around her opened a little, then faster, as she dodged bodies, looking for chances to gather speed. It wasn't until she reached the Pontalba Apartments on Jackson Square that she was officially in the race. Her eyes flickered to the digital sign flashing the time that had elapsed since the starting cannon had sounded. She made a mental note: one minute and forty-three seconds. She would subtract that amount from her finishing time and have an accurate picture of how well she had done.

Concentrating on the road ahead she began to pick up speed, but it wasn't easy. Not only did she have to politely maneuver her way around slower runners in front of her, she had to be on the lookout for the runners behind who were passing. She felt as if she were running on bubble gum, moving in slow motion when what she really wanted was to break free and make an uncontrolled dash for the finish line so many miles away.

Her time for the first mile was poor, but she had schooled herself to expect that, so by the time she saw the flashing numbers, she was resigned. Watching for potholes now instead of bodies, she increased her speed. The crowd was thinning. Those who were fleeter than she was were far ahead; those who were slower were behind her. She had found a place for herself, and as she passed a spectator group of tired old men clutching wine bottles near Julia Row, she realized that from that point on, the problem wouldn't be the other runners. It would be her own stamina and will to succeed. She wasn't tired yet, but she wasn't foolish enough to believe that she might not be by the time 6.2 miles had passed.

"You didn't get any water back there."

Lizette turned her head and saw her blond doctor-friend coming up behind her. She registered two thoughts. One was that, in motion, he was a dream come true. The second was that he was coming from behind her. She had made a better start than he had!

"Are you checking up on me?" she asked, forcing the words out between breaths.

"I was planning to lift you off the asphalt after you were flattened, but you took off like a shot." Chris was still amazed. Even with the dense crowds, he had watched the young woman weave her way through the other runners with the graceful agility of a gazelle. While he had gotten caught between a group of young teenagers, she had made a start any *B* entrant would feel proud of.

"After your warnings, I was scared not to run fast."

"How are your feet?"

"Tough as nails."

Chris grinned, matching his pace to hers. It was a good pace, fast enough to feel as if the miles were burning under the soles of his Nikes, slow enough to keep him from burning out. "They'd have to be tough to survive running in those shoes."

"The shoes are a sop to convention. At home I run barefoot."

He swallowed hard. The idea was outrageous, although there were Olympic athletes who swore they trained that way. Still, if the idea was outrageous, if, as a physician, he knew what it could do to her feet, why did it seem so provocative? His brain had flashed an instant picture of her, hair flying free, feet dainty and bare as she dashed through fields of golden California poppy and purple lupine, majestic mountain ranges behind her for contrast.

Of course this was Louisiana, not California. Not home. He tried to picture her running under towering live oaks, dodging curling strands of Spanish moss, but the image wouldn't come.

Mile two brought a smile to Lizette's lips. Her time was all she had hoped for and the scenery was improving. She watched as her protector veered off to the water station to grab a paper cup of springwater. She wasn't thirsty yet, although she was beginning to sweat out all the liquids she had consumed before the race. She suspected ten-kilometer races anywhere else in the country would be easier just because the humidity would be lower. She felt sorry for the out-of-state runners who weren't used to racing in a steam bath. They were going to be surprised at the difference it made in their times.

"You can drink it or I can throw it on you." Chris caught up to her and held out a white-and-blue paper cup.

"You're in the right profession. You have an inordinate need to take care of people." Lizette reached for the cup, and her fingers grazed his. They were long and sturdy, and she could imagine them soothing a forehead wrinkled in pain or holding the hand of a sick child. Doctors didn't really do those things anymore, though, did they? They were too busy programming computers to give diagnoses, or devising expensive, elaborate lab tests, or punching buttons on their telephones to order their latest Mercedes.

"If you don't take care of yourself," Chris warned, "you could end up in one of the twenty or so hospital beds at the end of the race. Running in this heat, especially dressed the way you are, is no laughing matter."

Dutifully she sipped the water, splashing the last drops on her face before she swerved to toss the cup on the growing pile by the side of the road.

By now they were beginning to pass yards filled with spectators. There was no excuse too flimsy to throw a party in New Orleans, and people who lived on the race route had used the opportunity to entertain friends. Lizette ran past trees decorated with crepe paper, groups of people with signs in one hand and festive go-cups of beer in the other, huge stereo speakers blaring the themes from *Chariots of Fire* and *Rocky*, and best of all, hoses aimed in the street for the runners to dash through and cool off.

She lost sight of the doctor after mile four. He had been running just ahead of her, and she had secretly enjoyed the sight of his firm buttocks flexing as his feet pounded the pavement. His body wasn't basketball-player slim nor was it weight-lifter muscle-bound. It was the body of a true athlete, firm and broad and muscular, the body of a man who could run with the Olympic torch and epitomize the Greek ideal of physical fitness. When she'd looked up after slowing down to take her turn in a roadside sprinkler, she'd realized he had disappeared, and somehow the finish line suddenly seemed very far away.

Chris realized he had finally hit his stride. His pace was comfortable and even. He felt good. "Has the winner crossed the finish line yet?" he shouted to one of New Orleans' finest standing at the junction of Napoleon and Prytannia by the aid station. At the policeman's nod, Chris grinned and waved, increasing his pace again after he'd grabbed his cup of water.

He'd pulled ahead of his curly-headed companion of a mile or so back, and now he wondered if she was still all right. She was fast, he'd have to give her that, but he suspected she was one of those runners who gave it everything they had at the beginning, incurring an oxygen debt they could never recover from until they were forced to a walk or a complete stop somewhere near the middle of the race. He ventured a quick glance behind him, but he couldn't spot her in the crowd.

It wasn't until he was assiduously passing a failing runner that he saw her. Apparently she hadn't slowed down for a drink, because she was several lengths ahead of him, running as if her life depended on it. Her shirt was soaked and plastered to her back so that he could see the straight line of her spine and the outline of her bra. Her curls were in wet, wild disarray, having long since escaped from the ribbon confining them. As he watched, she lengthened the distance between them by another three yards.

Chris put on a burst of speed. He was a runner who saved his best for last, in this case for the final mile or so of tree-shaded asphalt in Audubon Park. Now, however, it seemed more important to use that reservoir of energy to catch up with Miss America.

"I thought you were behind me," he said between pants when he'd finally made his way to her side.

Lizette was almost too winded to answer. She was still feeling good, but there was little energy or oxygen left to spare for anything except putting one foot in front of the other. "I was watching you run, then I took my eyes off you and you disappeared." As soon as she said it, she wondered what he would think. She was just glad she hadn't blurted out that her eyes had been riveted on his rear end.

Chris was encouraged. He had a feeling this wasn't a woman who flirted with every male over ten. She was entirely too classy to hang an I'm Available sign around her neck. If she'd been watching him, though, she might be interested, and that was good, because he was definitely interested himself.

"Not much farther now," he said after they made a sharp right, then a left, and the trees of Audubon Park became discernible in the distance. He hadn't meant to stay at her side after catching up to her again, but even when he felt adrenaline push him faster, she kept up. "There's another mile and a quarter to go when we reach the park, then we're home."

"I guess when we hit the park, we can really push." Lizette concentrated on holding herself back. She felt simultaneously exhausted and exhilarated. Since she'd never raced formally before, she had no idea if this fear that her body might come to a screeching halt with or without her permission was normal, but she did know that from here on out, her performance was anybody's guess. She felt like letting go and running at her top speed, but she wasn't sure that if she did there would be any speed to draw on.

"Wait till mile six, then let go." Chris gave her one quick glance, then forced himself to think about nothing except the road in front of him and the act of covering it as quickly as possible.

Lizette was doing the same thing. The park loomed in front of them, then they were on the ring road, hugging the inside curve to save distance. She counted steps, stopping her count at fifty to start again. Over and over. From the corner of her eye she could see that the doctor was still beside her. She wondered what would happen when they hit mile six and called on their last reserves of energy.

The finish line wasn't visible as they rounded the final curve to begin the straightaway. There was no time to admire stately trees or placid lagoons. Lizette called forth unexplored seeds of energy and began to run faster. The thump-thump of her own shoes was encouraging. She was still alive; she was still running. In fact, judging from the sounds she made, she was running well.

She felt an arm brush hers and saw the doctor pull ahead of her. It only made sense that he would; after all, his legs were longer, and he had obviously trained for the race. Still, the idea that he was going to beat her rankled. She no longer cared if she was running her personal best. She only cared that she was being left behind.

Where had that explosion of energy come from? She almost felt as if she were flying. Faster and faster she ran, buoyed by a runner's high she'd only read about. She wasn't tired anymore; she felt as if she could run a marathon with breath to spare. She was floating; the body surrounding the real Lizette St. Hilaire was a mere shell that no longer weighed her down. She was at the doctor's heels, then at his side again. She registered his startled expression as she pulled ahead.

Chris lengthened his stride and caught up with her. There were others racing beside them, but as far as he was concerned, she was the only runner on the track. He pulled ahead again, only to realize that directly in front of him were three runners who were moving slower than he was. He lost precious seconds as he maneuvered around them, and by the time he was back at top speed, his curly-haired running mate was beside him once more.

"We've...got to...stop..."

"Meeting like this," he finished.

The finish line loomed ahead. Adrenaline begat adrenaline begat adrenaline. Lizette had stopped counting steps. Now she chanted silently, I'm going to make it, I'm going to make it. Calling forth everything inside her, she put on one last burst of speed.

To the cheers of spectators, they finished just as the clock flashed forty-nine minutes and forty-three seconds.

There wasn't much breath for a self-congratulatory whoop of joy, but Lizette managed one anyhow. As she slowed down she felt a hand on her shoulder, and she turned, her eyes shining. "We did it!"

Chris realized he'd probably lost his good judgment somewhere on Prytannia Street when he'd watched a curly-haired beauty in flimsy little tennis shoes run her heart out. Still, he'd always believed in taking advantage of an opportunity. And if his good judgment was temporarily gone, that was an opportunity to take advantage of.

His hand tightened on the young woman's shoulder, and he pulled her to the side of the track. His other hand settled at the side of her neck and then moved up into her wet curls. Before caution could return, he bent and found her mouth with his.

Chapter Two

C ongratulations." Chris stepped back to get a better look at the young woman's face. He smiled at the surprise written clearly across it. "I'm sorry, but I promised myself if I came in under fifty minutes, I'd kiss you."

"When did you promise yourself that?" Lizette asked breathlessly. She wasn't sure if she was breathless because she'd just run 6.2 miles, or because she'd just been thoroughly kissed for the first time in more years than she wanted to count.

"About thirty seconds ago. If I'd thought of it earlier, I wouldn't have cut the time so close. We'd better start moving again. We need to cool down slowly." Chris started down the track past the finish line at a fast walk.

Lizette considered setting a meandering pace for herself and losing him in the crowd, but when he turned and shot her an infectious grin, she shrugged and went to his side.

They were halfway to the batture, the land between the levee and the Mississippi River, where the postrace celebration was to be held before Chris spoke again. "I'm Christopher Matthews, Chris to my friends."

She nodded. "Lizette St. Hilaire. Never Liz to friends or enemies."

Chris dropped one hand on Lizette's shoulder to steer her around a runner who had stopped in the middle of the track to remove a shoe. "So, what made you decide to enter the Classic, besides the fact that you knew you could do it with time to spare?"

She had entered the race because, for once, she had wanted to do something for herself. She couldn't tell him that, though. He would have to know her and know the life she led to understand what this had meant to her. She compromised on a small slice of the truth. "It was a whim. I was over at Security Sporting Goods a couple of weeks ago, and I signed up."

She didn't add that afterward she'd decided not to run, that she'd left the house this morning to do some shopping and ended up at the race instead. She didn't tell him what running the Classic was going to do to her overloaded schedule or her morale. "How about you?"

Chris didn't want to let her off that easily. "When you left your house this morning, you weren't going to run, were you?"

Lizette sighed. "Are we back to the way I'm dressed?"

He nodded.

"I don't own running shoes, running shorts or even a T-shirt more casual than this one."

"Do you always run in expensive gold jewelry?"

She rarely left the house without it. The jewelry had been given to her by Julian, and Julian's parents expected to see her wear it. When she'd parked her van to catch the shuttle bus to the race, she'd thought about storing her jewelry under her seat. New Orleans was a big city, though. She wouldn't have thought twice about leaving anything in the van in Port Ascension; being a St. Hilaire put an invisible safety net around everything she owned. But here there were no safety nets, and she felt safer wearing the jewelry.

"Good-luck charms," she said succinctly. "Now it's your turn."

"I run on a regular basis and compete when I can, but I'm not really a dedicated runner. I do it for the exercise and the fun."

"It *was* fun, wasn't it?"

Chris wished he knew why she sounded so wistful. "You're very good, Lizette. If you trained properly and started in the *A* section next year, you could be one of the top fifty women."

"I don't care if I place. I'm just glad I had the chance to run."

They crossed the railroad tracks at the levee and headed down the levee slope to the batture. The flat, green expanse had been transformed into a bright carnival of tents and tables. There were already several thousand people gathered to pick up their race T-shirts and their jambalaya and beer, rewards for covering the whole distance.

"Are you meeting anyone here?" Chris asked.

Lizette shook her head. "I was just going to pick up a shirt and go."

"Don't do that. This part's as much fun as the race. At least have some jambalaya." With me, he added silently.

The euphoria of the race was beginning to disappear. Instead Lizette felt a profound sense of peace and well-being from the long run, plus an unaccustomed current of excitement at being with Chris. It was only ten o'clock. If she stayed a little longer she could still get back to her van and do the shopping before heading back to River Oaks. Right now her son, J.J., would still be happily ensconced in front of the television set watching cartoons. Barbara, her best friend, had promised to watch him all day if necessary. Barbara would consider it a triumph if Lizette took another hour for herself.

"Jambalaya sounds good," she told Chris.

"And a beer to go with it?"

"Why not?"

"Why don't you wait for the jambalaya after you pick up your shirt? The line always moves slowly, even this early in the day. I'll get our beers and meet you there."

"Chris?"

He turned.

"You know you don't have to take care of me anymore."

"Don't I? Good. Now I can just enjoy being with you."

He watched her eyes turn a darker gold. It was the color they had been when he'd kissed her.

"I'll meet you in line." She turned, and he watched the sway of her hips as she moved through the crowd.

It was the last time he saw her that day.

Lizette listened to the van's windshield wipers slap back and forth. The sound was surprisingly like the sound of feet on asphalt. But she didn't need it to remind her of the race she had run earlier, or the race away from the celebration afterward.

Halfway through the jambalaya line she had realized how foolish she was being. Chris hadn't found her yet, and with the continuous stream of runners onto the batture, there was an excellent chance he might never find her.

Dr. Christopher Matthews. He wasn't from Louisiana. Lizette knew all the myriad accents of her home state, and Chris didn't fit anywhere. The slow drawl of Shreveport, the nasal lilt of Cajun country. He had the blond good looks of a Minnesota Swede or a California surfer, and an accent that sounded almost Midwestern.

Christopher Matthews. He had the warmest green eyes imaginable, and a smile that would melt butter. He wasn't a bad runner, either, and watching him run...well, that had been one of the high points of the race.

Chris Matthews. For all she knew he was a married man, a man with a live-in lover, a man with a steady girlfriend. He certainly wasn't a man who would go unnoticed by eligible females. At that point in her thoughts she had stopped and realized that, by all definitions of the phrase except the most important, she was an eligible female. She was a widow; the period of mourning had long since passed, and she was still young and healthy. What hadn't passed was a firm conviction that she never wanted to be married again.

Chris. If he was interested in her, he wouldn't be a man to take no for an answer. And there was no answer she could give him that was any different. She didn't want a husband; she didn't want a lover; she didn't even want another friend. Most of all, she didn't want another complication in a life filled with complications.

With only a dozen people ahead of her in line, she had turned and made her way out of the batture to Magazine Street, where she had caught the shuttle bus back to her van. Now, with the back filled with groceries, dry goods, garden tools and a new part for one of the harvesters, she pulled off the interstate to drive along curving River Road back home to River Oaks.

She had made the trip between the plantation and New Orleans so many times that she barely noticed the scenery—if scenery it could be called. With the surprise rain shower blurring the misshapen lines of chemical factories, oil refineries and sugar mills, she could concentrate on the occasional cow tethered on the levee and the patches of yellow chamomile and pink wild geranium. The rusted tin roofs of factory workers' shacks looked pleasantly rustic against the dove-gray sky, and the few swampy acres that no one had yet seen fit to drain and exploit were fecund oases, teeming with unseen life.

Then there was the sugarcane. Fields and fields of fragile green tendrils reaching for the sky. Leaves the color of money—if the grower was lucky.

Lizette found it humbling during grinding season every year to realize that she and her workers could labor almost around the clock, apply the latest technological advances plus a little harmless hoodoo and still be bested by Mother Nature and Uncle Sam. Hurricanes, freezes, sugarcane rust and smut, combined with inflation, rising production costs, increased interest rates and fluctuating fuel prices, made each year a gamble. The worst years were the ones where she realized she would have been more productive if she had stayed in bed for twelve months with the covers pulled over her head.

Everyone's cane looked good this year, and River Oaks was no exception. Lizette could only hope that nothing would change that.

She rounded a familiar curve in the road and passed the turnoff to Houmas House, a classic two-and-a-half-story Greek Revival mansion, once the crown jewel of a ten-thousand-acre plantation. Houmas House had represented some of the best that the plantation culture offered, a magnificent home, landscaped grounds, a view of the mighty Mississippi and acres of fields in cultivation. Now the home stood on twenty-five acres, a house alone. Plantation houses like it were scarcer than castles in England.

They hadn't been scarce once. Once River Road had been lined with plantation homes. Some, like River Oaks, had been more modest than Houmas House, but some, like Belle Grove and Nottoway, had been even more flamboyant. Belle Grove was gone now, but Nottoway existed, surviving partly—like Houmas House—on tourism dollars. Others existed, too, but most had fallen victim to hard times or fire or man's greed. The land along the river was valuable. That value hadn't been overlooked by the petrochemical industry.

River Oaks had survived the plundering of river land because of the courage of generations of St. Hilaires. Lizette thought of herself as the latest in a long line of St. Hilaire men and women testing their mettle against the dark forces trying to wrest the land from those who loved it.

The plot was worthy of the *Star Wars* trilogy. When the stresses of trying to run River Oaks occasionally overwhelmed her, she wondered how many more remakes of the basic story there would be before some St. Hilaire just handed the whole thing over to the evil empire and found something else to do with his life. Would it be J.J.'s generation? His children? Or some space-age St. Hilaire who tired of using the plantation to produce the world's supply of artificial sweetener?

The rain continued to beat against the windshield as she turned left off River Road and began to progress slowly toward the big house standing on a natural levee crest in the midst of a grove of oak trees. The road needed repairs, just like half the structures on the plantation, but it wasn't the potholes she was trying to avoid. Farther along this same road was the quarters, a cluster of ten tin-roofed cabins that housed River Oaks' workers. Some of the men had families, and more than once Lizette had been forced to slam on her brakes to miss a child or puppy who was racing down the road.

Apparently the rain had dampened enthusiasm, because today as Lizette pulled the van onto the green grass behind the house, no one was about, not even Shoo, the multibreed mutt who perpetually hung around the back door waiting for Marydell, the cook and housekeeper, to feed him scraps.

Lizette sat in the van and waited for the rain to slacken so she could make a dash for the house. Idly she played her favorite game. If this year's crop was a bumper one, what would she do to the house? Which renovation would come first?

Paint. The one-hundred-and-seventy-year-old structure needed paint worse than anything, except possibly a new roof. Neither was critical to the point of the building being irreparably damaged without it, but both the paint and the roof had been patched so many times that more of the patches than the original showed.

The house was French Colonial or West Indies style, two story, with the ground floor and first-story pillars built of brick, and the upper floor and pillars constructed of cypress. It consisted of six rooms, three in the front, with the main room in the middle, and three in the back, surrounded on all four sides by a ten-foot gallery—or balcony—incorporated into the line of the hip roof. As an extension of the roof, the front gallery formed an overhang that produced a front porch for the lower level. There were three doors in the front, each leading into one of the rooms, and three in the back. In addition, each room was graced with long French windows that extended from floor to ceiling. Except for the green louvered shutters, the second story was painted white.

The galleries served as hallways, because there were no interior stairwells or halls in the house, and only the wide outside stairs in the front and a smaller set in the back led to the second story. Pieces of the gallery railing were missing, which gave Lizette nightmares when J.J. and Ricky, his best friend from the quarters, played there. But she had already contracted with Ricky's father to fix it.

Her next worry after paint and a roof was the kitchen. Originally the house hadn't had an indoor kitchen. Like most of its contemporaries, River Oaks had had an outdoor kitchen, one far enough away from the house to protect it from fire and unnecessary heat on sultry summer days. In later years, after permanent protection levees had been built along the river and flooding was no longer a problem, a kitchen and dining room had been added on the first floor; most of that space, until then, had been used for nothing more than storage.

That had been in the early 1900s, and except for the addition of a new stove now and then and refrigeration as it came into vogue, nothing vital had been changed or added since. Ricky's mother, Marydell, threatened to quit on a weekly basis if something wasn't done to modernize the kitchen. Lizette couldn't blame her one bit. Cooking at River Oaks, like living there, was like waking up in a museum one morning and finding that someone had locked you in.

The rain seemed to be coming down harder. With a shrug, Lizette gave up the wait and opened her door. After jumping off the running board into a puddle, she sloshed her way into the house. Soaked, bedraggled and dead tired, she wondered, if Dr. Christopher Matthews could see her now, if his emerald-bright eyes would still be lit with interest.

Barbara Grafanier had at least one talent no one would ever dispute. She could sense a good story a mile away, and she knew how to dig for facts. Sometimes she wondered why she had decided to grow sugarcane instead of reporting for a newspaper. Now she gripped her knees with her hands and probed. "So tell me about this man!"

Lizette slipped a rose-colored cotton sweater on over her recently showered body and thought about her best friend's order. She was beginning to feel human again, and Barbara, with her usual unerring instincts, had decided this was the time to get the gossip. "What's there to say? I already told you he was just a doctor who struck up a conversation with me at the beginning of the race." Lizette turned and regarded her friend. "It was not the romance of the century," she added pointedly.

"Too bad."

"Under that tough exterior you're as mushy as a plate of grits, aren't you?"

Barbara grinned, her teeth gleaming white against her dark skin. "Caught."

"You need a man in your life. Maybe then you'd stop worrying about me."

"Somebody's got to worry about you. You don't." Barbara idly picked lint off the crocheted cotton bedspread on the mahogany tester bed where she was sitting.

"That's a full year of some poor St. Hilaire woman's life you're destroying."

"That's one of those myths about plantation life," Barbara said with a sniff. "This was probably made by one of my slave-woman ancestors who was taught to crochet by one of your slave-owning ancestors. Then your ancestor took credit for it."

Lizette laughed appreciatively. "How was J.J. today?"

"Fine, until his grandparents arrived, turned off the television set and sent him to his room to shine his shoes so he could go visiting with them."

Lizette sighed. "Marydell said he was over at her place playing with Ricky."

"He is now. When he got back I promised Sophia I'd make sure he stayed inside to take a nap. When they were out of sight I sent him down to Marydell's."

"Why did Sophia think he needed a nap?"

"To keep him away from Ricky, most likely. Or maybe he just wasn't the perfect little gentleman on their trip that they thought he should be."

Lizette regarded her friend with a troubled expression. Barbara was Lizette's own age, but her twenty-five years had taught her things that Lizette knew she herself would never learn. Lizette often wished she didn't have to listen to the gospel according to Barbara, but she also knew that if she didn't, she was going to be in the dark about a lot of things going on around her.

"What do they have against Ricky all of a sudden?" Lizette asked now. "Ricky and J.J. were friends before they could walk."

Barbara shook her head with just the faintest hint of disbelief. "Come on, Lizette. Be smart. J.J.'s in school now. Sophia and Jerome want better friends for him than some little black kid who won't ever be his social equal. They're going to wean him away from Ricky until he hardly remembers who he is."

Although the words had been said with no bitterness, Lizette knew that behind them were twenty-five years of personal frustration and disappointment. "Jerome and Sophia are old," Lizette said finally. "We aren't going to change them."

"I don't care if they change. I just don't want them changing J.J."

Lizette nodded, and she felt the weight of her life at River Oaks weighing her down, ounce added to ounce added to ounce. "So, if you didn't have to spend the day with my son, how did you spend it? Shopping? Is that a new blouse?"

"Do you like it? I thought red would be good. No one can miss me in the fields now."

"No one can miss you anyway." Lizette surveyed the red against Barbara's skin and nodded in approval. "It's a good color for you."

There were few colors that weren't good on Barbara, because, in Lizette's opinion, her friend was one of the most stunning women she'd ever seen. Barbara's hair was long and cornrowed until it divided into two braids that fell to her waist. Her hair was a glossy true black, while her skin was a rich café au lait. Her bone structure was magnificent and her face heart-shaped, much like Lizette's own, except that her chin was more blunted to proclaim the strength of character that had brought her so far.

Barbara's eyes were huge wells of ebony, even darker than her hair, and alive with intelligence and sensitivity. With her looks, drive and brains she could have modeled in Paris, acted in Hollywood or taught at Harvard. Instead she had returned to the place of her birth to become the River Oaks plantation manager. And anyone who knew the plantation system knew that that feat had been more difficult than Paris, Hollywood and Harvard combined.

When Julian St. Hilaire had died three years before, Jerome and Sophia St. Hilaire, Lizette's in-laws, had agreed to let Lizette hire Barbara. They hadn't wanted to; they still objected to her presence, her success, her accurate predictions about crops and world markets. But their prejudices against Barbara's race and sex had been overcome by their love of River Oaks, and in the end they had done what they knew they had to do for the sake of the plantation.

In her three years as manager, Barbara had begun to turn River Oaks around. In the process she and Lizette had firmed up the friendship that had begun when they were sixteen. But also in that process, Barbara had alienated Jerome and Sophia even more.

"Mom!" A six-year-old whirlwind came streaking into Lizette's room from the door off the gallery. "Ricky and me caught a bullfrog bigger'en Shoo. Can I put it in the *pigeonnier*? I'll keep good care of it, I promise. Ricky will, too."

"Not a lot of differences between pigeons and bullfrogs," Barbara reminded Lizette before she could speak. "Just big hind legs as opposed to wings. Think of it as part of the ongoing restoration."

"You're the restoration nut. Not me." But Lizette nodded in J.J.'s direction anyway. "All right, but first you have to give me a kiss. I haven't seen you all day. Remember?"

She held out her arms, and he flung himself at her, a wet, dirty bundle of little boy who smelled like a swamp in the rain and looked, according to photographs, exactly like his father had looked at the same age. Lizette pushed J.J.'s dark hair off his angular little face and wondered what his father would say if he could see him now.

"Have you had a good day?"

J.J. jumped back and looked at Lizette's sweater. "I got you dirty," he said repentantly.

"So you did. Now, how was your day?"

Relieved that he wasn't going to be scolded, J.J. launched into an excited chronicle of his hours with Ricky and, earlier, with Barbara. Conspicuously absent were any details about his trip with Sophia and Jerome.

"And did you go visiting with your grandparents?" Lizette prompted.

J.J. nodded, suddenly quiet.

"Anywhere fun?"

He shook his head.

"Well, I'm glad you and Ricky had such a good afternoon." Lizette ruffled his hair. "Better go take care of your frog."

J.J. was gone as suddenly as he had come, leaving a wake of silence behind him.

"He's a pretty great kid," Barbara said at last.

"I plan to keep him that way." Lizette walked to the French windows and stared out over the remnants of a thick stand of mulberries, crepe myrtle and magnolias.

Barbara joined her, and the two friends stood together and stared at the land surrounding them.

Chris stared at the passing parade of traffic on St. Charles Avenue. He wasn't really a city person, although he had lived the first eighteen years of his life in a North Beach apartment in San Francisco, not too far from Chinatown. He might have grown up with the whoosh of cars and the honk of horns; he might even have grown up with cable cars, cousins to the streetcar now passing his apartment. But whether the scene was vaguely familiar or not, Chris was unaccountably irritated by it.

There was something lonely about the swish of cars on a wet street. Something poignant. He hadn't expected the day to end this way. Not the rain, not the loneliness. If he hadn't already run almost seven miles, he would have put on his running shoes and jogged through the wet streets, relishing the raindrops on his heated skin. Now, however, there was nothing to do except watch the rain come down and wonder how he could have been stupid enough to lose Lizette in the crowd. Or how he could have been stupid enough to forget her last name. Or how he could have been stupid enough not to immediately get her phone number and address.

"St. Something or other," he said out loud. St. Clair? No, he didn't think that was right. St. what?

Trying to remember was no use. He'd been trying to remember all day. He just hadn't paid enough attention when she'd told him. Instead he'd been thinking about the way her lips had felt against his and the unaccustomed speed of his heart—a speed that had little to do with his run through the New Orleans streets.

He was going to have to let it go. Somehow he had lost her, and lost the chance to know her better. Somehow they had missed each other, and he had been left alone with two cups of beer and a drooping yellow dandelion that he'd spotted during his long wait behind a hundred thirsty runners.

There were other women in New Orleans. Countless other women. Women who didn't wear expensive jewelry or decorative little canvas shoes to footraces. Women whose hair was sensibly short and bodies sensibly clothed. Women whose eyes wouldn't turn the color of old gold coins if he kissed them.

There was Lizette.

Why was it only Lizette he wanted to watch the rain with?

Chris turned his back to the window and leaned against the sill, his arms folded across his chest.

"Lizette St...."

St. what?

Chapter Three

"Sorry, Doc. We struck out."

Chris gripped the telephone receiver in disappointment. "What do you mean, we struck out? She's not in the index?"

The man on the other end cleared his throat. "We had more St. Something or others than you can shake a stick at, but no Lizette St. Anything. Whoever entered her name into the computer probably put it under whatever follows St. It's a bad break for you."

Chris nodded dejectedly at the unseen speaker, but his voice was composed. "There's no other way of checking for it?"

"Not unless you remember her race number."

Chris shook his head. "I'm afraid I don't. Thanks for trying, Tony."

"If you think of anything else, I'll be glad to try again. But only because it's you," Tony added. "I wouldn't do this for anybody else."

"I know you wouldn't," Chris reassured him. "I'll call if I get another lead."

Chris hung up and sat at his office desk, staring into space. He had been so pleased when he'd thought he'd solved the problem of finding Lizette. Two weeks after the race, he'd remembered that a runner he had once treated for a bad sprain was one of the Classic organizers. Tony had given him a long lecture on confidentiality, but in the end he had agreed—just this once—to search the entry list for a Lizette St. Whatever it was.

The result was a big, fat zero.

A sharp rap on Chris's door was a welcome interruption. It wasn't going to do him any good to brood.

The door opened a crack, and the compassionate-first, efficient-second R.N. assigned to him opened the door. "There's a tennis injury in room A," she said, her eyes reflecting her concern. "A teenager. They just brought her in. Her knee locked in place, and she's pretty upset. I know your schedule's full, but can you work her in?"

"Yeah." Chris stood and stacked the papers on his desk into neat piles. "I think I'm going to have a lot of free time. More than I want," he added with a wry smile. "A lot more than I want."

Why would Christopher Matthews be the first thing she thought of when she awoke this morning? Had she been dreaming of him?

Lizette sat up and stretched, locking her hands high above her head. The movement pulled the sheer fabric of her gown over her breasts in a pleasantly sensual sweep. It only accentuated the feelings already pulsing through her body.

How strange that she had been thinking of Chris here, in the bed she and Julian had shared for the first months of their marriage. She felt a little like a child who had been caught daydreaming in church. Not that the bed was sacred.

The things that had happened in it hadn't been sacred, either—although she imagined that in a theological discussion, her priest might argue that point. Julian's lovemaking had been gentle and brief. Her role had been to be a fertile receptacle for his seed, seed that was to grow inside her to become their child, Julian's son, the heir to River Oaks.

Lizette had willingly accepted that role, just as she had willingly accepted Julian's lovemaking. Julian had been thirty to her nineteen on their wedding day, and before that he had guided her life for as long as she could remember. Lizette had always known that she was to marry Julian someday, although no one had ever come right out and said so until the moment he had proposed.

Still, she had been the obvious choice as wife to the next master of River Oaks, and she had relished the idea. She was a St. Hilaire, too, on her mother's side. The relationship was just far enough back in the family tree not to raise eyebrows and just close enough to assure the patrician blue of her bloodlines. Her father was descended from a line of planters whose ancestral home was now the site of a factory, but whose family name lived on in the small world of plantation society. She and Julian had been a perfect match.

Elizabeth St. Hilaire Stanhope St. Hilaire. "Lizette" from birth and only "Elizabeth" when Julian had been angry at her, which had been so rarely that she could remember each instance with startling clarity.

The most outstanding occasion had been the day just before their wedding when, in a fit of bridal nerves, she had asked him to postpone their marriage. She had needed more time—time to grow up, time to be sure she was doing the right thing, time to be sure she loved him. Julian, his dark eyes blazing, had given her an ultimatum. They could cancel the wedding or go ahead with it. There would be no postponement. He would wait no longer. He had told her that at thirty, he understood how quickly time could pass and how little there could be to show for when it did. Who knew how much time was left to them now?

His words had been prophetic. Months after their marriage had proceeded as planned, Julian had been diagnosed with a heart defect, a problem that had existed since birth but had never been recognized. She had been pregnant by then, and one day Julian had quietly moved out of their room. On the rare occasions when they made love in later years, she had been careful not to excite him, careful not to tire him.

There had been surgery and medication, long naps and enforced early bedtimes. Then, three years after the birth of the new River Oaks heir, Julian Jerome St. Hilaire, Julian had died in his sleep.

It hadn't been the marriage happily-ever-afters are made of; it had been more like an apprenticeship. Right from the beginning, Julian and his parents had patiently schooled Lizette in her duties to River Oaks. Jerome and Sophia had given the River Oaks deed to Julian on his wedding day, but even though they had moved into a remodeled overseer's cottage five hundred yards behind the big house, the elder St. Hilaires had never really given up emotional control of the plantation. With Julian's death, the ownership of River Oaks had passed to Lizette and J.J., and with her status as owner had come more problems than she had believed possible.

Three years as a widow, but sometimes Lizette still missed Julian. She missed his gallant smile, his handling of plantation affairs, his pride in their son.

She had known too little passion, however, to miss that. Or so she had thought until this morning. Why had she been dreaming of Chris? What had she been dreaming? Whatever it had been, the resulting pleasant ache inside her was a reminder of something she tended to forget. She was a young woman with a young woman's needs.

She would never see him again, but Dr. Christopher Matthews had taught her one thing. She was still alive. It was something to think about.

"How did the surgery go?"

Chris signed the orders he had just written on his newest patient's chart and handed it to a nurse, who disappeared down the hallway. He turned to his friend and colleague, Paul Waring, and smiled in greeting. Paul, a handsome man with skin the rich brown of mahogany and a neatly trimmed Afro, was dressed in a dark suit and high-top leather Reeboks. In Chris's opinion, Paul was the only man in the world with enough personal style to make Reeboks look like dress shoes.

"It went like I hoped it would," Chris answered. "I've got a videotape, if you'd like to see."

"I see enough bones and cartilage every day to pass, thank you," Paul answered. "Think she'll be playing tennis again?"

"In a couple of weeks, with almost full mobility."

"One of the lucky ones."

The two men started down the hall toward their offices. The Sports Medicine Center of New Orleans City Hospital was located on the third floor in a wing that had been recently renovated. The center staff was composed of Chris and Paul, who were both orthopedic surgeons, a certified athletic trainer, two licensed physical therapists and a variety of specialists who worked at the clinic as their skills were called for. A part-time psychologist and a nutritionist rounded out the team.

They passed through the large, cheerful reception area, nodding greetings to patients and staff. They continued past exercise machines and treatment tables, the cast room and examining rooms, until they reached their offices, two identical rooms directly across the wide hallway from each other.

"Do you have anything planned for the weekend?" Paul pushed his office door open before he turned back to Chris.

"Nothing. How about you?"

"I thought I might go up to Arkansas and do some canoeing. I wish we could both go."

"One of us had better be an easy phone call away," Chris agreed. "But thanks."

Paul nodded. "Well, you ought to make some plans, then. Won't do you any good to sit around all weekend."

"I'll line up something, boss." He touched a hand to his forehead in humorous salute. "I promise I will."

Chris was at his desk going through the day's mail when Paul appeared again. "Polly left this on my desk by mistake." Paul handed Chris an envelope.

Chris examined the return address. Marathon Foto. He shrugged as he opened the envelope. There in a two-inch-square proof was a photo of him at the Crescent City Classic finish line. Next to him, her head thrown back and her number plainly visible, was Lizette St. Whatever.

"I'll be damned. They took our picture."

Paul raised one eyebrow. "Extortion? Are we going to have to mortgage the center?"

Chris laughed. "Not hardly. Look." He handed the picture to Paul. "That's the woman I told you about. Now I can find out who she is."

"I forgot they did photos. The year I ran the Classic they caught me with a snarl King Kong would kill for." Paul handed the photo back to Chris. "If you catch up to her, do you want to go out for pizza Friday night?"

"I'll let you know when I'm ready to share her company. It won't be Friday."

"Well, at least I don't have to worry about how you'll spend your weekend." Paul turned toward the door. "I'll let your preacher worry about that."

"I have a feeling this is one lady who isn't going to worry anybody, except me." Chris reached for the telephone and dialed Tony's number.

An hour later he sat staring at the memo pad in front of him.

E. St. Hilaire. P.O. Box 273. Port Ascension, Louisiana. No phone number. E.? No wonder it hadn't shown up on the computer as Lizette.

"Where the hell is Port Ascension?" Chris punched a button on his telephone and waited for Polly, the receptionist, to answer. "Polly, do we have a map around here?" He listened to her answer through the crackle of their intercom. "Then do you know where Port Ascension is?" He waited again. "Can you find out for me?"

He hung up and drummed his desktop with a pencil until Polly knocked at the opened door. "It's a little town, not too far north, right on the river," she said, her eyes dancing with merriment under thick spectacles. "They grow cane up that way, and there are a lot of big factories. Is this about a woman, by any chance?''

Chris had known it wasn't smart to ask everyone in the center if they knew a Lizette St. Something, but in his quest for her phone number he had been willing to try almost anything. In his year in New Orleans he had discovered what a small town the city really was. Everybody knew everybody through somebody. Unfortunately, Lizette had been the exception.

"*The* woman," he admitted, twitching his eyebrows lecherously. "The *mystery* woman. Her name is Lizette St. Hilaire."

"St. Hilaire, huh." Polly seemed to be turning the name over in her mind. "I don't know why, but that sounds familiar. I'll ask around, if you'd like."

"Don't bother. I'm going to see if I can get her number and call. Then I can find out what I need to know."

In the end, however, the best he could do was a note to her post office box. According to the telephone information operator there were two St. Hilaires in Port Ascension. Neither of them had a listed number.

"Wait, Barbara. I'll check the post office box, then we can have lunch over at the Rainbow." Holding J.J.'s hand firmly in one of hers, Lizette touched Barbara's arm with the other. "Unless you don't want to be seen with me."

Barbara snorted. Both women were a little too young to remember a time when black people weren't served with white in Port Ascension, but neither of them was too young to remember the occasional angry look that had been aimed their way when their friendship had begun.

"I don't mind being seen with you, girl. I just don't have time for lunch. There are three big ugly men at River Oaks who'd like nothing better than to plant one female plantation manager in a row of cane. I'd better hustle on back with the truck and the herbicide."

"I know what the special is," Lizette taunted her.

"I don't care."

"Fried trout. Hush puppies." Lizette savored the next word, drawing it out slowly. "Coleslaw."

"Not nice, Lizette."

"Coleslaw like your mother used to make."

"Not nice at all."

Lizette had saved the best for last. "Pecan pie."

Barbara rolled her eyes in disgust. "Your treat?"

"I'll even deliver the herbicide myself. If they plant me in the cane, who'll sign their paychecks?"

"Let's go."

Lizette pulled J.J. along beside her as if he weren't resisting with every step. J.J. was angry that his mother had temporarily separated him from Ricky and forced him to go shopping. Her patient explanation that sneakers were hard to fit in absentia had apparently made no sense to him. She darted into the post office and unlocked her box, dropping the dozen or so letters in her purse, then rejoined J.J. and Barbara on the sidewalk.

"You know, Barbara," Lizette said at the door of the Rainbow Café, "the Rainbow has the best peppermint-stick ice cream. But I've heard that it tastes awful to rude little boys. Sort of like Mississippi mud, only worse. What do you think?"

"I think you're exploring blackmail as an art form today."

"Can I have some?" J.J. asked.

"He speaks!" Lizette squatted down to look J.J. straight in the eye. "You've been sort of a creep."

"I'm sorry. Can I have some ice cream?"

"May I have some, and yes, you may—if you eat your lunch and act like the little boy I love."

J.J. seemed to be trying to decide whether to let pride or greed rule. He stuck out his lower lip, but his pout quickly turned into a grin. "I want lots."

Lizette stood. "Lead on," she said to Barbara, sweeping her hand in front of her.

It wasn't until the pecan pie was a memory and their coffee was almost gone that Lizette thought about the mail. She pulled it out and riffled through it as J.J. finished his second bowl of ice cream. "Bills, bills, more bills, bigger bills." She tucked them away for the plantation accountant to handle. "Here's one from some place called Marathon Foto." She tore open the envelope and stared at the photograph of her with Chris.

Barbara peered over her shoulder and gave a low whistle. "You ran away from that? You need your head examined, girl."

J.J. peeked, too. "Who's that? He's got a scarf on his head like Tyrone wears over his mouth when he's burning cane."

"That's a bandanna, not a scarf," Lizette corrected, but her mind wasn't on her son. In her memory it was still April, and she was running fast and free, with Dr. Christopher Matthews beside her.

"You could call him," Barbara pointed out logically. "You know his name."

Lizette slid the photograph back into the envelope and put it in her purse. She finished going through the mail. The last letter was addressed in a sprawling, almost indecipherable script across a small envelope. The message inside was succinct. *Call me,* she read silently, while Barbara read over her shoulder. *I don't know how I lost you after the race, but I do know I wish I hadn't. Chris.* Below his signature were his phone number and home address. She folded the letter and put it with the photograph.

"And now you know his phone number," Barbara continued, as if she hadn't even paused. "You don't have any excuse not to call him."

"Who are you going to call?" J.J. asked. "The guy with the scarf?"

"Eat your ice cream," Lizette said absentmindedly. "Ricky's waiting for you at home."

"If you don't call him, I will." Barbara tapped her forehead with a fingertip. "The man's number is now permanently engraved right here."

But Lizette was lost in thought and didn't even hear her.

* * *

"I'm a surgeon, not a detective." Chris punctuated his statement by tossing a can of beer to Paul. He popped the top of another can for himself and leaned against his refrigerator to take a long drink. It was a Friday, and the two men had spent the early afternoon teaching a seminar. They had given themselves the rest of the afternoon off, and somehow the conversation had turned to Lizette.

"Seems to me you're as interested in this woman for the challenge as for the chemistry." Paul sprawled in one of the two chairs in Chris's kitchen, his six-foot-three frame covering every available inch of space in the vicinity.

"Not hardly. The only challenges I ever liked were on the ball field. I've never been the type to appreciate a cat-and-mouse chase." Chris took a long swallow before adding, "I don't appreciate this one, either."

"Then give it up. It's been what, almost two weeks since you dropped her a note? Either she's not at that address anymore and didn't get it, or she's not interested. Either way, she's out of the picture. Right?"

"Go ahead. Make it sound simple." Chris smiled ruefully.

"I've never seen you this way before. In med school you were always Mr. Cool."

"I don't know why this is eating at me. It just is," Chris admitted.

Paul was silent until his beer was almost finished. "Ever been up north of here to sugarcane country?"

Chris shook his head.

"My daddy used to go up every fall to help a farmer he knew with his harvest. The man had a little stand, way back on an inlet off a bayou up by Baton Rouge. This guy couldn't afford to grow much. He didn't have the money to buy equipment, so he'd hire people to cut it by hand. Ever cut sugarcane, Chris?"

Chris shook his head.

"A cane knife's about eighteen inches long. It looks like a machete, except it's got a hook on the end away from the cutting blade to pick up the cane and strip off the leaves. Swinging that knife was the hardest work I've ever done."

"You cut cane, too?"

Paul smiled. "From the time I was fourteen to the time I went off to school. In those days my daddy and I did just about anything we could to put food on the table."

Chris knew that Paul's family had been unable to help him through college and that he had put himself through on a basketball scholarship and hard work. Medical school and the lean, hungry years afterward had been accomplished with more scholarships—this time for his academic prowess—and government loans.

Even now Paul was still paying for the education that had changed his life so radically. He might tease about it, but he never complained. Once he had driven Chris by the housing project where he had grown up. Chris could see why Paul considered the money he owed to be a pittance compared to what the loans had given him.

"So what's it like in sugarcane country?" Chris asked.

"Maybe you ought to go see for yourself."

Chris considered his friend's advice. If he'd had Lizette's home address, he might have been tempted. But as it was, all he had was a post office box number. "I could drive up tomorrow, but what good would it do? I don't know where she lives."

"Want me to find out?"

Chris grinned. "Bet you can't."

"What's it worth to you?" Paul asked, crumpling his can and tossing it neatly into the wastebasket on the other side of the room.

"Dinner at Commander's?"

Paul shook his head. "Dinner and drinks."

"Dinner and one drink," Chris bargained.

"Dinner, one drink and dessert."

"Do I get to watch you at work?"

"Sure," Paul said magnanimously.

"Okay."

Paul stood, stretching the kinks out of his long frame. Chris followed him into the living room.

One phone call later Paul had the number for the Port Ascension post office. "Now listen carefully," he told Chris as he dialed. "You might learn something." He waited, lounging comfortably on the sofa as he did. "Is this the Port Ascension post office?" he asked.

Chris watched with interest.

Paul continued. "Yeah? Well, this is Hayes, over at the Gentilly branch in New Orleans. Yeah, I'm checking on a registered letter sent from here to a Miss Lizette St. Hilaire. We never got anything back on it, and the sender wants to know what's going on." He waited until a flood of conversation from the other end halted. "Yeah, I know this is irregular, but this guy is really tearing up the place trying to find out what happened." He covered the receiver. "What's her box number?" he mouthed to Chris.

"Two-seven-three."

Paul spoke into the receiver. "Well, this guy's not going to wait for the process, honey. I'll tell you what, the letter went to her private box number, two-seven-three. If you can give me her address we'll send another letter right out to her house." Paul held the receiver away from his ear. "Yeah, I know it's not done like that. But this guy's desperate. It's an emergency of some kind."

Chris wondered if he really were desperate. He must be, to let Paul play out this charade.

"Okay, if that's the best you can do," Paul said finally. "Thanks." He hung up.

"Well?"

"She wouldn't budge on the address."

Chris wasn't surprised, but he was disappointed. "I'll have a filet, medium rare."

"I don't recall promising you anything if I didn't get it. Besides, I found out something important," Paul said smugly.

"How important?"

"Lizette St. Hilaire picks up her mail 'most every Saturday morning, right before lunch. Miss Lucy Carroll of the Port Ascension Postal Service says you can set a clock by it."

"And?"

"And? Tomorrow, if you're serious about her, you'll be waiting at her post office box at eleven o'clock. If you decide not to go, I don't ever want to hear the lady's name again."

Chapter Four

So what was he doing lounging in a corner at the Port Ascension post office?

Chris looked at his watch: 11:02. He'd been there for half an hour. Miss Lucy Carroll herself had already asked him twice if she could help him. He imagined that the next time she felt moved to speak, it would be into a telephone receiver, and the sheriff would be on the other end.

He supposed he did look suspicious. How many big, blond men in canvas cargo pants and tropical-weight flight jackets hung out in the Port Ascension post office? Judging from the curious glances he'd received, not many.

He could have waited in his car, but it was parked across the street. The heavens had opened a little earlier and deluged Port Ascension with enough rain to make the Mojave bloom like an English country garden. Chris had come inside because he hadn't been sure he'd be able to see Lizette through his car windows. And, of course, seeing Lizette at all depended on whether she was foolish enough to go anywhere on a day like this one.

The post office door opened, and Chris lifted his eyes, expecting to come face-to-face with the Port Ascension law. Instead he straightened. "Good things come to those who wait," he said softly.

It was a motto just made for a rainy day in Port Ascension.

"Now look, J.J.," Lizette said with forced patience as the post office door slammed behind her. "I'm tired, I'm hungry and I'm losing my temper. Do you think we could talk about this after lunch?"

"Ricky's got one," J.J. said, his lower lip stretched out in a pout.

"Maybe he does, but that doesn't mean you have to have one, too. If you want a space gun that glows in the dark and shoots sparks at unsuspecting adults, you'll have to save your allowance for it. Now that's all I'm going to say on the subject." Lizette ruffled J.J.'s hair before she turned toward the wall of metal boxes secured with combination locks. "Let me get the..." Her voice trailed off as she saw Chris lounging in the corner by the row that held box number 273.

"Hello, Lizette." Chris pushed himself away from the wall.

"Chris." At lightning speed she discarded all the possible reasons why he could be there except the obvious one. "You don't give up easily, do you?"

"Not usually. Although even I get set back by certain things like not knowing names and addresses." He came to her side, but his attention was focused on J.J. "Hello, son. My name is Chris Matthews." Chris held out his hand.

J.J. drew himself up to his full forty-eight inches. "Mine is J.J.," he said, holding out his hand. "You're the guy with the scarf."

Lizette felt Chris's quick glance go right through her. "Scarf?" he asked J.J..

"Yeah. Around your head at the race with my mom."

"So you saw that picture."

"Did my mom call you? Barbara said she was supposed to."

Chris focused on Lizette's left hand, perched reassuringly on J.J.'s shoulder. Had she been wearing that narrow gold band on her fourth finger at the race? If not, why not? He found her eyes with his and saw that they were shadowed. "No, your mom didn't call me," he told J.J.. "I think she's been too busy."

"You shoulda called," J.J. berated his mother.

Without taking her eyes from Chris's, Lizette reached into her purse and pulled out her wallet. "J.J., take this and go buy the space gun over at Mack's. If I'm not here I'll meet you at the Rainbow for lunch. Can you do that by yourself?"

"Can I!"

"It's coming out of your allowance," she warned as he turned and fled.

"Thanks, Mom."

"So what kind of allowance do you and your husband give J.J.?" Chris asked with studied casualness. "Or is it a family secret?"

Lizette wondered how a two-inch photo could convey so little of the real man in front of her. It was funny, but her memories of Chris had been changed by the tiny snapshot. She had forgotten how big he really was, how blond, how golden his tan. And there was no photographic process on earth that could have duplicated the green of his eyes.

The photograph was a lie. Lies were amazing things, really. Sometimes they hurt or enraged, and sometimes they were kinder than the truth. No matter what the result, however, she was incapable of lying on purpose. Leaving after the race without telling Chris had been close to a lie. Wearing Julian's wedding ring was almost a lie. But pretending she was still a married woman was a definite lie, and she couldn't make herself go through with it, even if it would simplify things.

"My husband's dead," she said. "He died three years ago."

Chris nodded, unpleasantly surprised to learn that he could feel relief at another man's misfortune. But his relief was indisputable. "I'm sorry," he murmured, and he wasn't sure if he was apologizing for his feelings or consoling Lizette for her loss.

"So, how do you like the Port Ascension post office?" Lizette tried to smile. "Have you had a tour?"

"Miss Lucy volunteered something like that several times. I believe she was planning to tour me right through the front door if you didn't show up soon."

Lizette lowered her voice. "Never, never get on Miss Lucy's bad side. Your reputation can go like that." She snapped her fingers for emphasis.

"I'll remember."

"How long have you waited?"

Despite his intention of not making a move in Lizette's direction until he was sure she wanted him to, Chris reached up and pushed a damp curl off her cheek. He had rarely wanted to touch a woman this badly, and he had absolutely never wanted to touch one in the middle of a post office before.

"Don't you own an umbrella?" he asked, ignoring her question.

"Several. I wasn't paying attention to the weather when I left home."

"What were you paying attention to?"

Since she wasn't about to tell him that she'd been wondering if another note from him would be waiting for her in box 273, she just shook her head. "This and that."

"Is J.J. your only child?"

"Yes."

"He's quite a little guy."

"That he is."

"Are you engaged, spoken for, seriously attached or semi-involved with anyone else?"

"No. Is this a survey?" Lizette realized she was stalling.

"Something like one. Why do you still wear a wedding ring?"

"For J.J.'s grandparents."

Chris imagined her answer held a story much too involved to go into with Miss Lucy right around the corner. He would ask to hear it in the future. "The next question is the last. Why didn't you call me?"

Lizette sighed. "You'd have to understand my life to know."

"I've got all day."

"And I don't even have an hour. That's part of the problem."

"Hey, Mom!" The post office door slammed, and J.J. came running full tilt in their direction. "Look! I got it! They only had blue ones left, but now Ricky and me can tell which is which. Ricky's is red."

"Let me see." Chris squatted on the floor in front of J.J. and held out his hand for the package. "Very nice. Do you need some help getting it open?" he asked, handing it back to J.J.

"I tried in the store, but you gotta have scissors or sumpthin' to cut the cardboard. I'm gonna saw it with a knife at the Rainbow."

Lizette groaned.

Chris stood and rummaged in his pocket. "I've got something that will work better." He pulled out a leather case and handed it to J.J. "See what's inside."

"What's this?" J.J. pulled out a rectangular piece of metal about three by two inches. "It shines. I can see myself."

Lizette was intrigued, too, as much by Chris's ease with her son as with the strange object.

"It's called the ultimate pocket survival tool." Chris took it from J.J. and began flipping out various implements. "It's got a knife, scissors, magnifying lens..."

"Hey, let me see that!"

Chris obliged the little boy, first folding the knife and scissors back in. "Look at your thumb," he encouraged him.

"What else does it have?" J.J. wanted to know as he made his thumbprint larger and smaller by moving the magnifying glass back and forth.

"Let's see. A can opener, screwdriver, nail file and a ruler, there along the side. I can't keep track of all the other things it does." Chris took it back. "I'll flip out the scissors, and we can open your package."

"Won't that dull them?" Lizette asked.

"If it does, we pull out the magic sharpening stone in the middle, and J.J. here can sharpen them to perfection."

"Neat!"

Chris squatted back down and helped J.J. with the package as Lizette watched. She noticed the way he held back, letting J.J. do everything instead of doing it himself with much less effort. Most important, she noticed the way J.J. was eating up Chris's interest in him.

When had the little boy last had a man's undivided attention? Tyrone, Ricky's father, took the boys fishing sometimes, or taught them woodworking in the shop behind his house, but Tyrone was a busy man. In addition to Ricky he had three daughters and a wife who needed his time. Another of the River Oaks workers, Big Jake, was teaching J.J. about sugarcane, but his time was limited, too. J.J.'s grandfather, Jerome, believed that his own duty to his grandson was to teach him his proper place in life and his duties to River Oaks. Lizette was sure Jerome loved the little boy, but he loved the plantation and what it stood for more.

Lizette had never realized more clearly that J.J. needed a father. It was too bad she didn't need a husband.

"Look, Mom." J.J. held the gun out for Lizette to see, dropping the package on the floor as he did. Then he aimed the gun at the door and shot off a round of make-believe ammunition.

"Not in here, J.J. Miss Lucy will have a heart attack." Lizette watched as Chris picked up the package and tossed it into a nearby trash can. She compared the simple action to the lecture that J.J. would have gotten if Jerome had been there, or even if Julian had been. Like his father, Julian had been a firm believer that no child was too young to understand his responsibilities.

"I'll bet there are better places to talk than the post office," Chris said, his eyes still on J.J. but his words aimed at Lizette.

"We're going to lunch. Wanna come?" J.J. asked excitedly.

Chris swung his gaze to Lizette's. "Do I?"

The Rainbow Café, like the post office, was one of the nerve centers for the tiny town of Port Ascension. Along with the others, Mack's General Merchandise, the Fields of Cane supply store and Turk's Barber Shop, the Rainbow served as a major post for the dissemination of information. Lizette knew that if she and Chris had lunch at the Rainbow together, the gossip would reach River Oaks before she did.

But how could she say no? J.J.'s eyes were shining in anticipation, and although she hadn't made a decision, she suspected her own might be shining, too. Lizette wanted to spend at least this much time with Chris. Hadn't he been alive and well in her fantasies for the past several weeks, even though she had tried to exorcise him? Was it carved in stone that she wasn't to have male friends?

She was surprised by the rebelliousness of the last thought. What resentments were lurking deep inside her that she hadn't even known existed? And how deep was the well of her loneliness that she was going to ignore all warnings and ask Chris to join them for lunch despite the problems it might cause?

"Please come," she said at last. "J.J. and I would both like your company."

Chris hadn't known he'd been tense until he suddenly relaxed. He wasn't an aggressive man. Pursuing Lizette this way had been one of the most aggressive things he had done in a decade. In the last analysis, however, all he could do was show up at her doorstep—or in this case her post office box—and let her take it from there. He wasn't going to push himself on her—pushing wasn't his style. Still, he wondered what he would have done if she'd said no. He was glad he didn't have to find out.

"Do we have to walk far?" he asked, humor lighting his eyes.

"You have to be kidding."

"I was."

J.J. chattered the whole twenty yards to the Rainbow. He told Chris all about Port Ascension, about the school where he went, about River Oaks and Ricky. When he had finished the frantic recital, Chris's eyes looked glazed.

"A sugarcane plantation?" was all Chris could manage to ask before they stepped into the wood-frame building that housed the Rainbow Café and Turk's Barber Shop.

"Fifteen hundred acres. Half in cane, one quarter in soybeans, the rest fallow or in cover crops," Lizette told him. "I'm the resident Scarlett O'Hara. Without the hoopskirts."

Chris opened the appropriate door and let Lizette and J.J. pass in front of him. The Rainbow had been aptly named. Someone years before had obviously had a collection of nearly empty paint cans. They had emptied them on the roughly paneled walls, painting each board on one side of the room a different color. To finish the decorative scheme, someone had painted a wide, bold-enough-to-be-vulgar rainbow from one end of the room across the ceiling to the other.

Lizette watched Chris's expression. He looked stunned. "New owners bought the Rainbow about two years ago," she explained, "but when they announced that they were closing for redecoration, the whole town went crazy signing petitions. People don't like change in Port Ascension."

"I can see that."

Lizette laughed. "The new owners weren't stupid. They went ahead and left the color scheme and added these new chairs." She pointed to the multicolored vinyl-upholstered chairs at each table. "Just about everybody approved of that, I think, although I hear that a few people still won't set foot in the place because it's different."

"Is the menu the same, too?"

Lizette headed toward her favorite table, smiling at a waitress. "Hi, Becky." She seated herself before Chris could help and patted the chair at her right for J.J. "The basic menu's been the same since I've been coming here. The fat they use for deep frying is the same, too," she teased.

"That's what I smelled." Chris seated himself at her left, glad that the table was round. Lizette was wearing blue today, a deep royal blouse and a contrasting paisley-patterned skirt. Her damp hair was a riot of curls around her face and shoulders, and she was wearing only a touch of makeup. She was even lovelier than he had remembered. The drive and the wait had been worth it.

"What's the special?" Lizette handed her menu back to the waitress without opening it. "I've got this memorized," she explained to Chris.

"Creole chicken on rice, stewed okra and corn on the cob," Becky recited.

Lizette nodded. "Got any pecan pie today?"

"Peach, but I can put some ice cream on it for you."

"Sounds great. J.J., a hot dog or a hamburger?"

"Corn on the cob and peach pie with peppermint-stick ice cream," J.J. said firmly. He peeked a glance at his mother and clapped when he saw her nod her consent to Becky.

"I'll take the special." Chris handed his menu to Becky, too. "Skip the ice cream and pie."

"Where's your sweet tooth?" Lizette asked when Becky was gone.

"Firmly on hold, right along with my cholesterol."

"I knew it. A health nut. I'm surprised anything on the menu was acceptable," Lizette observed.

"I carry a secret stash of brewer's yeast and alfalfa sprouts with me everywhere I go. I'll sprinkle it over lunch when it comes," he said with a straight face.

"Really?" J.J. seemed amazed.

"Nah." Chris tweaked J.J.'s nose. "But I do watch what I eat. I want to grow up to be big and strong."

J.J. giggled. "You are grown up."

"Nah. I'm only ten. Didn't you know? I look older because I take care of myself so well."

"Nah," J.J. said in unconscious imitation of the man who was rapidly becoming his new hero.

Lizette smiled as the two males continued their exchange. She felt strange. She wasn't sure what was different until she realized that she was actually relaxed. Chris was relaxing to be with, although at the same time he set off little currents of excitement deep inside her. But he was so undemanding, so calm, so sure of who he was.

"What do you think?" Chris turned to include Lizette.

Lizette realized she had no idea where the conversation had drifted. "I'm sorry," she said with a half smile. "I was thinking about something else."

"What do you think about what J.J. ordered? Will he grown up to be as big as me if he just eats corn on the cob and peach pie with ice cream?"

"If we throw in a few Moon Pies and Mr. Goodbars to round it out."

J.J. laughed appreciatively when Chris groaned.

The corn on the cob was served in a puddle of butter. The Creole chicken had ingredients that only the cook could have identified—and then only under protest. The rice was white, overcooked and sticky. The okra was a sickly, slimy green and cold to boot.

"This looks great," Lizette complimented Becky. "And I'm starved."

Chris pushed the food around his plate, making little mountains and valleys with streams of butter oozing through them. J.J. had gotten up to scour the café for more salt for his corn. "Let's see what I know about you," he said as Lizette began to eat. "You're beautiful, intelligent, and you can run like the wind. You have a wonderful son, a sugarcane plantation and a bad habit of not answering your mail. You are also definitely not a gourmet."

Her sensual mouth curved into a grin. "And you are persistent, bossy, funny and a complication in an already complicated life. You're also a picky eater. That's a bad example to set for J.J. He already adores you."

"If I eat this stuff, *that* will be a bad example."

Lizette turned as the door slammed and luncheon customers began to take their seats. "In the next fifteen minutes this place will be full," she observed. "In less time than that everyone at River Oaks will know I'm sitting at the Rainbow Café having lunch with a stranger.''

"And?"

Lizette shrugged. "Doesn't that amaze you? Terrify you? Humble you? Something?"

Chris smiled as J.J. returned. "Do you want it to scare me away?"

There was little she could say with J.J. sitting next to her beaming at Chris. She changed the subject. "Where are you from? How'd you end up in Louisiana?"

"I'm from California, San Francisco originally. I came here last year when the Sports Medicine Center of City Hospital had a temporary vacancy. The director is a friend of mine from medical school."

"Temporary?" Lizette wondered why she felt so disappointed. She wasn't planning to see Chris after today, anyway.

"Yeah. One of their doctors is on maternity leave. I'm going back to California after Christmas to open my own practice."

"Who does a sports medicine doctor treat?"

"Anyone who walks in his front door." Chris grinned. "You know, runners who refuse to wear proper shoes and end up with sprains or shin splints, runners who eat high cholesterol junk food and end up with heart conditions, runners who refuse to drink during races and end up with heatstroke, runners who..."

"Enough!" Lizette smiled back at him. "Who besides runners?"

"Actually, I'm most interested in kids. When I settle down I'd like to work with secondary school athletes. I'm more enthusiastic about prevention than intervention."

"Kids like me?" J.J. asked, his mouth full of peach pie.

"Kids like you. Do you like sports, J.J.?"

"Like what?"

"Baseball? Soccer? Football?"

"I like catching frogs."

"That was next on my list," Chris said seriously.

"And I like climbing trees," J.J. added, "but I can only climb them if my grandmother doesn't see me. Ricky and me go out by his house and climb the tree in Big Jake's yard. Big Jake says we're not s'posed to, but he always walks away when we do."

"Big Jake can hardly read or write, but his diplomatic skills would make a foreign service veteran envious," Lizette told Chris.

"Big Jake's gonna show me how to drive a tractor," J.J. said proudly.

"I'd like to meet Big Jake." Chris turned to Lizette. "Am I going to?"

She knew what he was asking. Were they going to see each other again? Meet each other's friends? Spend time together? Was she going to invite him to River Oaks and into her life?

J.J. saved her from answering. "Can you come home and meet him now? I'm all done with my lunch."

"Not today," Chris said, sounding properly disappointed. "I've got to get back to New Orleans pretty soon." He signaled Becky and gave her a credit card.

"You live in New Orleans?" J.J. was obviously dismayed. "I thought you lived here!"

"New Orleans isn't so far away. Maybe you and your mother can come and visit me soon. I can show you where I work."

"Tomorrow?" J.J. asked.

Both Chris and J.J. turned to Lizette for the answer. She wondered if Chris understood how hard he was making this for her. Not only was he a powerful temptation on his own, now he had enlisted the support of her son.

"Not tomorrow," she said finally.

"Wednesday afternoon we close early." Chris's gaze held hers. "Maybe you and J.J. can come and tour the facility. Then I'll take you out to dinner afterward."

Lizette shook her head. "I'm busy Wednesday." She didn't know why she felt it was necessary to explain, but she did anyway. "I promised the plantation manager and accountant that I'd go over the books with them. It's going to take all day, probably even well into the evening."

"Friday?"

"J.J. and I always have dinner with my parents on Fridays."

"I see." Chris signed the receipt Becky had given him with a flourish and pocketed his card. He was glad that the interruption gave him time to swallow his disappointment.

Lizette ended the silence by pushing her chair away from the table. She stood and waited until Chris was standing, too, before she held out her hand. "Thank you for lunch."

He heard the next sentence, although she didn't say it out loud. *I was glad to see you again, Chris, but this has to be the last time.* He reached for her hand and held it a moment, wondering why he felt such a loss. Nothing had really happened between them, yet he felt bereft. Her hand was soft in the firm grasp of his, and he ran his thumb along the back of it before he dropped it. Then he extended his hand to take J.J.'s. He was surprised at how small and fragile it felt.

"It's been nice to meet you, son," he said quietly. The last word, nothing more than a nickname coaches loved to use with team members, suddenly took on new meaning for him. He had thought little of having children of his own and equally little of having a wife. This was a strange time to be thinking of either. Lizette had made it clear that she didn't want him in her life. Why then had a simple nickname given him such an acute ache in his gut?

"When we come and see you, would you like me to bring one of my frogs?" J.J. asked, having missed the vibrations between his mother and Chris. "I've got a c'llection."

"You do that." Chris dropped the little boy's hand.

"Goodbye, Chris." Lizette was surprised at how vulnerable she sounded.

"Take care, Lizette." Chris turned toward the door.

"Chris?" J.J. called.

He turned back to the table. "Yeah, son?"

"I won't have any dessert tonight."

Chris grinned. "Thataboy."

"I'll even eat salad." J.J. made a face.

"You do that." Chris's gaze flicked to Lizette's face. She looked exactly like he felt: empty, and surprised as hell about it.

Somehow his hope was renewed.

Chapter Five

Lizette stood in front of the big house, her shoulders heaving as she tried to catch her breath. The air she gulped was for all practical purposes steam, a hot, wet vapor that condensed the instant it reached her lungs. Only a lifetime of breathing air just like it kept her from giving up. There was oxygen there, if she could just keep breathing long enough to find it.

"Have a good run?" Barbara sat under the overhang of the front gallery, fanning herself with a newspaper.

"If anyone ever wants a good research project," Lizette gasped, "they ought to see if people in Louisiana are developing gills."

"Smart people in Louisiana don't go running out in the noonday sun," Barbara said placidly. "Mad dogs and Englishmen..." She stopped. "And lady plantation owners," she added a moment later.

"I didn't plan to run." Lizette sat down beside her friend and grabbed a section of the newspaper for herself.

"You never plan to. If you don't plan to run, then you don't think of yourself as a runner. And if you don't think of yourself as a runner, you don't have to admit that you need some sort of interest outside this throwback to the nineteenth century." Barbara gestured to the house and grounds surrounding them.

"Plantation manager and psychologist, too. What a bargain you are." Lizette thumped Barbara on the top of the head with her newspaper before she resumed fanning herself.

"I had to go into Port A this morning to pick up a new section of chain for one of the harvesters. I picked up the mail."

"Anything good?" Lizette asked with just the right touch of nonchalance.

"The usual."

"Hardly worth stopping for." Lizette reminded herself to continue waving her newspaper.

"Oh, there was one thing."

"Was there?"

Barbara smiled lazily. "A package from New Orleans."

"Probably the shirts I ordered from D.H. Holmes for J.J."

"I believe the package was from a Christopher Matthews."

Lizette stopped trying to appear nonchalant, but she was silent.

"If you don't want it, of course, you can send it back without opening it. You've got his address. And telephone number," Barbara added with a significant pause.

"What did you do with the package?"

"It's in on your desk in the office."

Lizette tried to imagine what Chris might have sent her. She had thought about him more in the week since they had said goodbye than she wanted to admit, even to herself. She couldn't forget the look on his face when she had made it clear that she wasn't going to pursue a relationship with him. Neither could she forget the deep sense of loss she had felt when he'd walked into the rain outside the Rainbow Café.

She didn't share any of those feelings with Barbara, who would be good for another lecture if she did. Instead she pretended nonchalance once more. "I've sat around long enough. I'm going to take a shower." Lizette stood up and stepped off the porch—directly into the path of her in-laws.

Jerome and Sophia St. Hilaire were perfect examples of people who, as they aged, grew to resemble each other. Jerome had never been a tall man, and now, at seventy, his stoop subtracted inches from his height. Sophia had never been a short woman, and her still-proud stance made her just as tall as her husband. Both had thick silver hair and olive-tinted complexions. The subtle machinations of time had blurred the dissimilar shapes of their faces and strengthened the similarities of their hawklike noses and thin lips.

If there had ever been differences between them on their view of the world, those had been blurred by time, too. On any issue Jerome could speak for Sophia, Sophia for Jerome.

Now Sophia obviously spoke for both of them. Disapprovingly. "You're soaking wet, Lizette. What have you been doing?"

"I went for a run along the road and the levee."

"Whatever for?"

Lizette reminded herself that Jerome and Sophia did have her best interests at heart, even though they sometimes expressed their concern in peculiar ways. And they were J.J.'s grandparents.

"I run for the fun of it," she said, trying to smile with real warmth. "Besides, if I didn't, I'd get fat on all that good food Marydell cooks."

"Better fat than dead from heatstroke," Jerome said sharply.

"That's certainly true," Lizette said diplomatically as she heard the scrape of Barbara's chair on the porch behind her.

"Good afternoon, Jerome, Sophia." Barbara came to stand by Lizette's side. "Hot for May, isn't it?"

Sophia nodded in Barbara's direction. "Too hot."

"Barbara, I noticed some of the boys out in the fields changing the way the plots are laid out. What's that all about?" Jerome asked. "Nobody told me anything about it."

Lizette jumped in to take the blame, wincing internally at Jerome's unfortunate use of the word *boy* for grown men. "That's my fault, Jerome. I forgot to mention it to you."

"Those plots have been the same size for as long as I can remember," Jerome went on, warming to his favorite subject. "Barbara, your daddy thought they were just right the way they were, and he was as good a cane farmer as they come."

"He sure was," Barbara said politely. "But Daddy didn't have multiple-row equipment to work with. If the rows are longer and the plots wider we can use our equipment more efficiently and minimize the number of turns on the headlands to get back into the row."

"I wish you'd discussed it with me first."

"I discussed it with Lizette." Barbara looked at her watch. "Big Jake ought to have that harvester repaired by now. I think I'd better go down to the tractor shed and see how he's doing."

Lizette watched as Barbara deserted her, although she knew that really wasn't a fair way to think about it. She and Barbara both knew that if Barbara stayed, she and Jerome would end up in an argument. Jerome still saw Barbara as the little gap-toothed, pigtailed charmer who had followed her father, Jim, all over River Oaks, asking questions and learning all he had to teach her about growing sugarcane.

Jim Grafanier, his father and his father before him had been River Oaks' overseers. The generations before them had been less lucky. They had been River Oaks' slaves. If the St. Hilaires were tied by blood to the land, the Grafaniers were tied to it by sweat and tears.

Jerome St. Hilaire was a man who increasingly lived in the past. At some point in his adulthood he had stopped adjusting to change. He and Sophia longed for a simpler time when lines were firmly drawn and roles easily maintained.

Jerome had been forced to accept Barbara as plantation manager, not only because Lizette had asked, but because River Oaks' survival had depended on it. Still, no one could force him to like it, or even to make the best of it. Never overtly rude to Barbara—because Jerome was a gentleman, and a gentleman was never overtly rude to anyone— Jerome nevertheless made his thoughts and feelings clear. Barbara was hired help, nothing more. He resented Lizette's personal relationship with her; he resented J.J.'s association with her; and he resented the fact that River Oaks was changing under her leadership—even if it was changing for the better.

"She presumes too much," Jerome said when Barbara was no longer in hearing distance.

"All she's required to do is talk to me before she makes any changes," Lizette reminded him gently. "I told you, I'm the one who forgot to mention it to you."

"We're going to go up to Baton Rouge this afternoon and visit the Hilldahls," Sophia said, brusquely changing the subject. "We'd like to take J.J. when he gets home from school."

"I'm sorry. He's spending the night with a friend in his class." Lizette tried to sound as sincerely apologetic as she could, but she knew there were few things in life that J.J. hated more than visiting Jerome and Sophia's friends in Baton Rouge. Even baths and trips to the doctor were looked on more favorably. She was glad she had arranged the overnighter.

"What friend?"

"Billy MacCleary."

"I don't know any MacClearys," Sophia said, frowning.

"They're new in Port Ascension. He's a foreman over at the mill."

"How well do you know them?"

"I've talked to Mrs. MacCleary several times on the phone, and Billy's visited us, so I met his father when he came to pick him up. They seem like a nice family."

"It's so hard to tell," Sophia worried out loud. "And J.J.'s such a sensitive little boy."

Lizette's private opinion was that J.J. was about as sensitive as a rock, at least in the ways Sophia meant. But she nodded understandingly. J.J. was all the St. Hilaires had left of Julian. If they were overprotective or overly rigid with him, it was because he meant so much to them. "He'll be fine," she reassured Sophia.

"Aren't you having dinner with your parents tonight?" Jerome asked.

The question thrust Christopher Matthews back into Lizette's mind. It had been ridiculously easy to call her mother and cancel their weekly Friday-night dinner when J.J. had received the invitation to Billy's. It would have been equally as easy to cancel it to spend the afternoon and evening with Chris.

She wondered what was in the package sitting on her desk.

"Lizette?"

She realized she'd been daydreaming. "I'm sorry. What?"

"Aren't you having dinner with Mary and Stephen tonight?" Jerome repeated.

Were they still only at that point in the conversation? Lizette wondered if somehow the afternoon had gotten stuck in slow motion. "No, I have some work I need to do," she lied.

"You work much too hard," Sophia said sternly. "Don't neglect Mary and Stephen. They worry about you."

Lizette squelched a strong urge to curtsy. She was only good for five minutes with her in-laws. Her patience ran out quickly after that. "I know they do. Will you excuse me? I was just on my way to take a shower."

"Yes, dear. You go ahead."

With a wave to them both, Lizette climbed the wide front stairway and disappeared into the house. The cool water of the shower helped her put the conversation with Jerome and Sophia in perspective. Nevertheless, she had to admit she was finding it increasingly difficult to respond lovingly to their complaints and demands, especially when J.J. was the subject. Lizette wanted J.J.'s childhood to be as normal as possible; she did not want him to be a little prince, cosseted, protected and sealed off from the real world. River Oaks was not the real world, although it was the only world Jerome and Sophia had ever known. There were days when Lizette knew that she had trouble putting things in the proper perspective herself.

Out of the shower, she dried off and put on a pale green skirt and knit shirt. She had work to do in her office, didn't she? Wasn't that why she was crossing through J.J.'s room and into the third bedroom she used as her office? Wasn't that why she was going straight to her desk?

Chris's package lay there. It was nothing more than a large, padded envelope with her name and address scrawled across it in typical doctor's script. She held it to her chest for a moment like a well-loved teddy bear.

Chris. It hadn't even been a full week since she had seen him, but she missed him already. Could you miss someone you hardly knew? Or was it the relationship they could have had that she missed? She was sure she had done the right thing by refusing his invitations, so why had she had to fight herself all week not to pick up the telephone and call him?

Almost reluctantly, Lizette lifted a letter opener and slit the top of the envelope. The reluctance wasn't from worrying what the envelope contained; it was the knowledge that once it was opened she wouldn't be able to open it again. She felt as if she was severing the final link to Christopher Matthews. He wasn't a man who would continue to butt his head against a stone wall. This was the last time she would hear from him.

Inside, wrapped in tissue paper, were running shorts and a matching mesh singlet. The shorts were brightly striped, and the singlet was white, with the solid fabric of the stripes repeated along the front for the sake of modesty. Pinned to the singlet was a race number.

"The Great Riverboat Race," Lizette read out loud. The race's date was the next evening. Frowning, Lizette felt inside the envelope for more information. There was no note from Chris, but there was a flyer about the race. It began at seven in the New Orleans central business district and ended at a wharf on the Mississippi, where runners would board a riverboat and spend the rest of the evening cruising the river to the tunes of a local jazz ensemble.

Apparently she had been entered in the race.

There wasn't enough paper in her office to list all the reasons why she shouldn't go. There wasn't enough time in the day to list them if there had been enough paper.

In the end, though, after Lizette had mentally reviewed the best reasons to throw out the number and send back the shorts and singlet, she had only one thing left to worry about.

She was going to have to find the time to buy some running shoes before tomorrow night.

Chris surveyed the crowd as he pushed against the brick wall of a storefront. With his knees slightly bent, one behind the other, he stretched slowly to warm himself up for the 5K race that would begin in ten minutes. He had already gotten his T-shirt and tied it around his waist. For the sake of the people around him, he would change into it at the race's end before boarding the riverboat.

Lizette was nowhere to be seen, but then, he had expected that. Next week sometime he would probably get a polite thank-you note for the running outfit accompanied by the outfit itself, or at least a strongly worded statement that he wasn't to send her anything else. It would be their final communication. But at least no one could say he hadn't given the whole thing his best shot.

Lizette had become an obsession, and obsessions weren't healthy. Chris knew from personal experience just how dangerous they could be. And since he'd had to learn the hard way, the lesson had carried over into all aspects of his life, personal and professional.

In medical school, while other students had vied for the best residencies, Chris had sat back and waited. He had wanted good training, not the most prestigious, and his attitude toward people had been similar. He never made contacts; he made friends. Through the years he had gained a reputation as a laid-back, comfortable, totally genuine guy who could be counted on not to be pushy.

So why had he been so pushy with Lizette? He scanned the crowd once more, craning his neck awkwardly. She was nowhere in sight.

"Hi there. Is it healthy to throw your neck around that way?" Lizette put her palms on the wall next to Chris and began to imitate his stretching motions.

Chris turned his head in the other direction. For a laid-back guy his reaction to Lizette was certainly out of character. He wanted to grab her and cover her face with kisses in welcome. With difficulty he restrained himself. "Don't you look wonderful."

"A friend sent me this. Do you like it?" She stopped pushing and held the singlet out to show it off.

"Someone has good taste."

"He certainly does." Lizette lifted her foot to show off her new shoes. They were white sneakers in the general style of running shoes, but even Lizette knew they were more decorative than functional. "What do you think about these?"

Chris grinned. "The best Port Ascension has to offer?"

She nodded. "It was either this or bright turquoise hightops. I didn't think turquoise would go with the shorts."

He grinned again. In fact, he was beginning to think he might not be able to stop grinning. "I'm going to kidnap you and take you shoe shopping someday soon."

"Thank you for the outfit and the invitation, Chris," Lizette said, sobering.

"I didn't think you'd come."

"Neither did I."

Chris put one foot against the wall and bent his head to touch his knee. Lizette followed his example.

They exercised in silence together until the race organizers began to encourage the crowd to line up. Compared to the Crescent City Classic, this race was small, populated by runners who raced on a regular basis for the exercise and fun. There were many such races throughout the spring. The beginning of June would signal the end of the largest number of them, and fall and cooler weather would see a resurgence in their number.

"Where do you want to start?" Chris asked, reaching for Lizette's hand.

She liked the way her hand felt in his. He had threaded her fingers through his instead of encasing them in his hand as some men would have done. She decided it was a symbol of partnership and sharing. Then she decided any woman who read symbolism into a man's most casual gesture had been alone too long.

They started about a dozen rows back from the leaders. Chris ran slowly in place, while Lizette retied her shoe. "Did you get a chance to warm up before you found me?" he asked, enjoying the sight of her bottom waving in the air in the striped running shorts.

"Weren't we warming up just now?" She straightened just in time to realize where Chris's eyes had been.

"We were stretching."

"What's the difference?"

"You should run a slow mile before you start the race."

"If I did everything right it would take the fun out of running."

"With no warm-ups and brand-new shoes to give you blisters, you don't have to worry about that," Chris assured her with a smile. "I'm not worried, though. I've seen you run. Remember?"

"Yes, I remember." Lizette's gaze locked with his, and for a moment she let herself enjoy the small intimacy as she had enjoyed holding his hand.

The starting gun sounded. In a matter of seconds they were both running. Lizette expected Chris to disappear ahead of her. She had outmaneuvered him at the Classic several times, and her excellent endurance had helped her keep up then, but there was no real doubt who was the faster in a shorter race. When she realized that he was pacing himself to stay with her, she touched his arm.

"You go ahead. I don't do well when it's this hot."

"Nobody does." They were making excellent time, but there would be no awards for him if he stayed with her.

Chris didn't care. His days of pushing himself to excel were over. Now he just enjoyed participating. And tonight he was enjoying Lizette.

They had run a mile and were halfway through the second before she spoke again. "I didn't tell J.J. I was coming. He would have wanted to come, too."

"You could have brought him. They had a one-mile fun run before you got here. We could have entered and run with him."

Lizette measured the tone of his voice. He sounded genuine. "You're all he's talked about since he met you."

"I liked him, too."

Lizette didn't add that she hadn't wanted to bring J.J. tonight. Tonight was for her. She felt like Cinderella escaping from the drudgery and routine of her days to spend one glorious night at the castle. Maybe she had been selfish, but sharing this with J.J., sharing Chris with J.J., had been out of the question. J.J. was spending the night with his grandparents instead.

They threw paper cups of water at each other at the beginning of the third mile, earning stares from other more serious runners. Lizette couldn't tell whether it was water or sweat dripping into her eyes during the final part of the run; she was only grateful the race was almost over. Instinctively she had set a pace faster than her normal to compensate Chris for running beside her. When the finish line appeared in the distance, she gave a weak cheer.

"Twenty-two minutes and thirty-one seconds." Chris slowed considerably until he was finally walking. Beside him, Lizette did the same.

When she had enough breath to speak again, Lizette grabbed Chris's arm to stop him. "What's your usual time?"

"A little better than that."

She changed her question, hoping for a more exact answer. "What's your best time?"

"Just a little short of sixteen."

She gave an appreciative whistle. "I really did slow you down."

"That was a couple of years ago when it was worth it to me to run like that. I trained hard for two months before that race, just to see if I could do it. Once I knew I could, I didn't bother again."

"Not very competitive, are you?"

"You don't know the half of it." Chris stripped off the bandanna that had held his hair off his forehead and used it to wipe his face. "Did you park nearby?"

"Not too far away."

"It can get pretty chilly out on the water. Did you bring anything to change into before the cruise?"

She took a deep breath before she delivered the bad news. "I don't think I'm going on the cruise."

Even as she said the words, Lizette wondered why they sounded so ambivalent. She knew she wasn't going on the cruise. She had made that decision on the drive to New Orleans. Sunday mornings were traditionally spent with Lizette's parents, Mary and Stephen Stanhope, and the St. Hilaires. She and J.J. rose early to join all four of his grandparents for morning mass, then they came back to River Oaks or went into Port Ascension to the Stanhopes' house for Sunday-morning brunch. Sometimes other River Road families joined them, or entertained them instead. Tomorrow she was doing the honors herself, and she would have to be up at dawn to be sure everything was ready.

"Why not?" Chris asked, careful to keep the disappointment out of his voice.

"I've got company coming for brunch tomorrow. In-laws and parents," she added quickly. "I don't want to get back too late tonight or it'll be hard to get everything finished when I get up in the morning."

"You'll survive on less than eight hours of sleep," Chris said gently. "What's the real reason, Lizette? Don't we know each other well enough by now to be honest?"

"That is the real reason."

He shook his head. "I don't think so. But I guess it's unfair to ask you for explanations you don't want to give."

"When I picked up my shirt at the registration tables before the race they said that the boat is going to be docked for a while before it sails. I'd like to come on board and have a drink before I head back," Lizette offered as a compromise.

Chris knew he and Lizette were making progress in their relationship, but he also knew that if he blinked he might miss it. For a moment he wondered if Lizette was worth this frustration.

"Look, I know I'm not making this very easy. I'll understand if you want me to just disappear." Lizette raised her eyes to his and steeled herself for his answer.

For a change Chris had the chance to do the rejecting, but no matter the problems, he didn't want to say a permanent goodbye. "If I wanted you to disappear, I would have let you. Any number of times."

"My life is complicated." Lizette wasn't sure if she was explaining or warning.

"Life generally is. When it gets so complicated you're not getting what you need from it, though, it's time to make a change."

"You make it sound so easy."

"It's never easy. Just worthwhile." Chris took her arm, sliding his hand down to thread his fingers through hers. "Someday I'll tell you how I know. In the meantime, I'd love to have you to myself on the boat for a while, but I don't want you walking to your car afterward without me."

Lizette hadn't thought about it, but it was getting dark. The streetlights were already on. She was disappointed; she wasn't ready to say good-night to Chris. They had hardly had a chance to talk. Nevertheless, she knew he was right. She pointed down a side street. "I'm about three blocks that way."

They walked in silence until they reached Lizette's van. At the door she turned to Chris to apologize, but as if he had sensed her intention, he shook his head. "Don't." He touched her lips with a finger. "I'm glad we had a chance to run together again."

Suddenly she understood her own ambivalently worded statement about the cruise. No matter what he said, how many times could she turn Christopher Matthews down without turning him away for good? Her life was complicated; that wasn't going to change overnight, if it ever did at all. Was she going to ask Chris to wait for one of those rare moments when she had no one else's expectations to fulfill?

When had she begun to believe everyone else was more important than she was? Worse yet, had she ever believed otherwise?

Before she could worry about it any more, she spoke. "I've changed my mind." She lifted her head a little in defiance of all the worried voices inside her. "If you'll wait while I change into my T-shirt, I'd like to go on the cruise with you."

How come? Are you sure? What changed your mind? Chris swallowed the questions fighting to escape. Instead he smiled as casually as he could. "Do you have anything warmer than those shorts?"

"I'll check and see. Amazing things get left in this van."

"I'm a block over. I'll come back and get you when I'm finished changing." He turned, but Lizette's fingers on his arm stopped him.

"Chris, I don't mean to be so difficult. I'm not playing games with you. Really."

"If I thought you were, I wouldn't have worked so hard to see you again."

Lizette rose on tiptoe and kissed his cheek. He tasted like salt and smelled like good honest sweat. She decided the combination was irresistible. "I hope I'm worth all the trouble," she said, moving away from him again.

"I have a feeling that may be the only thing I'm going to be sure of for a while." Chris stepped forward and gave her a brief surprise hug before he disappeared down the street at a fast jog.

Chapter Six

She had smelled sweeter and been better groomed at other times in her life, but when Chris returned, Lizette was presentable. She wore the gold Great Riverboat Race T-shirt she had stowed in the van before the race and a pair of faded blue jeans she always stored under a seat in case of an impromptu fishing trip with J.J. She had managed to clean up sufficiently with the aid of the moistened towelettes she kept for emergencies.

Chris looked wonderful, not at all like a man who had just completed a three-mile race. He was wearing baggy khaki pants that nipped in at his trim waist and a matching khaki jacket over his racing shirt.

"Are you really going to need this?" Lizette fingered the material of Chris's jacket. "I'm already regretting that I changed into long pants. It's hot."

"It won't be hot on the water. You should know that. Didn't J.J. say that you live on the river?"

"On the river, not in the middle of it."

Chris put his arm around her waist, and they began walking toward the wharf where they were to board. He smiled when he felt Lizette's hand slide around to rest lightly on his hip. "Tell me about River Oaks," he said, hoping he wasn't treading on forbidden territory, with his arm *or* his words. "What's it like owning a sugarcane plantation?"

"It's either a delight or a complete frustration, depending on the weather and the government." Lizette rested her head against Chris's shoulder and tried to remember if she and Julian had ever walked this way. With a stab of guilt she realized she couldn't.

"I gather it keeps you busy."

"It's a constant drain, but it's my life."

"Do you run it yourself?"

Lizette laughed. "If I managed River Oaks, it would belong to an oil company by now. When my husband died I knew as much about sugarcane as any young lady in cane country knows, and believe me, that's not enough to run a plantation."

"So some nice Simon Legree type runs it for you?"

"I imagine Barbara would get a good laugh out of that."

"Barbara?"

She explained. After all, Barbara knew everything about Chris. "Barbara Grafanier. She's my manager, and Simon Legree she's not. She's young and gorgeous, and she carries a two-way radio, not a whip."

"So at least one young lady from cane country knew something about growing cane," Chris said in approval.

"Barbara grew up at River Oaks, and she graduated from LSU in agriculture. She was the obvious person to take over the place when Julian died. Actually, she was the obvious person to take it over before Julian died, but no one was ever willing to say so."

"Male pride?"

"I suppose."

"I'd like to meet Barbara."

"I'm surprised you haven't."

Chris cocked his head. "What's that supposed to mean?"

"She's badgered me senseless ever since she found out about you. I expected her to call you at some point to deliver a lecture."

"A lecture?"

"Oh, something like . . ." She deepened her voice to imitate the rich timbre of Barbara's. "Dr. Matthews, I know Lizette's a first-class yo-yo, but if you'll just hang in there, she does have redeeming qualities."

"Such as?"

"Beats me."

"Was that you or Barbara talking?"

"Beats me," Lizette said with a laugh, turning her face up to his.

Chris was surprised at Lizette's transformation. Not only would he never have believed she owned jeans as tight or as faded as the ones she was wearing, he would never have believed she could be so relaxed. It seemed that once she had made the decision to enjoy herself for the whole evening, she was going about it with joyful determination.

They reached the wharf and showed their race numbers to board the riverboat. It was a white paddle-wheel steamer, one of the half dozen or so used for pleasure cruises up and down the Mississippi. Inside, the ballroom was crowded with race participants drinking free beer and soft drinks.

"Are you hungry?" Chris took Lizette's arm to steer her through the crowd.

"A little."

They each ordered a bowl of red beans and rice and took it out to the upper deck to eat it. Several whistle blasts later they were gliding slowly through the water with the lights of the city on either side of them.

Lizette moved to the railing to watch, and Chris followed her. "This is quite a river," she told him. "Too thick to drink, too thin to plow. Somebody said that once. I don't know who, but he caught the essence of it."

"I've found that you don't insult the Mississippi to a native." Chris leaned his back against the railing and watched Lizette gazing at the water.

"There's hardly any such thing as a native. The Mississippi goes through so many states and so many other rivers feed into it. In fact, it drains all the plains between the Appalachians and the Rockies. So in a way everyone east of the Rockies could claim the river." She turned her back to the water and leaned against the railing to finish her red beans. "When I was a little girl somebody told me that man was descended from some creepy little animal who crawled out of the sea. I went down to the river—I guess I wasn't old enough to know the difference between the river and the sea—and spent days watching to see if anything crawled out of it."

"Did it?" Chris watched the breeze bounce Lizette's curls against her cheeks.

"No. But finally I remembered something I'd learned from the nuns at school. Man was supposed to be created from mud. I decided then that maybe everybody was right, because the river sure had enough mud in it to create just about anything, creepy little animals and man, too."

Chris laughed. "Did you ever share that theological perspective with anyone?"

"Nope. Never did. Even as a kid I knew when to keep my mouth shut."

Chris took Lizette's empty bowl and dumped it in a nearby trash can along with his own. When he returned, she was watching the water again. He stood close beside her. "Have you always lived on the river?"

"Not on it, but near it."

"And you grew up in Port Ascension?"

"My great-great-great-uncle on my father's side founded Port Ascension when it was nothing more than a landing for flatboats from Kentucky. The 'Kaintucks' used to drift down the river to New Orleans, sell whatever goods they had to offer, break up their boats and sell them as lumber, then go back overland to Kentucky. My relative must have gotten tired of drifting, because he decided to settle in on the side of the river and offer some of those things the 'Kaintucks' needed by that point in their trip, namely whiskey, women and song."

"How disreputable, Miss St. Hilaire," Chris teased.

"My parents rarely admit we're related to him," Lizette said, lowering her voice. She turned and winked. "But frankly, he's my favorite ancestor. The others were disgustingly proper."

"So your Louisiana roots go back a ways."

"Did you notice a big brick house on the edge of town, with enough pillars to make you think you were on a movie set?"

"Can't say I did," Chris reflected. "It was raining so hard I didn't see much of anything."

"Well, that's the old Stanhope homestead. It used to be on a plantation east of River Oaks, but when some forward-looking Stanhope sold the land for a bundle of money, they moved the house. It's not really old enough to be of real historical interest, or well designed enough to be of architectural value, but my parents adore it anyway because it's big." She dragged out the last word.

"And you don't?"

Lizette faced him, surprised to realize as she did that they were only inches apart. "I used to pretend I lived in one of the little houses in town where the kids ran around in each other's yards and built clubhouses and waded in mud puddles."

Chris's hands settled at her waist. "And you didn't do any of those things?"

"I was more the doll-and-tea-party type." She slid her hands up Chris's arms to his shoulders. "What kind of kid were you?"

"The kind whose face was always dirty."

"No wonder you and J.J. got along so well."

"I seem to get along with his mother, too."

"Yes." Lizette was surprised at how natural it felt to stand this way. She didn't come from a family that touched easily, and during her marriage there had been little affection displayed openly. With Chris, however, this casual intimacy felt completely right.

"Are you cold yet?"

"No, but I can see I might be later," she admitted.

Chris stripped off his jacket and held it out to her.

"No, I couldn't," she protested.

"Either you wear it or I'll pull you inside it while I'm wearing it."

"Wouldn't we look funny." She slipped on the jacket, pushing the sleeves up her arm, only to watch the cuffs slip back over her hands once more. Chris grasped the cuffs and pulled her close. Then he rolled them up until her hands were visible.

"Now, where were we?" he asked, his hands at her waist again.

Lizette rested her palms on his shoulders once more. "Here, I think."

"And I was just about to kiss you." Chris spread his fingers wide and pulled her closer.

Lizette shut her eyes and waited.

"Is this a private party, or can anybody come?"

Chris turned at the sound of the familiar voice, his hands still at Lizette's waist. Paul stepped out of the shadows, a plastic cup of beer in each hand. "I thought that about now you two might appreciate something to top off the red beans. The chef makes them hot on this boat."

"What are you doing here?" Chris grinned good-naturedly at his friend, reluctantly moving away from Lizette to take a cup. Lizette took an extra second to muster up a welcoming smile.

"They called me at the last minute to see if I'd be medic for the race. Didn't you see me on the sidelines?"

"You think I was looking for you?" Chris toasted his friend before sipping the beer.

"I yelled when the two of you passed, but you seemed to be thinking about something else. Then I saw you downstairs, but I couldn't get to you through the crowd."

"Lizette St. Hilaire, meet Paul Waring." Chris watched as the two took stock of each other. "Paul, Lizette," he finished.

"I'm glad to know you," Paul said, apparently approving of Chris's choice. "I'm glad Chris finally caught up with you."

"Me too. Do you and Chris work together?"

"Paul's my boss," Chris told her.

"Can you keep him in line?" Lizette asked Paul.

"When he's not trying to chase down mystery ladies."

"You know, I never did ask how you found me," Lizette said, turning back to Chris. "Just how did you?"

"Perseverance," Chris said with a smile. "By the way, what's the E stand for in E. St. Hilaire?"

"Elusive," Lizette said with a toss of her head.

"Chris tells me you live up in Ascension Parish." Paul settled against the rail.

"Do you know Port Ascension?" Lizette asked. "Most New Orleanians don't go past the Orleans Parish line if they can help it."

"I can't say I've done more than drive by on my way somewhere else."

Lizette let her eyes drift to Paul's hands. Like Chris's they were long-fingered and broad. Best of all, there was no wedding ring in sight. She let her eyes drift slowly back to Paul's face. Her smile grew lazy and well satisfied. "I think you should do more than drive through. Port Ascension is definitely worth a stop."

"The grease at the local café should have a historical marker posted over it," Chris said, tongue in cheek.

"You missed all the sights that day because of the rain," Lizette reminded him.

"I saw Miss Lucy Carroll. Actually, Miss Lucy ought to have a historical marker posted over *her*."

"I can tell I've missed something special," Paul said with a mock-serious nod.

Lizette liked Paul and, better yet, she knew someone else who might like him, too. There was just one thing she needed to know. "Then there's no question about it. I think you and Chris should come visit. Bring your family. If you have one," Lizette probed.

Chris was surprised at the turn of the conversation. He had schooled himself to take his relationship with Lizette one step at a time. Now she was three steps ahead of him.

He hadn't expected an invitation to her home so soon. He wondered what was behind it.

Paul answered before Chris could say anything. "I don't have a family." His smile mirrored Lizette's. "Is the woman you're trying to match me up with pretty?"

Lizette's smile blossomed further at Paul's good instincts. "Very."

"And her daddy won't come after me with a gun?"

"Barbara might come after you with a gun if you don't treat her right. She can take care of herself."

"Barbara." Paul said the name approvingly. "I just might come."

"So that's what you're up to," Chris said. "A matchmaker in our midst."

Lizette had issued the casual invitation as a way to find out about Paul, but she had become more excited about the idea as they talked. When had she last invited friends to River Oaks? Friends, not people she had obligations to? Barbara would be amazed, but then, it was about time that Barbara was paid back for all the good advice she'd been giving Lizette in the past weeks. She pushed down the thought that she was just giving herself an excuse to see Chris again. She wasn't quite ready to deal with that. It was safer just to concentrate on introducing Paul and Barbara.

Lizette did a mental search of her calendar for the next week. "Would you happen to be free next Sunday?" she asked both men. "For dinner?"

They finalized plans to the strains of the jazz band that had begun the evening's entertainment in the ballroom.

"I'm going to go down and watch," Paul said when all the arrangements had been made.

"What about you, Lizette?" Chris asked when Paul had gone.

"I'd like to dance." Shyly she held out her arms in invitation. "Here? Or downstairs?"

Chris wanted to dance in the shadows, somewhere private, where he could hold her close and kiss her the way he had wanted to all night. But no matter what his state of ardor, he wasn't unaware of the fact that the music was only drifting upstairs in brief snatches. If Lizette was serious about dancing, it would have to be in the ballroom.

He stepped into her arms and pulled her close for a moment, anyway. She nestled against him, and they swayed to the music. Chris rubbed her back in slow circles and wondered how she could feel so good.

Lizette shut her eyes and imagined, just for that moment, that the evening was never going to end.

By the time they got downstairs the mood of the music had changed from dreamy blues to cheerful Dixieland. They danced on the crowded dance floor, then chatted with people Chris knew when they tired. It was only when he saw that the boat was heading back to the wharf that Chris separated Lizette from the crowd and led her upstairs again.

"I thought you'd like to watch us dock," he said.

Lizette touched his hair. "Did you?" She brushed blond tendrils off his forehead and followed the curve of his hairline down to his ear. She traced the edges of it down to the line of his jaw, stopping at the shallow indentation in his chin. "This has been a wonderful evening," she said huskily. "I'm not going to forget it for a long time."

Chris heard the message behind her words. She was making memories. He wondered if they were the kind you take out and cherish on a cold winter night, or the kind you share out loud during an intimate evening with a loved one. He wanted her memories to be the second kind, and he wanted to be that loved one.

At what point in their brief relationship had he fallen so hard? And why had he fallen for such a difficult lady?

Chris's hands crept up Lizette's neck, and he dug his fingers into the wealth of her moonlight-dappled curls. His thumbs caressed the soft skin under her chin, and he bent toward her, stopping just inches from her lips. "I'm not going to let you forget this evening," he told her solemnly. "I'm not going to let you go."

"You're invited to my house next weekend," she reminded him.

"Invite me into your life." Chris brushed her lips briefly with his. "You don't need to make excuses to yourself for spending time with me. Matchmaking with Barbara and Paul is fine, but do it because it's fun, not because you have to have a reason to be with me.''

''Am I that obvious?'' Lizette shut her eyes and leaned toward him as he brushed another brief kiss across her lips.

''How old are you, Lizette?''

''Twenty-five.''

''That's too old not to reach for what you want.'' Chris leaned back and waited.

Lizette opened her eyes and looked at him. ''And how do you know that you're what I want?''

''How do you now I'm not until you give us a try?''

''I don't want a man in my life. I'm not going to get married again. Not ever.''

He caressed her hair as he spoke. ''Was it that bad?''

She ignored the question. ''And I don't want a lover, Chris. I don't have time for one.''

''How much time does a lover take?''

Her lips turned up in a smile despite herself. ''As long as he needs,'' she said finally.

Chris laughed softly. ''How about a friend?''

''I can always use another friend.''

''Then we'll be friends.''

''I'd like that.''

''The kind of friends who aren't shy about showing their affection.'' He moved no closer, but his eyes kindled, and Lizette saw their warmth in the dim light from the cloud-covered moon.

''You don't want a friend,'' she accused him.

''No, I want a mature woman who knows her own needs and her own mind and isn't afraid to go after what she wants. But I'll take you instead. For now.''

How could she be insulted when his eyes were warm enough to set the deck on fire? Lizette leaned toward him and rested her hands on his shoulders. ''You must be crazy.''

''That's possible.''

''Or a real optimist.''

''Could be.''

''Or a man who likes pain.''

"Not a chance. Are you going to kiss me, woman, or are we both going to end this evening frustrated?"

She stretched up and touched his mouth with hers. "Like that?"

"If I was J.J., that would be a perfect good-night kiss."

"If you were J.J., you'd already be in bed by now."

"If the E in your name didn't stand for Elusive, *we'd* be in bed by now."

Lizette wondered if he was disappointed in her. But he didn't look like a man who was disappointed. In fact, she had rarely seen such approval in anyone's eyes. "Why did you work so hard to get me here, Chris? I disappeared after the Classic, I didn't answer your letter, I made it clear after I saw you last Saturday that I didn't want a relationship."

"Because we're going to be magic together."

"How can you know?"

"How can you not know?" He pulled her head slowly toward his.

She met him halfway.

It was all he needed. Chris made a strangled sound deep in his throat and slipped his arms around her to hold her tightly against him.

Despite Chris's warning, Lizette hadn't expected to feel this bombardment of sensation. The kiss was different than their kiss at the finish line. It was a soul-meshing intimacy that took everything she was and rearranged it until she was no longer the person she had been.

The deck rolled under her feet as the riverboat slid against the wharf, but it was nothing compared to the sensation of her life slipping out of control. There was no control left anywhere, only a glorious lack of control and a desire to see if it would take her somewhere she had never been.

Lizette opened her mouth for the invasion of Chris's tongue and pulled him closer still. She had forgotten a woman could feel this way against a man. Then she wondered if she had ever really known.

It didn't matter. She knew now. He was warmth and strength and sweet, sweet hunger, and his body and mouth were teaching her things she hadn't known she needed to learn.

Finally Chris stepped away. The riverboat whistle tooted two proud blasts and was silent. Other couples emerged from the shadows to prepare to disembark. He touched her lips with his finger. "One kiss, Lizette. That was just one kiss."

She heard the unspoken coda. *Think what we would be like in bed together.*

She couldn't think about it. She could hardly comprehend the possibility. Neither could she comprehend that in her years as a married woman nothing like this had happened to her. She had thought that at least in the early months with Julian she had understood arousal. Now she realized that she had understood nothing.

Think about what we would be like in bed together.

"It was just one kiss," she said, not quite meeting Chris's eyes. "Let's not read anything into it."

His smile told her that he couldn't be fooled. "Come on," he said. "I'll walk you back to your car."

She straightened her spine. "One kiss, Chris."

"Whatever you say," he said with a pleased laugh. "But we both know differently."

Chapter Seven

Mama." Lizette leaned over to kiss her mother's cheek. "I'm glad you could come. And Daddy." She kissed the air beside her father's ear as he went through the same polite ritual with her.

"We missed you at church, Lizette." Mary Stanhope extended her hand to J.J., who stood beside his mother, dressed in his Sunday best. "Shake hands, dear."

J.J. grasped her hand politely. "Good morning, Grandma Stanhope."

"Yes, I'm sorry we didn't make it this morning," Lizette told her mother.

"I understand you were out late last night."

Lizette didn't question where that piece of information had come from. She had noticed a bedroom light on in the St. Hilaires' house when she had driven in at midnight after the riverboat cruise. The light had gone off shortly afterward.

"I got in at midnight," she admitted. She admitted nothing else, although she knew her mother and father were waiting.

"Isn't that a bit late to be out roaming? What if your van had broken down?" her father asked after a long pause.

"It didn't." Lizette realized they were still standing on the gallery. She ushered her parents into the front parlor. "I thought we could have drinks up here before we go downstairs for brunch. Marydell made bacon-and-cheese canapés that will melt in your mouth."

"Ricky and me helped!" J.J. said proudly.

"Ricky and I," Mary corrected him.

"You weren't even there." J.J. giggled.

Mary smiled fondly at her grandson. Of his four grandparents, Mary was the only one likely to spoil him. "And did you wash your hands first?"

"Marydell made me."

"Marydell is a treasure. I always told Sophia I was going to hire Marydell away from her someday. And look, now she works for you," she told Lizette.

Lizette had heard the story many times before, but she still smiled. "If I don't get a new kitchen installed downstairs, I'm afraid Marydell might come and ask you for work."

"I'll be waiting."

"Grandmother and Grandfather St. Hilaire are here," J.J. told his mother.

Lizette went out to the gallery to greet her in-laws. As always, she wondered how they felt as visitors to the home that had been theirs for so many years. Actually, she would have liked nothing better than to trade houses with them. The remodeled overseer's house was comfortable and modern, with rambling roses blooming against the fence that surrounded it, and an arbor of wisteria and jasmine in the side yard.

But when she had suggested the trade after Julian's death, the St. Hilaires had insisted she remain in the big house. It belonged to Lizette and J.J. by right of inheritance, and the St. Hilaires were convinced they should live in it. Sometimes Lizette suspected that no matter how they professed to love the history and ambience of the big house, the St. Hilaires were happier in the comparatively modest overseer's home.

"Jerome, Sophia." Lizette shook hands with her in-laws. "You're just in time for Marydell's canapés."

"I even found something a little stronger than orange juice tucked away in a cabinet," Stephen Stanhope called to Jerome. "You just have to know where to look."

Lizette waited for her mother-in-law to follow her husband inside, but Sophia didn't move. "J.J. was worried about you last night," she said without any preliminaries.

"Why would he be worried?"

"He's not used to you leaving him alone that way."

"I didn't leave him alone," Lizette reminded her gently. "I left him with you and Jerome."

"But you weren't here. He's used to having you nearby when he stays overnight with us."

"J.J.'s a big boy, and he has to learn to be away from me." Lizette knew Sophia was using J.J.'s supposed unhappiness to express her own feelings about Lizette's date. J.J. had never been a child who clung. He was the first one on the school bus in the morning and the last one off in the afternoon. It was J.J. who had begged to be allowed to spend Friday night with Billy MacCleary and J.J. who had to be dragged back from Ricky's to eat meals at the big house.

"We expected you to come back earlier. It worried J.J.," Sophia insisted.

"Then I'm glad you were there to reassure him."

Lizette turned toward the door, but Sophia stopped her. "Perhaps it might not be a good idea for you to be gone again for a while."

Lizette was surprised that her parents and in-laws had pulled out all the stops so early in the game. Although no one had said anything, she knew that her lunch at the Rainbow with Chris was common knowledge. Now they suspected, and rightly so, that she had been with him last night. She had expected them to be worried. Chris, after all, was an unknown to them. She had not expected them to try to induce guilt quite so soon.

"I'm not going anywhere next weekend," Lizette reassured her mother-in-law. She saw the satisfaction in Sophia's eyes. "I'm having friends here, though," she continued. "For a barbecue. I think it's too hot for a sit-down supper, don't you?"

Sophia's satisfaction disappeared, replaced quickly by concern. "Anyone we know?"

"Well, you know Barbara, of course, and she'll be here. But you haven't met Chris or Paul yet. I hope you'll come over next Sunday night to welcome them."

Lizette watched Sophia process the new information. Idly she wondered if she would be like Sophia someday. Sophia had made River Oaks her whole life. Now her world was so narrow, so circumscribed, that anything outside it was a threat. Lizette's mounting irritation dissolved into pity, and then into fear. She didn't want to be like her mother-in-law. She wasn't that way already, was she? Was her reluctance to become involved with Chris just another form of Sophia's narrow-mindedness?

"Jerome and I will be here to meet your friends," Sophia said stiffly.

"I'm glad." Lizette put her hand on the older woman's arm. "You'll like them." If you give them a chance, she added silently. But even as she said the words to herself, she knew Sophia had already made up her mind.

Twilight was Lizette's favorite time of day at River Oaks. The shadows cast by the century-old live oaks blended into a unifying whole as the sun melted into the horizon. Crickets began their chirping, mosquitoes their humming, and the constant rush of cars along River Road was replaced by the occasional echoing cry of a screech owl.

At twilight, Lizette could imagine the gracious life that had once prevailed along the river—gracious, at least, for those in positions of wealth and influence. She could understand why the St. Hilaire family had hung on to River

Oaks so tenaciously through years of poverty and near-financial collapse.

There were still glimpses here of a time that was gone now, a time overly romanticized in novels, but a time when life was slower and small pleasures were woven into a rich canvas of days and months and years. Lizette knew that Barbara understood those feelings, too, not because her ancestors had led a life Barbara envied, but because the rhythms of the land called to her in ways the rhythms of city life never would.

At twilight Lizette often walked down to Barbara's just to share news of the day. Tonight, after spending most of the day with the Stanhopes and St. Hilaires, she needed Barbara's company more than usual.

"How was brunch?" Barbara sat in a rocking chair on the front porch of the little cabin that she used as combination living quarters and plantation office.

"Grits and grillades," Lizette recited, leaning against a porch pillar. "Oyster patties, watercress salad, ice-cream sundaes with crushed pralines."

"I wasn't asking for a menu."

"Well, let's see. What did we do for entertainment? My father told stories about Port Ascension politics, and Jerome told us about the time the Union army shelled River Oaks and missed every one of the windows."

"And Jerome told the story like he had been there," Barbara guessed.

"Julian could tell the story that way, too." Lizette tried to suppress a laugh. "I wonder if J.J. will be able to do the same thing. Heavens, do you suppose it's in the bloodlines?"

"What did they say about your date last night?" Barbara asked, getting right to the point. "That's what I want to know, and you know it."

"What My Family Thought of My Date Last Night, a thrilling drama by Lizette St. Hilaire," Lizette recited.

"River Oaks has gone straight to your head, girl. You're getting as crazy as everybody else who's ever lived in that house."

"Do you suppose the house is haunted?" Lizette's eyes grew round in pretend horror. "Do you think there's some evil River Oaks ghost who works his way into our souls?"

"That would explain a lot," Barbara said dryly. "The people who've lived there act like something besides good sense is working on them. Now, what did your family think?"

"What would you guess the family thought?" Lizette asked, sobering a little. She wasn't sure where her light-heartedness had come from. A large portion of it was left from last night, but she thought that some of it might have come from the way she had handled her parents and in-laws. She rarely stood up to them, because it was rarely important enough to bother. But asserting herself this time had left her feeling good.

"I'd guess they tried to make you feel guilty," Barbara said bluntly.

"You win the jackpot."

"Are you going to see him again?"

"My, my, aren't we nosy?"

"You look like you swallowed something alive and it's tickling your insides." Barbara stood and motioned her inside.

"I'm going to see Chris next weekend." Lizette sat down on Barbara's bed. While Barbara lit kerosene lamps to decorate the walls with flickering shadows, Lizette examined Barbara's latest additions to her own small re-creation of history.

Barbara's cabin itself was much like the other cabins in the quarters, where all the River Oaks workers lived who didn't have homes off the plantation grounds. The other cabins were grouped in rows along the main road leading from the riverfront past the big house. Beyond them was a dirt path leading to the ruins of the old plantation sugar-house, and just beyond that was Barbara's cabin.

The cabin had been built before the Civil War, and it was the only one still standing at River Oaks that had once been used by slaves. Barbara had done the renovations on it herself with the help of several of the men who lived in the quarters. The cabin was thirty feet square and divided into two large rooms, side by side, with a door leading into each room from the long front porch. Inside there was a central chimney with two flues, because the cabin had originally housed separate families, and they had done their cooking at the fireplaces. In more recent years, before the cabin had been abandoned, a primitive kitchen had been built along the back.

Barbara hadn't changed the basic structure except to replace pieces of the cypress board-and-batten siding. She had modernized the kitchen and added a tiny bathroom in one corner. The rusty tin roof had been replaced by one of cypress shingles, like those the cabin had probably possessed originally, and the outdoor privy had been reroofed, too.

Inside, the cabin walls had been insulated and covered with the natural weathered gray of old cypress salvaged from a demolished shed. Barbara had decorated the cabin with primitive pieces she had found in shops nearby. A bright patchwork quilt topped a polished brass bed, but next to it was a chest made from roughly hewn boards that had once belonged in a cabin much like this one at a nearby plantation. The walls were covered with paintings by an old Louisiana woman who had not forgotten what it was like when cotton and cane were still harvested by hand. One wall had a framed handbill advertising in French for a runaway slave.

Mixed in with the antique pieces were thoroughly modern touches. A stereo sat beside the chest; an air-conditioning unit perched in one window.

"I haven't seen this picture before." Lizette pointed to a painting of a river crowded with steamboats.

"It's new. So you're going out with the doctor again next weekend." Barbara's voice was silky and satisfied.

"No. That's not quite it."

"You said you were going to see him again next weekend."

"I am. You are, too. Chris and his friend." Lizette dragged the last word out as long as she could.

"What friend?" Barbara asked. Silky and satisfied had become suspicious.

"His doctor friend, Paul Waring. His *unmarried* doctor friend, Paul Waring."

"Let me guess. His *black* unmarried doctor friend, Paul Waring?" Barbara frowned at Lizette's nod. "You've taken up matchmaking these days?"

Lizette nodded again, unperturbed. "Do you know Paul?"

"Contrary to popular belief, all black people do not know each other. It's not like belonging to a fraternity."

Lizette burst into laughter. "I asked because you guessed he was black."

Barbara rolled her eyes. "Would I think he was some other color? Do I have a brain in my head?"

"He's Chris's boss. He's gorgeous."

"And you invited him here?" Barbara stopped to consider the ramifications of Lizette's invitation. "Do Jerome and Sophia know?"

"They do."

"And I'll bet they were thrilled to pieces."

"Do you care? I have to care, but you don't," Lizette reminded her.

"I only care for your sake." Barbara bent to pick a thread off the rag rug in front of the fireplace. When she straightened, she turned and faced her friend. "Living here is doing strange things to both our heads, Lizette. We have to worry about things that no one should even have to think about. Do you wonder sometimes if it's worth it?"

Lizette wasn't surprised at Barbara's question. "Lately I've been wondering every day," she said at last. "Maybe that's why I'm doing something different for a change."

"Being part of history and making something better out of my life than what was handed to me always seemed important...." Barbara stopped and shook her head. "But I just don't know anymore. Sometimes I think that ghost you were talking about has gotten to me, too."

"I know Lizette's gorgeous, but you're sure she has a sense of humor?" Paul looked down at his white linen slacks.

Chris laughed, his eyes flicking over his friend before he turned them back to the winding road in front of him. "She has a sense of humor. Besides, what else do you wear to supper at the old plantation house?"

"How about a suit and a tie?"

"You are wearing a suit and a tie," Chris pointed out. "A white suit and tie. So am I."

"And white shoes and white socks, and when I get out of the car I'm supposed to wear a white panama."

"And you'll feel right at home when they serve us drinks out on the old front porch."

"We look like the Bobbsey Twins in a *Saturday Night Fever* remake."

"I just wanted Lizette and Barbara to know we'd gotten in the spirit of the whole thing." Chris laughed at the disgusted sounds coming from his friend's throat. "Besides, the suits will be great icebreakers."

"Icebreakers? Like the time you wore a gorilla costume when you made rounds in the pediatrics ward?"

"I was a hit," Chris reminded him.

"You were until the head nurse called security."

"I can guarantee that Lizette won't call security."

"And Barbara?"

"I'm sure Barbara will be polite."

"I've always gone for polite women," Paul said with sarcasm. "That's always the first thing I ask. Excuse me, miss. Are you polite?"

"Are you sure we're on the right road?" Chris asked as they passed another giant industrial complex. "I was expecting something a little more scenic."

"This is twentieth-century Louisiana. The plantations are holdouts from another era."

River Road meandered along the levee-obscured river for another mile. Just at the point where Chris decided to find a place to pull over and consult a map, Paul pointed out the landmark Lizette had told them to watch for. "It's three-eighths of a mile after the ruins of that house."

"Get your panama." At the appropriate spot Chris slowed and turned right onto a blacktop road marked with a simple wooden sign. "River Oaks," he read out loud. "Damn, Paul. Look at this place." Chris parked his Honda Accord under a towering oak tree next to Lizette's van and cut off the engine.

"All it needs is a Smithsonian sign on the front lawn." Paul made no move to open his car door.

Chris knew he was viewing his competition. The jubilation that had been building at the thought of seeing Lizette again was gone. Had he wondered why she was so reluctant to begin a relationship with him? She had told him over and over again that she had no time to give him. Looking at River Oaks, he finally understood what she had meant. Lizette could pour her whole life into the plantation, twenty-four hours a day, seven days a week for the next sixty years, and it would only be a minute portion of what River Oaks needed.

"It needs a For Sale sign," he said grimly.

"You don't just call your local realtor and list a plantation. You don't sell history." Paul opened his door and swung his long legs to the side to stretch before standing.

Chris did the same, but he slammed his door in frustration. "Ever compete with history?"

Paul looked up and saw Lizette standing on the front gallery. Beside her was one of the most beautiful women he had ever seen. He whistled softly. "I think I just might get that chance."

Chris spotted the two women, too. He wasn't sure what he had expected. River Oaks was caught in a time warp. Maybe he had expected to see Lizette in hoopskirts. Maybe he had expected to see Rhett Butler by her side—although River Oaks certainly wasn't an imitation of Tara. What he hadn't expected to see was a thoroughly modern woman in a casual flowered skirt and white camisole. And he hadn't expected the knockout standing next to her, either.

"Simon Legree in red clamdiggers and a tank top," Chris said softly. "Are you glad you came?"

"If anything like that had showed up in the cane fields when I was a boy," Paul answered, "I never would have made it to med school."

On the porch, Barbara lifted her head in welcome, but her words were for Lizette alone. "Do you believe those suits?"

"I think it's endearing." Lizette smiled broadly at the good humor evidenced by the stereotypical white-planter's garb. "But we'd better find out how to make mint juleps fast. I can see they're expecting them."

"They're not moving," Barbara pointed out. "Think they're having second thoughts?"

"I think River Oaks is a bit much for the poor boys." Lizette raised her arm and motioned for the two men to come up to the house. She lowered her voice still further as the men started up the walk. "What do you think of Paul?"

"I think I should never have let you talk me into wearing California casual. Is a man like that going to look at a woman in pants and a T-shirt?"

"It's not a T-shirt, and he's already looking. Is he looking!"

"Now I know how my great-great-great-grandmother felt when they put her on the block to sell her downriver to River Oaks."

"Gallows humor, Barbie? You must be nervous."

Barbara smoothed her pants over her hips. "If he starts checking my teeth I'm getting out of here."

"I don't think it's your teeth he'll want to check out." Lizette put her arm around Barbara's back and applied not-so-subtle pressure. "Let's go down and meet them. Then you pick some mint while I get out the cookbook. We'd better fulfill their fantasies."

"You can fulfill any of Chris's fantasies that you want," Barbara said evenly, "but personally, I think I'm going to take it easy with the man walking beside him. He's too much like a fantasy himself."

Chapter Eight

"Chris." Lizette leaned forward and kissed Chris's cheek, then turned to Paul and extended her hands. "And Paul. Welcome to River Oaks." Stepping back, she introduced Barbara to both men, enjoying their reactions. If the men's expressions were any indication, the evening was going to be a good one.

"I like the suits," Lizette said after the first polite forays into conversation had ended. "You're truly Southern gentlemen at their finest, but you forgot your canes."

"I broke mine trying to learn to twirl it." Chris smiled to let her know he was teasing.

"Well, you're in cane country now, so don't worry." Lizette serenely lifted her eyes to heaven as everyone groaned at her pun. "Anyway, as gorgeous as you both are in the suits, you might want to leave your coats somewhere. Barbara and I planned a barbecue before we knew it was going to hit ninety today. I'm afraid we're going to be out- side most of the time."

The two men took off their coats and, without consulting each other, stripped off their ties and unbuttoned the top two buttons of their shirts. Paul piled his discarded clothing in Chris's arms, and Chris started toward the car. "Lizette?" He stopped and motioned with his head. "Why don't you come with me?"

Lizette was torn between going with Chris for a few private moments or staying with Barbara to help smooth her conversation with Paul. When she glanced at Barbara, however, Barbara and Paul were examining each other like two people who had already passed the point of awkwardness. Shrugging, she followed Chris.

"I think they're going to get along," she said when she and Chris were out of earshot. "Don't you?"

"I think you can stop fussing over them anytime now and concentrate on me."

Concentrating on Chris was as dangerous as it was easy. Still, Lizette couldn't have stopped herself. She tried to remember if she had ever seen a more attractive man. The white shirt and pants set off the golden brown of his tan and the sun-kissed blond of his hair. His green eyes were focused on her; they danced in silent laughter at her frank appraisal.

"Was I fussing?" she asked. "I didn't mean to."

"They're grown-ups."

"I feel responsible."

Chris imagined that Lizette spent most of her life feeling responsible about something. "This is quite a place," he said, tamping down the impulse that made him want to sweep her off her feet and carry her far, far away.

Lizette smiled. His assessment was a masterpiece of understatement. "Quite a place," she echoed.

"Are you going to give us a tour?"

"Do you want one?"

Faced with the choice, Chris wasn't sure. If he already felt overwhelmed by the obstacle River Oaks presented to their relationship, how would he feel after he had seen it all?

Lizette sensed his ambivalence. "You need to see River Oaks," she told him. "You'll understand me better. You'll understand my life."

"Do you want me to understand so that saying goodbye will be easier for both of us?"

She didn't answer until they reached his car. He opened the back door and piled the coats and ties neatly on the seat. When he shut the door and turned, Lizette was only inches from him. She put her hand on his arm.

"I'm not sure why I invited you here. But it wasn't so we could say goodbye easier. I didn't want to scare you off. Maybe I just wanted you to see what we're both up against."

He pushed a curl behind her ear, then stroked her cheek for a second before he dropped his hand. "Do you own River Oaks, or does it own you?"

She answered without hesitation. "River Oaks owns me."

"And you can't change that?"

"How can I? St. Hilaire blood flows in my veins, and it's even stronger in J.J.'s. This plantation is who we both are."

"Someone's sold you a bill of goods."

Lizette wondered how Chris could say something so cynical and yet still regard her with nothing less than approval in his eyes. "Maybe you're the one who's been sold a bill of goods. What's the point of living if nothing's important to you? Isn't there anything in your life that you feel this passionately about? Anything that's bound you to it body and soul?"

For a moment his eyes flickered with something very close to pain. "Not anymore."

"Anymore?"

"There was once. I learned the hard way about obsessions."

Lizette realized how little she knew about Chris. She had told him more about herself than she had learned about him. "Was it a woman?" she asked, hoping it hadn't been. She had been married herself, but she realized the thought of Chris's obsession with another woman made her unexpectedly jealous.

"No."

"Will you tell me about it sometime?"

"I will. But I'll tell you this now. Obsessions all take the same road, Lizette. You begin by making small sacrifices, and before you know it, your whole life is demanded of you. Is anything in the world worth that?"

Gold eyes locked with green ones. "How did we get so serious?" Lizette asked finally. "I asked you if you wanted to take a tour, and the next thing I know we're talking about ruined lives."

"Once I was the world expert on ruined lives." Chris draped his arm around her shoulders. "I just don't want you to have that same honor."

Lizette shivered. "Let's call a moratorium on serious discussion and have a good time tonight."

Chris pulled her closer and wished he could pull her so close that nothing would ever come between them. He started toward the house. "Well, that's a good sign, anyway."

"What?"

"People who are completely obsessed with something never have time to enjoy themselves."

"So there's hope for me?"

"How many times this week did you feel guilty about this invitation because of what it would do to your schedule?"

Lizette poked him with her elbow. "Never mind!"

Chris whistled "You've Got to Stop and Smell the Roses" all the way back to the house.

From the porch under the gallery Barbara stopped in the middle of a sentence and watched Chris and Lizette's approach. "He's not going to hurt her, is he?"

Paul had been so mesmerized by every word Barbara spoke, every move she made, that for a moment he was completely lost by the sudden conversational shift. "Hurt who?"

"Lizette."

"Is taking care of Lizette part of your job here?"

"Of course not."

"She seems like a big girl to me."

Maybe she had worried that she'd be too dazzled by Paul's male beauty, but Barbara realized she hadn't really looked him straight in the eye since he had been introduced to her. Now she did. "Lizette's my friend. There isn't anything I wouldn't do for her."

"Then I'd advise you to leave her alone. Chris is the gentlest man I know. She's safe with him."

"Her husband seemed gentle, too, but he still bled every drop of spirit out of her. She's just recovering."

"How about you?"

"What do you mean?"

"Are you recovering from something?"

Barbara smiled at Paul for the first time. "They make black people tough in this part of the world, city boy. We don't have to recover from anything, because we don't get hurt."

"And you don't run away easily?"

"If I ran away easily, I wouldn't be at River Oaks. And I'm still here, aren't I?"

"You are. Why?"

Her smile widened. "Damned if I know. It has something to do with Lizette and something to do with this god-forsaken piece of earth."

"Well, I'm glad you're here."

"Why?"

"Because I might never have met you otherwise."

Lizette rested her head against Chris's shoulder, aware that the position was beginning to feel natural. They had finished their walk in silence, watching the tableau on the porch with interest. If either of them had entertained any doubts about introducing Barbara and Paul, those doubts were now at rest.

"Are you two ready for something to drink?" Lizette called when she and Chris were almost to the house.

"Mint juleps?" Barbara's voice was heavy with distaste.

"I was thinking more along the lines of a cold Dixie beer," Lizette admitted.

"Hallelujah."

The sun was still turning the air to steam and baking the earth dry when they started around the big house. "We'll take you to see everything a little later," Lizette promised the men as they rounded the corner, heading toward what had once been the immaculately kept formal gardens. "Just as soon as the sun sinks a little lower."

Lizette had filled an old black cast-iron kettle that had once been used for boiling sugarcane with ice, soft drinks and beer, and they chose drinks, splashing one another with water from the melting ice before they wandered into the gardens. They settled on stone benches under live oaks with branches so low the Spanish moss hanging from them formed a canopy.

"Where's J.J. today?" Chris asked, pulling Lizette against him.

She snuggled contentedly in his arms when she realized that Paul and Barbara were sitting back-to-back, their weight distributed so that they were perfectly balanced against each other.

"Spending the night with my parents. During the summer he takes turns on Sundays visiting his grandparents."

"They both live in Port Ascension?"

"Julian's parents live right here on River Oaks."

"That's convenient."

Lizette had rarely thought of the St. Hilaires' presence that way. "Sometimes," she said cautiously. "Anyway, you'll probably get to meet them tonight."

"Why doesn't that surprise me?" Barbara asked.

Lizette looked up and saw two slow-moving forms coming toward them through the oaks. "In fact, Julian's parents are going to be here in a minute," she said. Flustered, she pulled away from Chris and stood. She smoothed her skirt self-consciously until she realized what she was doing. She forced herself to be still. Chris rose, as did Paul and Barbara, and the four waited in silence to meet the St. Hilaires.

Jerome and Sophia were dressed to receive guests. Lizette knew immediately that they had expected her to dress more formally, too, and that they were distressed by her lack of judgment, both in dress and demeanor. The St. Hilaires were completely eloquent without having to say a word. It was all there in the arching of eyebrows, the sweep of eyelashes, the tightening of lips.

Lizette made the introductions and watched as Sophia first, then Jerome, shook hands with Chris and Paul. The handshakes were just long enough to be polite. "Please join us," Lizette invited, gesturing to a third bench. "It's cool here under the oaks."

"I don't believe so, dear," Sophia said, waving regally at a fly. "Our dinner will be ready in a few minutes. Then we're driving into town for the evening." She paused to make her point. "You'll be eating soon, won't you?"

"We're cooking out," Lizette reminded her mother-in-law. "We'll probably start in a little while." She watched Sophia's repertoire of rebuking facial expressions again. It wasn't even necessary to try to guess what Sophia disapproved of. She disapproved of everything: Lizette's guests; the amount of time Chris and Paul would be spending at River Oaks; the casual atmosphere. But most of all, Lizette knew that Sophia disapproved of the death of her son. Lizette could forgive Sophia anything because she understood that.

Goodbyes were as perfunctory as the handshakes had been. Lizette and Barbara settled back on their respective benches, but the two men stood still until Jerome and Sophia were almost out of sight. When Chris finally sat back down beside her, Lizette wondered if she was imagining that his arm was tighter around her waist than it had been before.

"I'm afraid the heat's hard on them," Lizette apologized. "Summers here can be difficult for older people."

"And as hot as it is, you're going to make us barbecue." Chris buried his nose in Lizette's hair and inhaled its lemony fragrance.

"I wanted you to feel at home."

"At home?"

"Ask her what she knows about Californians," Barbara said from the next bench. "She's an encyclopedia."

"I can't wait."

"Californians are all blond and tanned," Lizette began, trying to shake off the malaise produced by the St. Hilaires' visit. "They surf, skateboard and attend encounter groups, but never church. They only eat meat if it's grilled outdoors, but they prefer restaurant soyburgers served by a waiter who is either an aspiring actor or a member of a commune led by little green yuppies from Mars. They protest against cutting down redwood trees, but every one of them has a redwood deck with a hot tub, which they'd fight to the death—nonviolently, of course—to protect. They save beached whales, but ignore air pollution. Curious people, Californians." She finished to the sound of the men's laughter.

"How much time have you spent in California?" Chris hugged her tighter.

"Lizette watches television," Barbara answered for her. "It's her umbilical cord to the real world."

Lizette turned so that she was facing Chris. "Anyway, since you're our guest tonight, Barbara and I have prepared a meal to make you feel right at home."

"And how do you know what I like to eat?" Chris asked, his mouth close to her ear.

"I watched you at the Rainbow. I saw you pick the sausage out of your red beans on the riverboat. I've got your number, Christopher Matthews."

Chris was delighted that she had paid so much attention to little details about him. "This I'll have to see."

While the men started a fire in the hibachi Lizette had set up under the back gallery, she and Barbara went inside to put the finishing touches on the rest of the meal.

"I wish you hadn't said my name in connection with this dinner," Barbara said, grimacing at the salad Lizette took from the refrigerator. "That's got to be the most disgusting mess I ever saw."

Lizette had to admit that the tofu salad that she'd made earlier resembled milk-flavored Jell-O held together by a few canned bean sprouts and a sprinkling of parsley. She averted her eyes from the bowl. "Chris is a health nut, and it stands to reason Paul is, too. They'll probably love it."

"Did it occur to you when you got *A Hundred and One Ways to Live Longer or Die Trying* off the bargain table at that bookstore in Baton Rouge that it might have been there for a reason?" Barbara took the crystal bowl out of Lizette's hands and dumped its contents into the kitchen garbage. "I've got the ingredients for a real salad growing in the garden behind my cabin. What other brainstorms did you have?"

"Touch my chicken and you die." Lizette pulled a platter of marinated chicken parts out of the refrigerator.

Barbara stared. "What happened to the skin?"

"Better ask what happened to an hour of my life this morning. Marydell refused to do it."

Barbara narrowed her eyes. "This took you an hour? You spent one hour taking the best part off the chicken?"

"Hard to believe, isn't it?"

"What'd you put on it?"

"Ginger, soy sauce, sesame seeds, oil..."

"Let me get this straight. You spent one whole hour stripping the skin off the chicken to get rid of the fat, then you sat it in a pan of oil all day?"

"Next time you cook."

"I think you're in love. And what do you mean, next time?"

Lizette ignored the first sentence and went right for the second. "You're trying to pretend you don't think Paul Waring is one of the handsomest men you've seen?"

"I didn't say that. But what's that got to do with cooking?"

"And nice?" Lizette continued.

"He's nice."

"And interested in you?"

Barbara was silent.

"Well?"

"Do you really think so?"

Lizette knew capitulation when she heard it. "It'll be a while before the coals heat up enough to cook. Why don't you take him down to your cabin and let him help you pick the salad?'' On impulse she spun to face Barbara, throwing her arms around her for a hard hug.

''What was that for?'' Barbara hugged her back, then stepped away.

''I don't know.'' Lizette watched Barbara until she disappeared through the door. ''Barbie,'' she called.

''What?'' Barbara stuck her head back into the kitchen.

''Go easy on the poor guy.''

Lizette was rinsing the bowl to prepare it for Barbara's salad when she heard Chris's voice behind her.

''Here I thought we'd have fried chicken, biscuits and collard greens served out on the veranda.''

She turned and saw the long, lean length of his body resting against the door frame. For a moment she just stared. It seemed so incredibly right for him to be there in her doorway. Somehow he had already insinuated himself into her life, and he was fast insinuating himself into her heart.

''Not here, you wouldn't. You have to go up the river a ways for that. This was a Creole plantation. More likely you'd have gumbo, roasted game hens with pecan stuffing, sweet-potato bread with cane syrup. And in Louisiana it's a gallery, not a veranda.''

''I like watching you.''

She smiled. ''Do you?''

''I like the way you move. I always expect to see you break into a run.''

''I frequently do when no one is around to see.''

He stepped into the room, skirting the long wooden table in the middle to get to her side. He leaned against the sink as she dried the bowl. ''Will you run with me sometime? Through the cane fields?''

''I'd like that.''

She set down the bowl, and the next thing she knew she was in his arms. ''And when we're in between rows of cane as tall as we are, will you let me pull you into my arms like this and kiss you?'' he asked, his back to the sink as he pulled her to him.

She leaned against him and wound her arms around his neck. "I might kiss you first."

"What a forward thought, Ms. St. Hilaire."

"I might kiss you first now."

"Your daring knows no bounds."

"Then again, I might not."

He laughed softly and brought his lips to hers. He stroked her back as he kissed her, and she relaxed against him with a sigh. The tensions of the day drained away, replaced by an aching, building pressure in the places where her body lay against his. His hands slipped down to her waist and then up beneath the camisole, caressing her satin-smooth skin, inch by inch, as if he expected her to pull away at any moment.

And why didn't she? She was standing in the kitchen granting Chris more intimacies than Julian had asked for until their wedding night. Yet all she could do was wish for more. When his hand found her breast she was awash with feeling, drowning in sensations she didn't even remember. She turned to the side, allowing him easier access, and forgot about everything except the newness, the wonder, of this.

Chris learned the shape of her breasts with his fingers as he had learned them with his eyes so many times before. She was perfectly proportioned and more responsive than he would have dreamed. He could feel her heart thunder against his fingertips and her flesh grow warmer. Her mouth was soft and sweet and almost innocent, not like a woman who has never been kissed, but like a woman who has never been kissed well and is just learning the delights that await her.

If he had ever thought that he could turn and walk away from Lizette, now he knew he had been fooling himself. He hadn't wanted a serious relationship any more than she seemed to, but in the impetuous pursuit, he had become the pursued. Pursued by love and caught unawares.

Lizette was the one to end the kiss. She straightened a little, and Chris smoothed his hand to her waist and then down over her hips. Never had he met a woman who needed a man to go so slow with her, and never had he wanted more to forget the preliminaries. Loving Lizette was going to test whatever self-control he had learned in his thirty years.

"We're standing in my kitchen necking like teenagers," she said, blinking as if she had just awoken from a dream. She stepped away from him, straightening her camisole self-consciously.

"I wonder how many other couples these old walls have seen doing the same thing."

"Very few. Up until the twenties this was a storage area, and there weren't even any walls down here."

"Love among the crates and barrels."

"Let me show you the rest of the house. Barbara can show Paul when they get back. She knows more about River Oaks' history than I do."

Chris shook his head at her evasions. "Do we have to pretend that nothing just happened?"

"Well, it's easier than discussing it."

"We don't have to discuss it, either. Come here and let me put my arm around you. Walk beside me when you show me the house."

Lizette slipped her arm around his waist. "You're a hard man to turn down, Chris Matthews."

"I hope so," he said, turning his head to kiss her curls. "I sincerely hope so."

"The last of the lettuce and the beginning of the tomatoes." Barbara held up a tomato so ripe it looked ready to burst.

"How many people do you feed off this garden?" Paul squatted down on his heels to separate the leaves of a squash plant to hunt for its yellow bounty.

"Everybody too lazy to grow their own, which means just about everyone."

"And you do all the work yourself?"

"No. I hire Ricky and J.J. to weed it. Big Jake runs the tiller between the rows for me now and then in exchange for fresh tomatoes, and Marydell waters and fertilizes for her share. Mostly I just sit back and watch it grow."

"How much time do you have to sit back and watch anything?"

"About two minutes, right before bedtime."

"Either you like working hard or you're just used to seeing black people in these parts run themselves into the ground."

She laughed and tossed the tomato at him. His hand snaked out and caught it just as it started its trajectory to the ground.

Since they had shared brief life stories already, Barbara knew where his theories came from. "When you cut cane back on the bayous," she said, "you were just there at the busy time. Grinding season is crazy. But the rest of the year isn't too bad. The cane just grows, we fuss over it some, it grows some more. It's a better life than living in a city, packed into apartments with no sunshine, no fresh air."

"Are you making fun of my life?" Paul shot her a seductive grin.

"I was watching you just now. You're just itching to get your fingers into the dirt and grow something yourself."

"My grandpa's a farmer. He's got a nice little piece of land up in Tennessee. The best memories I have are of going up there and helping him at harvest time. We'd sit out on his front porch in the evening, and he'd tell me stories you wouldn't believe."

"I'd believe." Barbara started toward her cabin and motioned for him to follow. "If your grandfather had land, why did you live in a housing project in New Orleans?"

"Grandpa had twelve sons and daughters. My father went south to find work and did—once in a while. He did his best for a man with no education to speak of. All his kids turned out right."

"Except you." She laughed and covered her face when he threatened to toss the tomato back at her. "I didn't mean it!"

He followed her up the rickety back steps of the cabin, through to the kitchen. "This place is something else."

"Go ahead. Ask me why I live here."

"I'd guess you're trying to stay in touch with something, some part of your roots."

She searched his face, pleasure in her eyes. It was rare that anyone understood her motivation.

"Tell me," he invited her. "In your own words."

She turned to the sink to begin washing the vegetables. "I get so sick of tourists in their big tourist buses driving along River Road to gawk at the few big houses that are left. The plantation mansions were a part of this country's history, but just a little part of it. Black people were a part of it, too. When slavery was at its peak there were over three hundred thousand slaves in the sugarcane parishes. We're the ones who gave our lives and our freedom for this land. There's nothing romantic about what happened to us here, but people need to understand it. And black people need to be proud that we survived, even thrived, when we had half a chance."

"So what's your plan?"

She turned, and the vegetables were forgotten. "How did you know I had a plan?"

"I can read it in your eyes and in every line of your body. I'm interested."

"Do you want to see?" Barbara dried her hands on her jeans.

"I want to see." Paul followed her through the door of her office.

Barbara bent over the big desk, which had once graced the office of an Ascension Parish sugar mill. She opened the bottom drawer and drew out a three-foot-long document, rolled and secured with a rubber band. The rubber band landed on her desk.

"I haven't shown this to a single soul, but here's my dream for River Oaks." She traced lines with her fingers as she talked. "I want to make part of the acreage into a working museum. We'd grow cane just like they did before the Civil War, but we'd use the new varieties, to avoid as many problems as we could. We'd use mules for plowing and for carrying cane in carts to our own sugar mill. The first grinding mill was right here. We could build a small, simple reproduction and mill our own cane.''

"Who'd do all the work? Wasn't that why they had slaves?''

Barbara nodded. "Children. School kids. See, my idea is to make this part of the curriculum for all the river parish schools. The kids would come here for a few days in the fall during grinding season and for a day or two in the spring while the cane was still growing. They'd live right here, in the quarters. Most of those houses are empty, because our workers would rather live off the property. We could convert them into dormitories. And then, if I had my way, we'd put the kids up for a night or two in the big house so they could see the differences in the way people lived. We'd rotate, so they could be planters, overseers, workers and sugar makers in the mill.''

"There would be a lot they couldn't do." Paul couldn't take his eyes off Barbara's face. It glowed with excitement.

"Sure. We'd keep the operation tiny, and we'd hire adults to do the main bulk of the work or anything too dangerous. I can't imagine turning a classroom full of kids loose with cane knives. But they'd get the feel of it, Paul. They'd live their heritage. You can bet not one of them would ever take those little packets of sugar at restaurants for granted again.'' She lifted her gaze from the drawing and met his. "What do you think?''

He stretched out his hand and wrapped his long fingers around her wrist. The drawing fell to the desk. "I think, in all my life, I've never met anyone quite like you.''

She tilted her head. "Is that supposed to be good?''

"Better than good.''

"Tending toward great?''

"Tending toward perfect." He lifted her hand and brought it to his mouth for a kiss before he dropped it. "Got any room in your life and your plans for a sports medicine doctor who can cut cane with the best of them?''

"It depends on how fast he works.''

"In the cane or in your life?''

"Both."

"I can work real fast when I have to." He paused. "And I think I may have to."

Barbara's smile was the only answer he needed.

Chapter Nine

Still hung over, Doc?"

If Chris was hung over on anything, it wasn't on the two beers he had imbibed at the barbecue at River Oaks the night before. It was on love. Hung over on love. There was a country-western songwriter in Nashville looking for that title. Chris lifted his head from his hands and stared at Polly. "Don't tell me. An emergency just walked through the door and Paul's already gone home for the night."

Polly's smile was sympathetic, though her eyes were anything but. "Sorry, but it does seem to be an emergency of sorts."

"Tennis elbow? Skater's ankle? Football player's knee?" Even as he muttered the words, Chris stood and stretched. "Dottie's gone for the day?"

"Just you and me and the emergency, and I'm leaving."

Chris checked his watch. It was later than he'd thought. "I shouldn't see him alone. We'd better send him..." He paused. "Him?" he asked.

"A her and a him."

"Two emergencies?"

"A Ms. Lizette St. Hilaire and her son, J.J." Polly laughed at Chris's expression. "She doesn't look like a woman who just drops by, so I suspect it's not out of line to call this an emergency."

"How long have they been out there?"

"Not long. You can pick 'em, Doc, I'll give you that. And by the way, I remembered why St. Hilaire sounded so familiar."

Chris knew he didn't have to prompt Polly. He went to his closet and took out his sports jacket while she finished.

"The St. Hilaire family is old Louisiana. Creole Louisiana. They've got one of the few plantations on the river that's been in the hands of the same family since it was staked out and cultivated."

Chris nodded. "I was there last night."

"What was it like?"

What was River Oaks like? Chris shrugged into his jacket. River Oaks had been like a dream. Possibly even a nightmare. River Oaks was acres and acres of sugarcane and soybeans, with miles of dirt road crisscrossing them. It was the quarters with their two-room cabins and front yards swept clean of everything, including grass and weeds, and the ruins of the sugarhouse, the endless outbuildings, the massive harvesting and transporting equipment.

What was River Oaks like? It was Barbara's slave cabin, half history and half real world. And it was the big house. The big house. Even the title set it apart from everything else. Yet the house hadn't been the immaculate mansion he might have expected. He remembered the kitchen, with its rough brick floor and ancient appliances, the upstairs, with its fifteen-foot ceilings and its peeling paint, room after room sparsely furnished in antebellum antiques the Yankees hadn't seen fit to carry off during "The War."

What was River Oaks like? It was a museum in need of a sponsor. A century in need of a death knell. A prison in need of liberation.

"It was quite a place," he said, unconsciously repeating the words he had said to Lizette the night before. Chris straightened his tie, then thought better of it, unknotting it and stripping it off to toss it on his desk. "I'll lock up, Polly. Have a good evening."

"You too, Doc."

Chris could hear J.J.'s voice as he started down the hall-way. He had wondered if he would ever see the little boy again. Lizette had been evasive about making plans for future dates. Had that only been last night? He had left River Oaks wondering if it was the last time they would be together. Yet here she was, no longer running away, but running toward him. He liked it better this way. Much better.

"J.J., we're just going to say hello and then leave. I'm sure Chris has plans for the evening." Lizette smoothed J.J.'s hair back from his forehead. She still couldn't believe she was sitting in the waiting room of the Sports Medicine Center. The last time she had done anything this impetuous she had been run in the Crescent City Classic.

And look how that had turned out.

"Chris'll wanna see us," J.J. reassured his mother. "He likes us."

"He's right." Chris stood in the doorway. "I do."

Lizette lifted her gaze and let good feelings fill all the hollow places inside her. Her doubts fled. Coming here hadn't been impetuous. It had been necessary. "Do you have room in your schedule for a six-year-old boy and his hundred-year-old mother?" she asked.

"I have room for you and J.J. Always."

"You're not a hundred years old," J.J. scoffed at his mother. "You're twenty-five."

"I think your mother means that today she feels like she's a hundred." Chris saw Lizette's slight sigh and knew he had guessed correctly.

"I'm feeling younger by the moment," she assured him. "I'll feel even younger if you'll let us take you out to dinner."

"My treat. You fed me yesterday."

"Was that only yesterday?" Her voice was wistful.

Chris didn't want to ask Lizette what was wrong. He suspected that whatever it was, she wouldn't want to talk about it in front of J.J. "Would you like to look around first? I think there are some things here J.J. might like to see."

"Like what?" J.J. wanted to know.

"Like exercise machines. Flex your muscles for me." Chris squatted down and felt J.J.'s biceps. "Mmm...I think you need a workout, kid."

Lizette and J.J. toured for most of the next hour. Chris sat the little boy on a Cybex machine to measure the muscle strength in his arms and legs, then he showed him how a stress test was done on a treadmill, with the mask and electrodes that could respectively measure oxygen intake and heart rate as he ran. He showed him a brief film on nutrition and sports, and another on common injuries, although J.J.'s biggest thrill was operating the projector. Chris ended by taking a high speed film of J.J. running, explaining afterwards how the film could be analyzed by a computer at a biomechanical laboratory to measure force, speed and stride length.

In the cast room he let J.J. experiment with dipping strips of plastic-impregnated cloth into water and fashioning them around a ruler to make a pretend cast. The result was a free-form sculpture.

"He's having such a good time," Lizette told Chris as J.J. added another layer. "He's your friend for life."

"I hope so." Chris rested his arm across her shoulder.

"I never knew there was so much to sports medicine. How can you stay current?" She moved a little closer to him.

"Like everything else, it's getting more and more specialized, but then, this is the age of computers. Information's at my fingertips any time I need it."

"You said you wanted to work with kids. How does all this fit in?"

"Well, I'd like to have a regular orthopedic practice and see anyone who came through the door, but I'd specialize in working with kids who've been injured. There's a lot that can be done in the way of prevention if you become a respected part of a community. More than one out of four sports accidents can be avoided if the right kind of safety precautions are taken."

"And you'd rather do that than work with professional athletes?"

"If we don't take care of kids when they start out, none of them will ever become professional athletes."

"Do you realize that I hardly know anything about you?"

Chris found the back of Lizette's neck with his fingers and lightly massaged it. By now J.J.'s ruler was nothing more than a thickening white bulge. "What do you want to know that you don't already?"

"How about your life story over dinner?"

"How about my life story over appetizers? It isn't very eventful."

With a promise to J.J. that he could take his cast off the ruler someday with the high-speed saw, Chris locked up the center, and they started toward his car.

Since J.J. had never been there, they decided on the Riverwalk, a glass-enclosed gallery of shops along the Mississippi in what had once been the International Pavilion of the 1984 Louisiana World Exposition. In addition to luxury shopping, there were also numerous food stands set up along the walkway, and tables overlooking the river. Since there were a variety of possibilities, everyone could be happy.

J.J. immediately settled on pizza, Lizette on barbecued ribs and Chris on wonton soup and sushi. They ate at a light-flooded table next to a window.

"Begin," Lizette commanded, waving her sparerib like a magic wand.

"Begin what?"

"Your life story."

"Do you have any kids?" J.J. asked helpfully.

"That would be a good place to start," Lizette agreed, the sparerib almost to her mouth.

"No kids. No wife, ex or otherwise."

"You should have kids. You could take 'em to work every day, and they could have fun!" J.J. grinned around his pizza.

Chris ruffled his hair. "My life story. Well, I've told you most of it before. I was born in San Francisco. My father was an engineer with the state, and we lived in San Diego and Eureka, as well as Fresno, where I graduated from high school. My folks live in San Jose now, where they'll probably stay until Dad retires."

"Can I have some more lemonade?" J.J. held up an empty paper cup.

Lizette opened up her purse and took out a dollar bill. "Do you remember where you got it?" J.J. pointed at the correct booth and she nodded. "Can you get it by yourself?" He took the dollar and scampered off.

"Talk fast," Lizette said with an apologetic smile. "When J.J.'s just with me like this, he has trouble staying quiet."

Chris wondered why Lizette would feel she had to apologize. J.J. was a normal little boy with a normal little boy's curiosity and liveliness. "Hey, I may not have kids of my own yet," he reassured her, "but I do know something about them. J.J. can talk all he wants. I love to listen to him."

"You mean it, don't you?"

Chris frowned. "Yeah. Is that such a surprise?"

"I guess I'm not used to men who like children when they *are* children," she said cryptically.

"What about your husband?"

"Julian loved J.J. He was proud of J.J. But he liked J.J. best when he wasn't in the same room with him." She wiped her hands on her napkin and avoided Chris's eyes. "Maybe all J.J.'s energy reminded him of his own illness. I don't know. But J.J. was expected to be quiet and polite around his father. That was pretty hard on a toddler. I don't think he remembers much about Julian, and that might be just as well."

"Were you expected to be quiet and polite, too?"

Lizette looked up sharply. There was no humor in Chris's eyes. He was completely serious, and more than a little angry. "I was just expected to be me."

"The you who breaks out into a run whenever she gets a chance, or the you who gets anxious when her in-laws make her feel like a trespasser on her own property?"

"You don't know me well enough to draw any conclusions about my life, Chris."

"I think I know you as well as anyone in the world," he said evenly. "Except maybe Barbara. I know the person you want to be, though I'm not even sure you know that person yet."

"I got it." J.J. came running back toward the table, a giant cup of lemonade in his hand. "And he gave me money back. See?"

Chris turned at the sound of the little boy's voice just in time to see an accident about to happen. With a shouted "Watch out," Chris leapt out of his chair and sprinted toward him, but even his athlete's speed and coordination couldn't stop J.J. from skidding on the freshly mopped tile and tripping over his own feet.

J.J. was in Chris's arms, sobbing, by the time a horrified Lizette got there. "He's all right," Chris reassured her. "I got here quickly enough to cushion his fall."

"My lemonade," J.J. sobbed.

"You're all wet." Lizette dabbed uselessly at Chris's sports coat with a napkin. "I'm sorry."

"I'm not worried." Chris stood up, J.J. still in his arms, and started back to the table. "You sit here, son, and I'll get you another lemonade. You'll be thirstier than ever after all that exercise."

J.J. hid his face on Chris's shoulder until his tears trickled to a stop. "With ice," he said at last, after a series of hiccups.

Chris smiled and set him down in his seat. By the time he returned, J.J. was nibbling on his pizza. "One lemonade. The man said he was sorry you fell, and that this one was free."

J.J. beamed, obviously feeling more like the hero of a melodrama now than the stooge. "I'm sorry you got lemonade all over your coat when you saved me."

Chris tried not to smile at the thought of "saving" the little boy. Apparently he had assumed gargantuan proportions in J.J.'s eyes. "Coats can be cleaned," he said.

"So can floors. That's why I fell!" J.J. laughed at his own joke.

"J.J., eat your pizza and drink that lemonade. Chris, back to your life story." Lizette started on her dinner again. "We were in San Jose."

"Well, I'm glad J.J.'s back, because this is the exciting part, and I didn't want him to miss it."

J.J.'s eyes got big, but his mouth was so full of pizza that he couldn't say a thing.

"When I graduated from high school, I decided that I didn't want to go to college. I wanted to be a professional baseball player."

J.J. said something that sounded like "Muggwhump raider?"

Chris grinned. "That's right, a baseball player. I'd played all through school, and I was the local all-star, so I tried out for a minor league team and made it. It wasn't a great team—in fact it's not even in existence anymore—but after a while I made it to a better one, and then a better one."

Lizette was fascinated. She didn't have any trouble imagining Chris as a professional athlete. Every line of his body radiated health and vigor. His movements had coiled-spring intensity, and his coordination was superior. She could easily picture him on a ball field playing... "First base?"

"Third, sometimes left field."

J.J. swallowed. "How come you're a doctor, then?"

"One day I was practicing with another player and a ball tipped the middle finger of my left hand." Chris held it up. "See? It's crooked."

"Hey, that's neat." J.J. tried to put his own in the same position, but he couldn't.

"I didn't want some doctor to put me out of commission for the rest of the season. It was almost over, and I'd done really well. I was hoping that a major league team was going to ask me to sign a contract. So I ignored the finger. By the time I went to do something about it, it was too late. I'd ruptured the flexor tendon, and nothing could be done to correct it at that stage."

"But it doesn't seem like such a serious problem," Lizette ventured. "I never even noticed it before."

"Maybe if I'd already been starring in the major leagues something could have been done to work around it. But probably not even then. My catching wasn't as good, even when the pain disappeared, and anybody could see I held the bat funny, especially scouts from the majors. So before I knew it, baseball wasn't an option for me anymore."

"How old were you?"

"Twenty-one. And I didn't know anything about anything except baseball. I'd lived it, slept it and breathed it up until that point. There was nothing else in my life."

"Obsession." Lizette said the word on a drawn-out breath.

"Exactly."

"Will you teach me to play baseball?" J.J. asked, finishing his last mouthful of pizza.

"You bet." Chris patted the little boy's hand affectionately. "Anytime you want."

"Now?"

"Anytime but now."

"What did you do after you realized baseball wasn't going to be your career?" Lizette could imagine the disappointment he must have felt, yet look where he had ended up, and who he had become. He obviously wasn't a man who had turned bitter when his dream died.

"I did what most middle-class young adults do to avoid reality. I went to college, the University of California at Santa Cruz. After the first year, I began to like it. After the second, I stopped mourning. After the third, I decided I wanted to become a doctor and specialize in sports injuries. I figured I had the necessary credentials. Anyway, I went to medical school in Boston and interned at Massachusetts General. Paul was two years ahead of me, and after he got the job here, he asked me to come for a year to cover for a doctor on leave. After she comes back I'll probably buy into a practice around Santa Cruz and settle down. And there you have my life story."

"Where are the women?" Lizette slurped the last of her Coke without taking her eyes from it. "There wasn't one woman in your story."

"I mentioned my mother. I know I did." Chris lounged back in his chair and rested his hands on his chest.

"Why do I have the feeling I just heard the expurgated version?"

"What piece of information are we after here? Do you want to know if I'm a healthy, normal male with a healthy, normal male's instincts? You know the answer to that one already."

Lizette pushed her cup away and flicked a crumb off the table. "No, that wasn't the piece I was looking for."

"Do you want to know if I've ever been in love?"

"That's closer."

"Do you love my mom?" J.J. asked, his eyes bright with interest.

"Your mom is very lovable," Chris answered smoothly.

"Your mom is very embarrassed," Lizette said. "Eat your pizza."

"It's gone! I want a brownie."

Lizette fished in her purse for another dollar and pointed to the right booth. "Walk this time," she cautioned J.J. "Before you say a word about his diet," she told Chris when J.J. was out of earshot, "let me remind you that you're eating raw fish. No one who eats raw fish can say a word about what other people feed their children."

He reached for her hand and covered it with his own. "He's a fine boy, Lizette. You're doing a wonderful job with him."

The starch in her spine melted. She turned her hand palm up and wove her fingers through his. "The only time I spoil him like this," she admitted, "is when we're out together. At home we eat most of our meals with his grandparents, and they're so strict that if he doesn't clean up every last pea on his plate he doesn't get dessert. I guess I try to make up for it when we're alone."

His fingers tightened around hers. "Isn't that hard on you?"

"They're good people, and they love J.J. They just don't remember how it was to be young."

"And your husband didn't, either."

Lizette had said as much earlier, but now, hearing the words from Chris's mouth, they sounded more ominous somehow. "I'm not sure Julian was ever young."

Chris was beginning to understand what that must have done to her. And what was living at River Oaks with Julian's ghost and Julian's parents doing to her now? What was it doing to the way she was raising her son? "Why did you come to see me today?" he asked. "I left your house last night wondering if I'd see you again at all."

"I just wanted to see you. I guess it was silly."

"Never silly. Did it have something to do with Sophia and Jerome?"

Lizette thought maybe he'd been right. Maybe he did understand her better than anyone else in the world. Anyone except Barbara, who had sent her here in the first place with a "Get away from this place, girl, and think for a change. Jerome and Sophia St. Hilaire aren't God and the Virgin Mary. You don't have to throw yourself at their feet!"

Lizette looked to see where J.J. had gone. Brownie in hand, he was watching a whistling clown who was giving away balloon sculptures to the children in a circle around her. "They have a lot of expectations for me," Lizette said at last, turning back to focus her eyes on the table. She realized its Formica surface would be forever ingrained in her memory. "When Julian died, I was the only one left to keep River Oaks going. And I have to do that for J.J. It's his inheritance I'd be throwing away if I didn't."

"And?"

"And Jerome and Sophia reminded me this morning, quite explicitly, that getting involved with an outsider..."

"An outsider?"

"Someone who doesn't understand about River Oaks—"

"Are there any insiders?" Chris interrupted. "Besides the St. Hilaires, I mean?"

"I guess there are men who would be prepared to carry on the River Oaks traditions, men I've known socially for years from other plantation families."

"And Jerome and Sophia want you to marry one of them?"

Lizette shook her head. "I'm sure they'd rather I didn't marry at all. At least, not until J.J. is old enough to take over the plantation himself. Of course, they're not crass enough to tell me that. They just reminded me that a doctor from California is not one of us. I'm supposed to rethink my relationship with you."

Chris sat back and withdrew his hand. "And have you?"

"In some ways they're right," she went on. "I've known from the start that this is crazy. I've got River Oaks like a ball and chain around my neck, you've got a new life waiting for you in California. That's why I was so hesitant to see you at first."

"In what ways *aren't* they right?"

"You make me happy." Lizette looked up from the table and met his eyes. "I love being with you. You're good for me, and for J.J. When you're gone I'll like knowing that you're walking around somewhere on the same planet I am. When Jerome and Sophia left today after our little talk, the only thing I wanted to do was cry on your shoulder. So I came to see you." She smiled a little. "Did you know there was a weepy woman under this poised facade?"

"I guessed."

"I'm sorry I dumped this on you." The only sign of the tears she wanted to cry was a small, impatient sniff.

"You can dump anything you want on me. Anytime. Forever."

"And vice versa."

"So we're going to keep seeing each other?" He grinned when she nodded. "J.J. will keep spilling his lemonade on me, you'll sniff once in a while when you get sad and sigh when you get angry, we'll run races together, and I'll hold back to finish with you, we'll kiss some more, and eventually we'll go to bed together?"

"Yes." She nodded again, then her eyes widened. "What?"

"Yes or what? Which is it?"

All thoughts of tears were forgotten. Lizette stared at Chris for a full minute, then her lips turned up in a smile that made his flesh harden with desire. "Yes to almost all of it."

"Which part was a no? I have to prepare."

"Easy. No to the part about holding back to finish with me when we run. I intend to beat you someday, Christopher Matthews. Fair and square."

Say **Yes** to romance

AND YOU'LL GET:

---

4 FREE BOOKS
A FREE CLOCK/
CALENDAR
A FREE SURPRISE GIFT

NO RISK • NO OBLIGATION
NO STRINGS • NO KIDDING

EXCITING DETAILS INSIDE

Say YES to free gifts worth over $20.00

Say YES to a rendezvous with romance, and you'll get 4 classic love stories—FREE! You'll get an attractive digital quartz clock/calendar—FREE! And you'll get a delightful surprise—FREE! These gifts carry a value of over $20.00—but you can have them without spending even a penny!

FREE HOME DELIVERY

Say YES to Silhouette and you'll enjoy the convenience of previewing 6 brand-new books delivered right to your home every month before they appear in stores. Each book is yours for only $2.49—26¢ less than reatil, and there is no extra charge for postage and handling.

SPECIAL EXTRAS—FREE!

You'll get our monthly newsletter, packed with news of your favorite authors and upcoming books— FREE! You'll also get additional free gifts from time to time as a token of our appreciation for being a home subscriber.

Say YES to a Silhouette love affair. Complete, detach and mail your Free Offer Card today!

FREE—COMBINATION CLOCK/CALENDAR.

You'll love your new LCD digital quartz clock, which also shows the current month and date. This lovely lucite piece includes a handy month-at-a-glance calendar, or you can display your favorite photo in the calendar area. This is our special gift to you!

If offer card is missing, write to:
Silhouette Books 901 Fuhrmann Blvd., P.O. Box 1867, Buffalo, NY 14269-1867

DETACH AND MAIL CARD TODAY

RUSH! FREE GIFTS DEPT.

First Class   Permit No. 717   Buffalo, NY

BUSINESS REPLY CARD

Postage will be paid by addressee

Silhouette Books®
901 Fuhrmann Blvd.
P.O. Box 1867
Buffalo, New York 14240-9952

NO POSTAGE
NECESSARY
IF MAILED
IN THE
UNITED STATES

Chapter Ten

"Whose idea was this, anyway? Between the heat, the humidity and the carbon monoxide, I'm going to keel over and die right here." Lizette realized that for someone who was threatening to die on the spot, she sounded ridiculously energetic. She should at least have stopped and panted between sentences.

"Then you're lucky you're jogging with a doctor," Chris answered, unconcerned. "I'll do a little C.P.R., throw you in the shower, and then we can still go out for dinner."

"Just promise you won't drag my unconscious body to a sushi bar."

"I was thinking more along the lines of a little place I know that serves tofu salad with bean sprouts."

"You've been talking to Barbara!"

Chris shook his head. "Paul told me."

"I'm not sure we should have introduced our best friends. Now we have no secrets."

"I've never liked secrets." Chris jogged in place on the median—or neutral ground, as it was called in New Orleans—for several steps until Lizette caught up to him. The sun was just going down, and the sky over St. Charles Avenue was suffused with a golden glow that cast a haze of wellbeing over the mansions lining the street to either side of them. Lizette's face was bathed in the same glow, and with her curls bouncing wildly to the rhythm of her new running shoes, he couldn't imagine a lovelier sight.

In the three weeks since Lizette had made a conscious decision to continue seeing him despite the warnings of her inlaws, they had been together on half a dozen occasions. Chris had been back to River Oaks twice, once for a picnic with J.J. and Lizette, and once for a formal Sunday brunch with Lizette's parents and the St. Hilaires. He'd rather do anything than go through another experience like that one, but he had done it for Lizette and, if called on, would do it again.

Lizette had needed him beside her. Chris was used to being needed on a professional level, but on a personal level he wasn't. Baseball, college, medical school, residency, all had served to make him concentrate on his own life, his own needs. Now, when his first thought in the morning was of Lizette and the last thought at night was of her, too—not to mention a growing number of thoughts in the middle of the night, in the form of increasingly erotic dreams—he wondered how he could have lived such a selfish existence.

Chris supposed it had been comparatively easy; after all, his was the generation whose motto had been Me First, and yet now, with his life meshing with Lizette's, he was surprised that anyone, himself most of all, could have believed that Me First was the path to anything except loneliness.

He was in love, and he hardly knew what to do about it. He was in love with a woman so tied to her roots and her duties that loving him back was impossible. And yet—and yet he saw signs of love, not the least of which was her refusal to break off their relationship. She was standing up to pressures at home, continuing to see him even though she had to wade through oceans of disapproval to do so.

He told himself that hoping and looking for signs that Lizette was falling in love, too, was childish. Despite that piece of good advice, he found himself watching her carefully, dissecting every conversation, even reading his horoscope. He still had enough presence of mind to laugh at the last, but just barely.

"Getting winded, Chris-to-pher? I don't mind turning back if you can't take any more."

Chris shot Lizette a warm grin just before his hand stretched out to slap her bottom. "I can run for miles. I can run for days."

"I can't. I think I'm getting a blister. It's these shoes you made me buy. I was fine until I was forced, *forced*," she repeated louder, "to buy expensive running shoes."

"Those shoes fit perfectly. I fit them myself, remember?"

"I'd rather run barefoot."

"This isn't a cane field, Lizzie-love. You're in the middle of a busy street, in danger of being run down any minute by a predatory streetcar. You have to wear shoes." Chris jogged in a half circle and started back down the other side of the streetcar tracks. "Come on, we'll head home."

Home. It sounded so natural for the two of them to head "home." Lizette wondered what was happening to her. When she had decided to continue seeing Chris, despite the friction it was causing at River Oaks, she had schooled herself not to expect anything to come of their relationship. Nothing *could* come of it. The relationship was a temporary one, built on mutual attraction and genuine admiration. She expected them to be friends for life, to send Christmas cards and occasional letters, and to think of each other fondly in the years to come. Theirs would never be a relationship where they went "home" together.

And yet it sounded so natural. So right.

The things they would share in a home sounded natural and right, too. She hadn't wanted a lover; she'd had no reason to believe that she needed one in her life. Now she knew differently. She needed Chris in every way, and each time she was with him, she found she needed him more.

The problem was that she didn't know how to tell him. She'd had little experience with any man except Julian, and he had taken the lead in all things. Lizette knew Chris wanted her; she also knew that he was waiting for a sign that she was ready for him. They were at an impasse, and the tension was heightening unbearably.

They jogged on, their feet slapping the grass on the neutral ground in a steady, unrelenting rhythm. Lizette could feel sweat collecting under the bandanna Chris had given her to tie her curls back from her forehead. She wondered if they were jogging to stay physically fit or to work off some of the energy they didn't seem to be able to work off any other way.

"We're almost there. How's your foot?"

Lizette realized she had forgotten about the alleged blister. There was nothing wrong with her foot. The rest of her body was a different story. She was tired, hot and frustrated. The first two could be cured by a cool shower. The third? The third was a different story entirely.

"It's fine," she assured Chris. "And I may not even need C.P.R. if you'll just move the house a block closer for me."

Chris slowed to a walk, grabbing Lizette's hand to force her to walk, too. "We need to cool down."

"I don't want to cool down. I want to collapse."

"You can collapse in my apartment. On my bed."

The idea sounded promising. "After a shower," she warned. "A long shower."

"I'll flip you to see who gets in first."

"I'm your guest."

"Funny thing, you don't seem like a guest." He squeezed her hand. "You're more important than a guest."

More important than a guest, less important than a lover. Lizette wondered exactly where that left her. "Does that mean we still have to flip for the shower?"

"You've got it."

Inside Chris's apartment, Lizette flopped into a plush armchair and rested her head. "I'm comfortable. You go ahead. I don't think I'll be able to get up for a while, anyway."

"I'll get the water running for you."

"You mean you were just bullying me out there?"

"I mean all of a sudden that armchair looks good to me."

She pushed herself up and headed for the bathroom. "I'll call you when I'm done."

"No hurry."

Chris liked the idea of Lizette standing in his shower, drops of water running down her shoulders and breasts, clear, cool water gliding down her hips to be caught in the dark triangle of hair between her legs. He imagined he would never stand in his shower without thinking of her there, sleek, warm, lovely—and totally unattainable.

He wanted her as he had never wanted any of the other women in his life, women who had been so available. Lizette seemed oblivious to his desires. When she was in his arms she responded wholeheartedly, yet she never initiated so much as a kiss. And it was always Lizette who pulled away, straightened her clothes and looked bewildered, as if she couldn't imagine what was happening to her.

She'd been a married woman. She was the mother of a six-year-old child. Why, then, did he feel he needed to go slowly? Why, then, didn't she give him more encouragement?

Why, then, was she standing in his shower, driving him crazy until he was sure that even if she came in, right that minute, and offered herself to him, it wouldn't be enough. He would never get enough of her.

He sat in the armchair, feeling the pleasant aches of a man who has just exerted himself physically and the unpleasant aches of a man who requires a different kind of exertion and doesn't expect to get it. He wondered if there was a water temperature that would soothe one type of ache and rid him of the other. He doubted it. As a physician, he was sure the magic attributed to cold showers was malarkey.

"Chris?" Lizette poked her head through his bathroom doorway. "Are you ready? I'll leave it running and change in your bedroom."

"Fine." He watched her emerge, swathed in a huge bath towel. There was nothing uncovered, nothing provocative—unless you counted the long length of her legs and the unmarred expanse of her shoulders and arms. Her hair was a wet tangle of dark curls, and her eyes were huge against her rose-flushed skin. He groaned.

"Come on. Get up. You'll feel better. I do." She warmed him with her smile, then crossed the hall to his bedroom. The door closed behind her.

Now he would have the image of Lizette naked, in his room, to deal with, too. Even now she was probably unwrapping the towel, stroking it over her glorious body. She was probably sitting on his bed to dry her feet, threading the towel between each perfect toe. He was glad she wasn't there to see what the thought of that did to the fit of his running shorts.

In the bedroom, Lizette smoothed her hand over the comforter covering Chris's bed. It was a dark brown, almost the color of her hair, and his pillowcases were a narrow brown-and-beige stripe. It was a comfortable bed, a contemporary bed of polished teak and straight, elegant lines. The rest of his furniture matched it. There was no history here, only a statement of who Chris was. He was a man who liked comfort, who preferred simple things of quality, who lived in the present.

It was no wonder, really, that he had decided not to risk a more intimate relationship with her. Whenever he came to River Oaks it probably hit him like a lightning bolt how different they were. He was being smart. They didn't need to complicate their lives.

As she unwrapped the towel she caught sight of herself in Chris's dresser mirror and wondered if he found her attractive. He seemed to. Sometimes she would catch him looking at her, his eyes blazing with something she liked to imagine was desire. Was she desirable? Had she been desirable at nineteen, when she and Julian had married? Had it been his illness that had cut short their physical relationship, or had it been disinterest on Julian's part? Maybe she didn't have the necessary credentials to interest a man. Maybe her breasts were too small, her hips too narrow, her legs too long. Maybe she needed to do something with her hair to make herself more appealing.

Then again, maybe she should stop worrying and be satisfied with what she had. What was the point in trying to be more appealing? She had been correct when she told Chris there was no room in her life for a lover. There wasn't room for anything except River Oaks and J.J. And those long, restless, lonely nights.

"Damn!" Lizette gripped the towel and began to rub it roughly over her body, as if by doing so she could erase her feelings.

"Lizette? Are you all right?"

She sat down on the bed, chagrined that Chris had heard her. What was the matter with her? Where was her self-control?

"I'm all right," she called through the door. "I stubbed my toe. Did you need to get in here? I'll be out in a minute."

"Take your time."

She wanted to get out in a hurry. Chris's bedroom was no place to be right now. Quickly she slipped on underwear and the skirt and blouse she had brought with her, then ran a comb through her hair. "Come on in." She opened the door and stepped into the hallway. Right into Chris's arms.

"I didn't know you were there," she said breathlessly. He was wearing the blue terry-cloth robe that had been hanging behind his bathroom door. It was belted loosely around his waist, and there was a wide expanse of chest visible for her to admire. Clean, male chest, with drops of water still clinging to the sprinkling of golden hair that covered it.

Chris put his hands on her arms to steady her. It seemed to him that the color had drained from her cheeks. "Maybe you did overdo it on that run," he said with a frown. "You look pale, and you're trembling."

Lizette thought Chris's hands were trembling, too. She lifted her eyelashes and met his eyes. "I feel fine."

"Do you?" He couldn't seem to make his muscles work. He knew his hands were supposed to drop to his side, that he was supposed to walk past her and close the door. *Hysterical paralysis.* He couldn't move. "Funny thing, I don't."

"What's wrong?"

"I feel like backing you into the bedroom."

"Do you?" The wispy sound of her voice was a surprise. She cleared her throat.

"Backing you into the bedroom and onto my bed."

She wondered if he was reading her mind. Had she somehow communicated her own feelings? He had given her precious little encouragement in the last weeks. Why now? She wondered if he thought she expected this, if somehow he had detected her needs and, in that warm, giving way of his, was ministering to them.

Or maybe he was just teasing her, as he had teased her at the Riverwalk. He had talked about making love to her then. She had as much as told him that she would be willing. Maybe this was just talk, too.

"I'm all dressed now," she said, trying to keep just the right light touch, so he could back down gracefully. "You're too late."

"When I was a kid, my father had a movie camera, and he took pictures of my friends and me every chance he got. Our favorite part was when he played them backward. There was this one movie where I was getting dressed after swimming in our pool. He would show it backward, and my clothes would just melt away until I was standing there in my swimming trunks. Then I backed into the pool and disappeared in the water."

"It sounds like a real scream," she said, not smiling.

"Let's see how funny it is. Do everything you just did, except do it backward. I'll watch and report."

"I think you've had too much sun."

His hands glided up her arms to her neck, and then up to her curls. He pulled her head against him, and his hands began to travel along her back. "I've had too much waiting," he said thickly. "You've taught me more about waiting than any woman I've ever met. If I'm not good at it anymore, you'll have to forgive me."

Her arms slid around his waist, and she sighed. She sighed again, wondering as she did at the sheer power in that small exhalation. She felt like a pressure cooker whose release valve begins spouting steam seconds before a blowup. "I didn't think you wanted me," she said in a small voice. "I stood in your bedroom and looked at myself and thought maybe you just didn't find me appealing."

His hands halted their caresses. Not appealing? "What else could I have done to show you I wanted you? Hire a skywriter?"

"You never pushed me. You always stopped before..."

"Before we made love? The key word there is 'we.'"

"Didn't you know I wanted you? Couldn't you tell?"

"No more than you could, evidently."

"Even in a democracy somebody has to take the lead." She laughed, and the joyous tinkling sound of it filled the room. "What a pair we make! We'll never understand each other."

"Maybe we'll understand more than you think after tonight."

She drew back a little to search his eyes. "Maybe we will."

He waited, his hands still. She waited, too.

"Show me you want me," Chris said at last. "When tomorrow comes, I don't want you to pretend to yourself that I took the decision away from you."

She could be swept away. All it would take would be a caress, a passionate kiss. But take the lead? It was beyond her.

Chris saw the dismay in her eyes. "You can't make a mistake," he said, drawing her a little closer. "Nothing you could do would be wrong."

She tried to convince herself that Chris wouldn't reject her. She laid her head against his chest and tightened her arms around his waist. And she remembered.

Another man, another night, almost another lifetime. Julian had come home from the hospital, and the doctors were optimistic about his recovery. Along with his prescriptions and exercise schedule, she had been given the news that she and Julian could resume a normal relationship just as soon as he felt like it.

She had waited patiently as he grew stronger. She had been pregnant with J.J., and as Julian grew healthier she grew larger and, in her own mind, unattractive. He took to going out often, proving his increased vitality. At home alone she had needed his support, his admiration, his touch. Finally, one night, she had decided that perhaps Julian was afraid to approach her. Perhaps he was afraid that she no longer found him attractive because of his illness, or that she had lost interest in him because of her pregnancy.

Young and impetuous, she had gone to his room wearing the most attractive nightgown she owned. He had gently, firmly told her to go back to bed. "When the time is right, I'll come to you," he had told her.

Deeply ashamed that she could have put him in such an awkward position, she had gone back to her room. She had chastised herself for not waiting. Julian would come to her as soon as he felt well enough. She would never ask again; she would spare them both that humiliation.

But it was only months later, after J.J.'s birth, that he had come to her, and by then she understood the truth. Julian was only in her bed because he wanted another child. She had learned her place; it had been ingrained in her by her in-laws, and by Julian himself. She had accepted his occasional lovemaking, but there had been no joy in it. His rejection, his kind and gentle rejection, had eclipsed all the joy forever after.

Lizette had never felt anger at that before, but now it poured through her in hot, fierce waves of anguish. She clutched Chris tighter and felt him quiver. "The bastard," he ground out.

She hadn't even realized she had spoken the memory. It had been so clear, so crystal clear, as she relived it. She hadn't even known she was describing it to Chris.

"It wasn't my fault," she said, and the words held no question. How could she have ever believed it was? How could she have let Julian convince her that she had no rights, no needs to be satisfied? How could she have settled for so little, like a brood mare that waits patiently for the stallion that has been chosen to impregnate her?

"I was so young!" She pushed herself away from Chris, and her eyes were blazing. "I was such a child!"

"Maybe that's why he married you."

She would search for the answer to that later. Now, however, her anger had carried her to a new plane. She threw her head back, and every angle of her body cried out her defiance. "There's no reason a man wouldn't want me."

"No reason." He clenched his fists at his side.

"There's no reason you wouldn't want me."

"We can safely say that."

She crossed her arms and grasped the hem of her shirt, stripping it off in one quick motion. Her bra was lacy and almost nonexistent. Chris could see the thundering beat of her heart in the veins of her neck and the rapid rise and fall of her chest. His mouth went dry as she unclasped the small scrap of lace and it fell to the floor.

"And there's no reason you wouldn't find me desirable," she continued.

He swallowed hard, clenching and unclenching his fists.

Her hands went to the button of her skirt and then to the zipper. Her skirt joined the growing pile of clothing at her feet, followed quickly by her half-slip. Then she slowly smoothed her hands over her hips, catching the silk of her panties with her fingertips and smoothing them down her legs until she was naked before him.

"And there's no reason you would reject me," she finished.

"No man would reject you," he said, stressing the word *man*. "Not unless he was very frightened of being a man."

"Well, I'm not frightened of being a woman."

And what a woman she was. Had he ever believed that his fantasies of her could be near reality? He had never seen a woman as beautiful. He had never realized one existed. His hands went to the belt of his robe, and he untied it slowly, as he drank in the details of her body. Her breasts were full and round, with dark, cherry-tipped centers. Her waist was narrow, her stomach flat, her hips flaring gracefully down to firm, slender runner's legs. Her skin was ivory and rose-flushed. He imagined it heating beneath his gaze.

His robe fell to the floor, and he saw her curious examination change to approval and then slowly to wonder. "You're not frightened of being a man," she said softly, stepping closer to him. "And you want me."

Chris kissed away what he was afraid might be an expression of gratitude. Silently he cursed the soul of Julian St. Hilaire.

In his bedroom he left her for a moment to fumble in his dresser drawer. He threw a small, foil-wrapped square on the bed. "I want you," he told her. "I don't want you pregnant."

Lizette smiled, grateful that he understood what that would have done to her. He sat on his bed and held out his arms. She came into them, and they fell backward onto the brown comforter, their bodies immediately entwined. He had thought to go slowly with her, to reassure her, but now he knew that the only reassurance she needed was his passion. He murmured endearments as he filled his hands with her flesh, moving them quickly over her as one fulfilled need provoked another. He tasted her skin, tasted again and again, until she was moaning against him as her body sought a solace it had been so long denied.

He denied himself nothing of her. She was innocent in ways that seemed impossible, yet he gave up nothing for her innocence. He was a gentle man, but she needed his strength. He had that to give her, too.

He had strength and love and the patience to let her take what she wanted from him. Her hands traveled over his body, lightly at first, shyly, then more intimately, until she knew him as he knew her. He knew that forever afterward he would remember the feel of her fingers exploring his flesh with a delicate passion that more than once was almost his undoing.

Her mouth was sweet and hungrier than he ever could have imagined. He left it only to come back for more again and again, until they were both dizzied from the drugging ecstasy of their kisses. Then he suffered the torment of her mouth seeking to know him more intimately. Her hair brushed his body as her lips did, and he felt the soft caress of her breasts as they moved against him. He was surrounded by the clean fragrance of her and the sound track of two hearts beating together.

Finally he pulled her beneath him, holding his breath as her long legs wrapped around him in unconscious frenzy. He protected her, then entered her slowly—his one concession to her years of celibacy—but once he was inside her, his control was gone. He moved, and she melted around him until there were no boundaries, no barriers. He heard her cries and felt them in his own throat. He felt her release begin and knew it was his, too. They were taken by the storm of passion that sucked them violently in, then, finally, cast them out. Changed.

Afterward Lizette pillowed her head on Chris's shoulder and wondered if the body nestled so close to his really belonged to her. In a way, it wasn't hers alone anymore. No one could share herself so fully and not give some portion of her body and soul into her lover's keeping.

"Are you awake?"

Lizette wasn't sure how to answer Chris's whispered question. Her eyes were certainly open. But she was awake in other ways, too, and for the first time ever. She was awake to her body, awake to what she had to give a man, awake to the love she felt for Chris. Did all women feel this way when they'd just been loved well? Or was she just finally awake to the truth? She was in love with Christopher Matthews, and what had just happened between them was the greatest expression of that love imaginable.

She felt his hand glide over her hair to touch her cheek. She turned her head to kiss his fingers. "I'm awake." Well and truly awake, she added silently.

Chris found himself incapable of commenting on what had just occurred. He settled for the mundane. "I think I promised you dinner."

"You did."

"I don't think I want to get out of bed."

"Would you get out long enough to answer the door?"

He laughed, and the rumbles resounded against her ear. "I might."

"We could order pizza. You could have bean sprouts on your half."

"I'll settle for mushrooms." He turned to his side and brushed her hair back from her cheek to see her eyes. "Will you stay the night?"

She could think of a thousand reasons why it wouldn't be wise. Not one of them was good enough. "J.J.'s with my parents."

"I know."

"I'll stay. I'll drive back early in the morning, before he gets home."

"I'll make it worth your while."

"Of that I have no doubt." She lifted her head to kiss him, lingering until her heart beat faster. "I'll try to be worth the effort."

"Somehow I'm not worried."

She kissed him again, then settled beside him once more. "Somehow I believe you. And it's the best feeling in the world, Chris. The very best."

Chapter Eleven

Lizette was a mile from River Oaks before she let herself think about the consequences of staying at Chris's house all night. She had no regrets. How could she regret something that had left her feeling reborn? No, she wasn't sorry she had spent the night with Chris. She knew the night would be a memory she would bask in for years to come.

Unfortunately life, like the United States government, seemed to have a built-in series of checks and balances. If she spent one perfect night with the man she loved, then she would have to pay for it. She had no doubt that Sophia and Jerome St. Hilaire would be the ones to exact the price.

At least they couldn't complain that she had caused them a sleepless night. Out of consideration for their feelings she had phoned River Oaks to explain that she would not be home until morning. Marydell had answered the telephone, and Lizette had left the message with her, asking her to let Sophia and Jerome know that she was all right. She had made no excuses, nor did she intend to. Surely a twenty-five-year-old widow was old enough to have some privacy, some secrets.

There would be fallout, however. There would definitely be fallout.

The fallout was waiting on her front gallery.

In Lizette's memory neither Sophia nor Jerome had ever risen this early before. She wondered if they had been to bed last night, or whether their vigil had begun with her phone call. She had left Chris's apartment without waking him, and now she badly needed a cup of coffee and a shower before facing her in-laws. The lack of both almost seemed more important than the confrontation that was to come.

Lizette parked the van and shut off the engine. With the fabric bag containing her running clothes in one hand and her purse in the other, she stepped down and walked toward trouble.

Jerome stood when she climbed the stairs, but Sophia remained seated on the small wooden pew that had once belonged in a country church not far from River Oaks. Somehow it seemed appropriate for Sophia to be sitting on the pew, as if she were waiting in church to do her Christian duty. There was nothing funny about the image for Lizette. Her hands were clammy. She wasn't looking forward to what was coming.

"Lizette." Jerome nodded.

Lizette nodded, too, and turned to her mother-in-law. "Sophia."

Sophia nodded. "We've been waiting for you."

"I can see that."

"We'd like to talk to you," Jerome said.

"Then let's go inside, where we'll be more comfortable." Lizette opened the door in front of the stairway and held it while Jerome and Sophia preceded her into the parlor.

The parlor seemed the most appropriate place for their conversation. Like the rest of the big house, Lizette had never felt it belonged to her. It belonged to the pre-Civil War St. Hilaires, who had furnished it to their taste. She sat on a settee upholstered in handwoven tapestry and felt as though she were defiling history. Sophia sat across from her, and Jerome stood by the marble fireplace.

"Lizette, what would Julian say about your behavior last night?" Sophia began when everyone was settled.

For a moment Lizette wasn't sure she had heard her mother-in-law correctly. "Julian?"

"Your husband."

"I know who Julian is . . . was."

"I believe he would have been shocked, just as Jerome and I were."

Seconds ticked by as Lizette tried to organize her thoughts. "Julian is dead," she said finally, wondering if she really did have to remind them.

"Julian would have been terribly ashamed of you."

"Julian would never have had to be if he were still alive."

"Julian left you the greatest inheritance a woman could ever expect!" Jerome turned to face Lizette. "And you have jeopardized it by last night's behavior."

Since Louisiana inheritance law would have made it impossible for Julian to do anything other than leave her River Oaks, Lizette ignored the first part of Jerome's statement. She was sure reminding him would be fruitless, anyway.

"What have I jeopardized?" she asked instead. "Who's going to sit in judgment of me? I'm a grown woman, and this isn't the nineteenth century."

"More's the pity." Sophia leaned forward and her dark eyes flashed with anger. "If it were, you might understand your duties."

"I understand my duties."

"Not if you stay out all night, then drive your van down River Road at dawn heading back from New Orleans, you don't. Didn't you realize there might be people who saw you leave yesterday and then saw you coming back this morning? Do you suppose they believe you were just delayed? That your shopping took longer than you thought?"

Lizette had a sudden vision of night watchmen at the big complexes on River Road noting her coming and going in their logbooks. "Lizette St. Hilaire passed on her way to New Orleans to meet her lover. Lizette St. Hilaire returned.

Comment: That must have been some night.'' For a moment she had to wrestle with hysteria-laced laughter. ''I don't think people care, if they even noticed at all,'' she said after she had forced herself to be calm.

''Your parents know where you were last night,'' Jerome said. ''They're as concerned as we are.''

''If they know where I was, it's because you chose to tell them.''

''We let them know because we're worried about you and J.J. both. You have a son to raise and a role to fill here. You can't do either if your energies are directed elsewhere.''

Despite her anger at the St. Hilaires' lecture, Lizette could understand their feelings. Perhaps understanding their feelings was a curse; life might be simpler if she didn't. But she had been raised to think as they did, and although she wouldn't let guilt intrude on what she and Chris had shared, neither was she willing to discount Jerome and Sophia's point of view entirely.

''I'm very fond of Chris Matthews, but in no way will he interfere with my duties here or my raising of your grandson.''

''Dr. Matthews isn't right for you!'' Sophia stood and began to pace back and forth in front of the settee. ''He'll never understand what River Oaks requires. He'll never be an appropriate stepfather for J.J. Can't you see that he's nothing but a divisive force? He's going to tear River Oaks apart before he's through, and you're going to let him.''

Understanding flew out the floor-to-ceiling hand-rolled windows. ''I don't want to talk about this anymore!'' Lizette stood, too. ''Since neither of you is concerned about my feelings, I see no point in discussing this further.''

''We care—'' Jerome began.

Lizette held up her hand. ''If you do, you'll drop this, then. If and when you can prove I've neglected J.J. or River Oaks, I'll be glad to talk some more. In the meantime, if Chris comes here to share some of what little free time I have, I'll expect him to be welcomed. That's all I'm going to say.'' She nodded, then left them alone to consider her words.

Barbara was sitting on Lizette's bed filing her nails when Lizette walked into her bedroom.

"I'd say," Barbara began with no preliminaries, "that you did pretty well. Of course, I could wish you'd been a little more direct, a little angrier, but still, considering it was the first time you've ever stood up to them, you did fine." She continued filing her nails without looking up.

"I'm living in a fishbowl!"

"I believe that's what Sophia was trying to tell you."

Lizette dropped into a green velvet lady's chair, so named because it had been built when hoopskirts were in vogue. It was wide enough to drape the hoops over the edges, but not soft enough to be comfortable. "So you heard the whole thing?"

"With my ear to the door in J.J.'s room. One thing about my family. Nobody ever had to eavesdrop. When we had a fight in our house, everybody got to hear it. Too bad the St. Hilaires didn't yell a little. You could have yelled back, and everybody could have gotten this off their chests."

Lizette tried to imagine a Stanhope or a St. Hilaire yelling. It was unthinkable. "Then you know where I was last night?"

"Your activities were left to the imagination. Everyone was so polite." Barbara chuckled and looked up at Lizette for the first time. "Just don't tell me you're sorry you spent the night with Chris. If you're sorry, I'm going to pack up and leave this place."

"I'm not sorry, and don't you dare leave. When you go, sanity goes, too."

"You could leave. We could go together."

Lizette knew Barbara was baiting her. "This is J.J.'s home. It's his heritage. I have to stay."

"What about Chris?"

"Chris will go back to California at Christmastime, and I'll stay here."

"Julian would be proud of you."

"I don't need this, Barbara." Lizette rested her head on the carved wooden frame at the back of her chair. "You hardly knew Julian."

"If I hardly knew him, it was because he didn't approve of our friendship."

There was no way Lizette could dispute that. She and Barbara had been friends since high school, when Barbara had been the first black girl to enter the exclusive convent school Lizette attended. The years of Lizette's marriage had been the only years since that time that the two women hadn't been close. Julian had never denied Lizette Barbara's company. He had just made it uncomfortable for Barbara to visit on her breaks from college, and impossible for Lizette to find the time to visit her.

"I don't think it was you he disapproved of. He just expected me to be here...."

"At his beck and call. The lord and master," Barbara scoffed. "And if you think it didn't have something to do with the color of my skin, girl, you've got tunnel vision or amnesia. I grew up here, remember? Julian St. Hilaire liked me just fine when I was a barefoot little overseer's daughter chewing on sugarcane on the front porch of our house. Everybody here liked me just fine until my folks forced the race issue and enrolled me in a school no black girl was supposed to attend. Nobody liked me after that. Me or my family."

"I liked you."

"How come?"

Lizette wondered why the conversation had taken this turn and, even more, why it never had before. For nine years neither of them had ever questioned their friendship out loud. It just *was*, like the sunshine that beat down on endless rows of feathery green cane, like the rain that washed nourishment and life-giving moisture to the cane's roots, like the cold air of autumn that gave the cane its sweetness.

"Why shouldn't I have liked you?" Lizette asked at last. "You walked into class one day, and I thought how strange it was that everyone had made such a fuss. You didn't smile much that first day, but I caught one and I thought, 'I'd like to know how she can smile at all, considering the way everybody's acting.' The next day..."

"The next day you came over to sit with me at lunch. You said, 'My name's Lizette Stanhope, and if you just keep on trying to smile and ignore everything else, I'll teach you how to get around Sister Mary Rose.' "

"You never did get the hang of it. Sister Mary Rose stayed on your tail till the end of the year."

Barbara pocketed her nail file and stood. "Sister Mary Rose is long gone, but you and I are friends in spite of everything, including Julian. I'll stay at River Oaks as long as you need me here, but the day I don't think being here does either of us any good, I'm walking."

"If I thought you were just staying here for me, I'd fire you on the spot."

"I've got my dreams, too."

"Is Paul one of those dreams?"

Barbara demonstrated the smile that had been under discussion. "You might say he figures in."

"I envy you that freedom."

"There aren't any bars on these windows."

"Only because they weren't in fashion in 1817. Women knew their place without them."

"Some women still do, or think they do." Barbara looked at her watch. "This woman's got a date with a drainage machine out at the back swamp."

"Thanks for being here."

"Gadfly at your service."

Lizette stood at the window and watched her friend hurry down the back stairs. If Barbara ever walked away, she wondered what River Oaks would be like without her.

"Now don't rest the bat on your shoulder. Hold it up just a little." Chris demonstrated with an imaginary bat. "See?"

J.J. nodded, but the bat just didn't seem to want to leave his shoulder. "It's awful heavy!"

"And it's awful hot!" Ricky yanked off the baseball cap Chris had brought for him and used it as a fan.

"You two boys want to call it an afternoon?"

J.J. and Ricky looked at each other and shrugged. It was hot, and baseball was hard work. Shoo settled the issue by leaving the shade of a nearby tree to collapse on Ricky's feet. "Guess we'd better take ol' Shoo up to the house and get him some water." Ricky edged his feet out from under the prostrate mutt.

"Ol' Shoo to the rescue," Lizette called from the shade Shoo had vacated.

"If you want to try again later, when it cools down, I'll be here." Chris pulled J.J.'s hat over his eyes.

"Yeah!" both boys said in unison.

Chris watched them amble off, Shoo close behind, before he joined Lizette under the tree. He stretched out beside her, turned to his side so they were face-to-face. "Short attention spans."

"Try telling them they can't have something they want and then see how long they can keep after you."

He grinned and reached over to tweak her nose. "That's just males in general. Look how long I kept after you."

Lizette was just so glad to have Chris at River Oaks, to be spending a lazy Fourth of July with him, that she didn't bother to remind him that his persistence had only been part of it. Her own attraction to him had been part of it, too. "Think either one of the boys is going to be a star?"

"I sincerely hope not." Chris lay back and folded his arms under his head. "Sports should be fun, not the be-all and end-all of life."

"The be-all and end-all of life sounds much too serious for a hot summer afternoon." Lizette stretched out beside him.

"If we could see the clouds I'd make you tell me what you see in them."

"If we could see the clouds, we'd be too hot to talk." Lizette pointed overhead. "We can make do. Interpret the branches and Spanish moss for me."

"I'll never see Spanish moss again without thinking of River Oaks."

"Do you know how it got its name?" She didn't wait for an answer. "The French called it *barbe espagnole*, Spanish beard. That was an insult, of course, so the Spanish retaliated and called it *peluca francesca*, Frenchman's wig. I guess Spanish moss stuck when the French finally gained control of this part of the country."

"I know the Indian legend about how Spanish moss came to be."

Lizette didn't. "How?"

"It's said that an Indian girl was being married, and in the middle of her wedding ceremony, she was killed by an enemy tribe. The mourning family cut off her hair and spread it on the limbs of the oak tree over her grave. The hair turned gray and blew from tree to tree. It's supposed to be a tribute to all lovers who aren't fated to live out their love."

"Where did you hear that? It's so sad."

"A woman I know told me."

"I'll bet she was just trying to soften you up."

Chris laughed and reached for Lizette's hand. "Soften me up for what?"

"The good things in life. You know, marriage, kids, a mortgage."

"By telling me a story about Spanish moss?"

"She wanted you to think of her every time you weren't together and saw Spanish moss on a tree."

"It didn't work," he reminded her.

"You're a hard case, Chris-to-pher."

They lay on the ground, their fingers entwined, listening to the calls of mockingbirds and cardinals.

"I missed you this week," Chris said after a few minutes of silence. "When I woke up Monday morning and you were gone, I wasn't even sure if the night had been real."

"If it wasn't real, we were both fooled."

"You didn't call."

"I had some thinking to do."

"If I hadn't called and invited myself out today to teach J.J. how to bat, would I ever have seen you again?"

"Yes." Lizette turned and propped herself on one arm. She touched his cheek, then drew a line with her finger to the tip of his chin. "Definitely." Leaning over, she touched her mouth to his.

Chris threaded one hand through Lizette's hair to keep her there a moment. "Is it going to be a long, hot, lonely summer? Or are we going to spend it together?"

"What about the woman who tells you Indian legends?"

"I could swear I'm seeing gold eyes turn to green."

"I just want to know where I stand."

"There's only you."

"I like the sound of that."

That much, but no more. Chris knew she wasn't ready to be told the truth, that he loved her and wanted her to be the only woman in his life for the rest of his life. He was willing to take it one step at a time. He tugged her curls, then let her go. "Then I can look forward to more lazy days in the shade with you?"

"Lazy days in the shade." She paused as she settled back beside him. "Lazy nights in your apartment," she finished nonchalantly. "Sounds like the way to spend a summer to me."

He reached for her hand, and once again they listened for the calls of the birds, although neither one of them heard more than their own hearts beating.

J.J. and Ricky returned in a little while, carrying glasses of iced tea courtesy of Marydell. The two boys waited impatiently while Chris and Lizette finished drinking, then dragged Chris off to see their frog collection. Lizette meandered up to the house to check on the dinner preparations.

By the time Chris joined her, the sun had set far enough in the sky to encourage them to change into their jogging clothes for a run through the cane fields.

"I saw your in-laws when I was with J.J. and Ricky," Chris told her when they had jogged a mile by weaving in and out of the rows at the farthest end of the St. Hilaire holdings.

Lizette nodded her head to the rhythm of the breeze-tossed cane towering to each side of them. She was sorry that even here, where the tall cane blocked the sight of River Oaks, the St. Hilaires had to intrude. "I thought they were gone for the day."

"Did that have something to do with my invitation?"

"If it did, it was only for your sake."

"They're having a hard time getting used to you with another man."

It wasn't a question. "Were they rude?" Lizette asked.

He countered without answering, and that was answer enough. "Did they give you any trouble about staying with me last Sunday night?"

"They were concerned."

Chris had never felt so protective of anyone before. He wanted to take Lizette back to the big house, pack her suitcases and whisk her away from River Oaks forever. Her own sense of duty was bad enough, but pressure from the St. Hilaires was going to be almost impossible for her to surmount.

He didn't want to upset her with the details of his exchange with the elderly couple. Jerome and Sophia had been cold to the point of rudeness, and Chris had seen the battle lines being drawn. But even though he didn't want to worry Lizette, he was concerned about the way the St. Hilaires treated their grandson. His protective feelings toward Lizette seemed to extend to J.J., too. He hadn't liked what he'd seen. He tested his observations.

"They gave J.J. a hard time. His shoes were muddy. I gather they don't want him near the swamp behind the house where he and Ricky catch frogs."

"Losing Julian has made them overprotective of J.J.," Lizette explained. "I think they'd die if they lost him, too."

"The swamp seemed like a fairly innocuous place to me."

Lizette didn't know what to say. She agreed with Chris in theory, yet she understood Sophia and Jerome's concerns. J.J. was all they had left. "I let him go there," she admitted after another row of sugarcane was behind them. "I just ask him not to make a point of it when his grandparents are nearby."

"Is that like telling J.J. not to let them see him climb the tree in Big Jake's yard?"

Lizette was surprised Chris remembered that story. "Do you memorize everything we tell you?"

"Nah." Chris turned his head and shot her a grin. "J.J. and Ricky reminded me when we were up in the top of the tree today."

Lizette wasn't sure where she got the breath to laugh, but she did. That was one sight she wished she could have seen, but it wasn't so hard just to imagine. Chris would look perfectly at home in the big oak with a little boy on either side of him. She tried to imagine Julian in the same place. She couldn't. Julian would have been under the tree ordering J.J. down. The thought was sobering.

"Getting tired?" Chris saw the strained look on her face and misinterpreted it.

"A little." Lizette slowed down. "Must be the heat." Even as she said the words, a breeze drifted between rows to cool her sweat-dampened skin.

"Let's walk. We've still got to have dinner and drive into Baton Rouge to see the fireworks tonight. I don't want you exhausted."

"You're sure you want to do that?" Lizette gratefully walked beside him.

"J.J. and Ricky are counting on it."

"Hey, are you here to see me or them?" she teased. "I'd hate to think my real competition comes from two six-year-olds."

"Come here, you." Chris put his hands on her shoulders, and all thoughts of exercise were forgotten. "I'll show you who I came to see."

"You don't want to kiss me." Lizette looked down at her sweat-soaked shirt and shorts. "I'm wet and smelly, and my hair probably looks like I stuck my finger in a light socket."

"I don't, huh?" He tugged her closer. "I like you best this way."

"Impossible."

"Put your arms around me."

She did. He was as disheveled as she was, and his skin felt slick and smooth under her exploring fingers. The golden hair falling over his red bandanna was boyishly appealing, and she blew on it gently to watch it dance in the fading light of day.

"Ah, Chris, I like you any way at all," she said, bringing his head down to hers.

She could feel his immediate arousal, and although hers wasn't as easy to define, it was just as strong. They kissed and held each other in the tightest of embraces until she pulled away. "There's a place we could go," she said shyly.

He knew what she meant, although the where was still a mystery. "I want to make love to you," he assured her, "but I couldn't protect you. I'm not prepared. I didn't think we'd have a chance."

"You don't need to worry. I'm taking care of it myself."

He hugged her tighter, pleased that she had made such a conscious decision to be his lover. "Where could we go?"

"Back this way." She began a slow jog and then picked up speed.

"Helps to have a goal, doesn't it?" he called after her, jogging along in her footsteps.

Their goal was the site of a primitive sugar mill, the first mill built on the St. Hilaire property. It had been an animal-powered grinding mill, unlike the more recent one Chris had already seen near Barbara's cabin. That newer mill, which was now only a sixty-foot brick chimney and a huge crumbling foundation, had been steam-powered and state-of-the-art until economics had dictated that it be closed down in the 1920s.

"There's nothing left of this one, really." Lizette stopped to catch her breath. "For a long time we didn't even know why this space hadn't been cleared and planted with the other fields. Then Barbara found some old documents explaining what had been here."

Now willow trees had grown into a small thick grove, sheltering the spot that had once been the focus of the plantation's financial success or failure. It was an island in a sea of sugarcane.

"Why didn't they cultivate this area once the new mill was built?" Chris asked, drawing Lizette into his arms.

"There's a story, more a rumor than anything else. Someone was killed at the mill. A woman, we think. Afterward none of the slaves would come near this place no matter what they were threatened with. They swore there was a ghost.''

''What do you think?''

''I think there is.'' Lizette lowered herself to the tall grass and held up her arms to him. Chris sat behind her and pulled her back so she reclined against him. ''When I was first married and needed to be by myself I'd come here,'' she continued. ''It's very private. Even though no one remembers why, most of the workers at River Oaks would just as soon avoid this spot. So when I came, I'd have it all to myself. Sometimes, at twilight like this, I'd hear noises, as if a woman was weeping. I used to feel that we comforted each other somehow.''

Chris forced Lizette to look at him. His eyes were sad. ''Do you know how lonely that sounds?''

''I didn't feel lonely here. After a while, though, I had to stop coming. Julian thought it was dangerous. I'm not sure what he was afraid might happen, but I couldn't risk upsetting him, because of his health.''

Chris imagined that Julian had been right, at least from his point of view. Too much time alone might have been dangerous for Lizette. She might have begun to see just how imprisoning her marriage was. ''And now you've brought me here.''

''I knew you'd understand this place.'' She twined her arms around his neck and pushed him to the grass so that she lay on top of him. ''I've thought of us together here so often that it's almost a memory.''

She slid her hands under his shirt and helped him pull it over his head. Then she did the same with her own. They finished undressing slowly, tasting and touching without leaving each other for an instant.

When she fell to the grass and joined her body with his, Lizette was conscious of nothing except the miracle of Chris inside her. Later, though, when they lay satiated in each other's arms, she heard the soft sighing of twilight's breeze through the willow trees.

The woman did not weep that night.

Chapter Twelve

July disappeared. One day Lizette climbed out of bed knowing she had the whole glorious month of July to look forward to, and the next day July had vanished and August had taken its place. Or at least it seemed that way.

Worse yet, before she could truly mourn July's passing, August seemed to be threatening the same rush to oblivion.

Summer wasn't normally a season that sped by. Summer had always been a slow progression of sultry days, when the only thing moving was the cane reaching toward the sky, threatening to spear any low-hanging cloud that got in its way.

This summer would have been that way, too, if Chris hadn't come into Lizette's life. Now, instead of days of adjusting thermostats, drinking endless gallons of iced tea and slapping away swarms of mosquitoes for entertainment, she had time with Chris to look forward to.

And the time was going too fast.

In July they had spent days together both in New Orleans and at River Oaks. They had taken Ricky and J.J. to the Audubon Zoo and the Children's Museum, and they had gone without children to some of New Orleans' finest restaurants and night spots. At River Oaks they had jogged through the sugarcane, climbed to the top of the levee to watch for ships and spent long evenings catching the slightest river breeze from seats on the front gallery of the big house. In the first days of August they had done much the same, adding an overnight fishing trip with Paul and Barbara and the boys to their growing list of shared activities.

To Lizette, Chris now seemed a part of River Oaks. He would never *be* River Oaks the way Julian had been, but neither was he a stranger to the workings of the plantation and its rich history.

Chris had learned about the cycle of sugarcane and the gamble of growing it from Tyrone and Big Jake, who, because they liked him, were willing to tell him more than he ever needed to know. With a surgeon's skill he had helped her scrape deeply into the paint of a section of woodwork in the parlor to find the original color so that it could be matched when money was available for the never-ending job of restoring the big house. He had stood by her side while she wished for rain and commiserated with her when the rain she had wished for exposed new leaks in the roof. He had even silently borne the brunt of Sophia and Jerome's hostility without complaint, as if that, too, were part of learning about her life.

Chris would never have that special feel for River Oaks that those who had been born to it had, but Lizette hoped he was beginning to understand her own commitment. If he could grow to appreciate the richness of the heritage that was J.J.'s and the knowledge that she and J.J. were just a link in a chain that stretched into two centuries, then he would understand why she couldn't leave the plantation. Not even for him.

While Chris had been learning about River Oaks, Lizette had been learning about Chris. He was every bit a man, and yet he had qualities she had never known a man to have. He was patient. He could sit with J.J. while the little boy fished or caught frogs and never once show by word or gesture that he was bored or frustrated. He was patient with her, too. He didn't push her to change; he let her move at her own pace and make her own discoveries. Even in their lovemaking he made few demands except that she help him find ways to please her.

He was also gentle. Julian had been gentle, too, but Chris's gentleness was different. Now Lizette realized that Julian had treated her like a precious pet who was best controlled and trained by delicate handling. Chris was truly gentle, not because he wanted her to conform to standards he had devised, but because no matter how he felt about the decisions she made in her life, he believed he had no right to make other decisions for her.

Lizette was so in love with Chris that sometimes it overpowered her. Her love had grown during all the days of July, and now that the hours of August had begun to tick away, it was still growing. Nothing had changed; she still knew that River Oaks was her destiny, but more and more she found herself wishing that somehow she could find a way to have everything she wanted. River Oaks, Chris, J.J.—and a life that was fulfilling for each of them.

Trying to think of ways to have it all had almost become a game for her. It was a game she was playing on the second Saturday of August when Chris's car pulled in next to her van.

She walked out to meet him, wondering if two pairs of eyes were trained on them from the remodeled overseer's cottage. Without giving the matter too much thought, she draped her arms over Chris's shoulders and gave him a lingering welcome kiss.

"Good morning to you, too." He slipped his arms around Lizette's waist and wished—not for the first time—that all their good-mornings could be said side by side in bed together.

"I ate already. You're late."

"I had an emergency this morning."

"Is everything all right now?"

"Just a simple fracture, but it was someone I'd treated before, and she wanted me, not the doctor on call."

"Pushover."

"Yeah. I'm a pushover for gorgeous females."

She narrowed her eyes. "Gorgeous females?"

"Gorgeous females with dark curly hair and fascinating smiles."

"Maybe you should have stayed in New Orleans with the one there. It would have saved you a drive."

"I don't think her mother would approve."

"Mother?"

"She's eight. She's a walking accident waiting to happen, too. This time skateboarding, last time gymnastics. I don't know if I could afford her."

Lizette laughed, and they walked up to the house, arms around each other's waists.

"Where's J.J.?"

"My mother took him to the circus in Baton Rouge."

"How do you want to spend the day?"

"How do I want or how am I going to?"

"Sounds ominous."

She opened the front door to the downstairs, and Chris followed her inside. "First I'm going to feed my man," she began.

"I like the sound of that."

"And then I'm going to take him to a place like none he's ever seen before. A place filled with suspense and mystery and intrigue, a place where time stands still and the present becomes both the past and the future."

"You should have gone to the circus with J.J. As the ringmaster."

"I did pique your interest, didn't I?" She led him into the kitchen and motioned to a chair at a small table by the only window in the room. "What'll it be? Sugar-coated cereal, sugar-coated pastries? Sugar in your coffee? Say no and I'll think you're trying to sabotage my livelihood."

"Have you ever thought about growing something else here? Like wheat germ, or sunflower seeds?"

"How could I ever face the world if I owned a wheat germ plantation?"

Chris watched Lizette bustle around the antiquated kitchen. He knew she did very little cooking herself, but he also knew she enjoyed cooking for him when he came. At times like these he could almost imagine them living a normal life, taking care of each other in the thousand and one ways that a husband and wife did, finding excuses to demonstrate a love that just grew stronger over the years.

The summer had taught him more than just the workings of River Oaks. It had taught him the strength of his feelings for Lizette. What it hadn't taught him was how to ensure that those feelings would have a chance to grow for the rest of their lives.

"Eggs have cholesterol," she said, setting a plate in front of him. "Bacon has nitrates and nitrites. Coffee has caffeine. The bread for your toast was stripped of all its vitamins and minerals when it was processed, and grits are well-known not to contain anything worthwhile at all, not even flavor. Enjoy your breakfast."

"It looks wonderful." Chris put a hand over his plate when she approached with the salt and pepper shakers.

"But I forgot to season the eggs," she explained.

"Thank God."

Lizette had her second cup of coffee while she watched Chris eat. Despite everything, he seemed to be enjoying his breakfast. She never tired of watching him do anything.

"So, tell me more about history and intrigue and whatever," Chris asked, looking up to smile at her. He knew she was watching him. He liked what it said about their relationship.

"I have to spend the rest of the morning in the attic."

"In this heat?"

"It's not nearly as bad as it sounds. The attic is more like a barn than anything else. The rafters are so high you can't even count the hundred-year-old cobwebs hanging from them. There are dormer windows, too, so that gives some cross ventilation."

"Why do you have to go up there in the first place?"

"Sophia asked me to. The River Road Historical Society is having a fund-raiser tea, and they'd like us to try and find costumes for some of the ladies to wear."

"Hoopskirts and bustles?"

"I don't think anything that interesting is left up there. Sophia's loaned a lot of clothing to a museum in New Orleans already. I think we'll probably just find touches for costumes the ladies re-create themselves. Things like lace collars and shawls. Anyway, I said I'd look."

"And you want some help?"

She rested her hand on his. "Would you mind? I could use some help moving things around. And . . ."

"And?"

"I'm afraid of mice."

His mouth twitched. "Promise to jump into my arms and throw your arms around my neck when you see one?"

"I promise."

"Then I'll do it."

The attic was everything Lizette had said it would be. The walls were layered with old newspapers to provide insulation, and the newspapers themselves were material for a museum collection.

Chris paused in the doorway. "I'm in a time machine. Going back . . . going back . . ."

"I came up here one night last year during a thunderstorm," Lizette told him. "The electricity had been knocked out, and I thought I smelled smoke. I was carrying a lantern, and the wavering light against these walls was something out of an old horror movie. There were even bats flying between the rafters. I haven't been back up since."

Chris ran his fingertips over a wooden trunk by the stairs. They didn't get dusty. "Somebody's been here."

"It's Barbara. She comes up whenever she has a chance. She's a history buff, and this place is a gold mine."

"What does she look for?"

"I'm not sure, exactly. Maps, diagrams of some of the old buildings. I know she's interested in the way cane used to be grown on this plantation. I guess you could say it's her hobby."

Chris lifted the top of the trunk and saw stacks of carefully preserved papers. "Are you a historian, too?"

"I guess not. I think I live too close to my history to want to explore it in any more depth." Lizette crossed the floor and stopped at an armoire with its pulls missing. "I don't think my fingernails are long enough to budge this. Got your handy-dandy survival tool?"

"Always." Chris flipped out one of the blades and gently pried open the door. "Success."

"Oooh... Look at this." Lizette pulled out a salmon-colored garment of the sheerest cotton. She held it against her shorts and blouse. "Somebody's nightgown. It's all hand-stitched. And look." She put it back and took out a velvet robe of the same salmon color. "Ostrich-feather trim."

"Are you sure River Oaks didn't supplement its income during Prohibition with a little distillery down in the cane fields and a few easy women on the second floor?"

"The big house would have made a wonderful bordello!" She hung up the robe. "I'm surprised some enterprising St. Hilaire didn't think of it. You're right about the period of the clothes, though. Definitely twentieth century. I don't think the River Road ladies would approve."

The attic was huge, and there were boxes, chests and dilapidated armoires throughout. Chris imagined he and Lizette might be there all day. "What's next?" He turned to a large trunk and lifted the cover. "Old military uniforms?"

Lizette peeked over his shoulder. "World War I."

Chris shut the top. "You have some idea where to look, don't you?"

She led him farther inside. "When Julian was still alive I used to wish I had a daughter to come up here with me. I never wanted J.J. to be a girl, but I would have liked to have had a daughter, too. J.J. gets bored immediately unless he's outside."

"So you wanted more children?"

She hesitated. "Not badly enough to let myself get pregnant again."

Chris remembered the first night they had made love and her story about Julian. He remembered that she'd said Julian had wanted another child and had tried erratically to conceive one. "Did Julian know you were using birth control?"

"Julian never asked. I guess he assumed I wanted nothing more in life than to produce little St. Hilaires. It just never came up for discussion."

"And yet you wanted a daughter."

"After J.J. was born I saw that raising a child here wasn't going to be easy. The expectations are so high. I wanted a daughter, but, well, it just didn't seem like a good idea."

Chris had imagined Lizette with their child. In fact, it had become a recurring fantasy. He already thought of J.J. as his son, a delusion that could have serious consequences someday, since J.J.'s flesh-and-blood relations, the Stanhopes and St. Hilaires, had very different ideas on child raising than he did. But the fantasy of Lizette with a child they had created together was even more dangerous. That fantasy meant a life with her, and a marriage. There was too much standing in the way to believe that would happen easily, if it happened at all.

Still, a little girl of their own. A little girl with his blond hair and Lizette's curls, his green eyes and Lizette's heart-shaped face. A little girl with J.J.'s energy, Lizette's grace, and his undying love.

Lizette seemed to read his mind. "Do you want children, Chris? You said something once that made me think you might."

"I'd like children if they were yours."

She swallowed hard. It was an idea too wonderful and too dangerous to consider. "Imagine what an awful big brother J.J. would be. He's such a tease."

"He's a normal six-year-old."

Lizette pulled the wooden knob on another armoire and it came off in her hand. The door swung open anyway. "Oh, look!" She lifted out a faded fawn-colored garment and shook out the folds. "A cape." She pulled it around her shoulders. It was made of silk and trimmed with embroidered violets and pleated ruffles. "I wonder how old this is?"

"Is that the kind of thing you're looking for?"

She shook her head. "Probably not. It's too fragile, anyway."

They found treasure in the next chest. It was a repository of accessories from the late nineteenth century. There were small hats trimmed with jet and plumes, a Persian lamb muff, fans, parasols and ladies' high-button kid boots in sizes much too small for modern feet.

The next chest yielded a lace shawl, the next box a taffeta crinoline.

"This should do it," Lizette told Chris, who was lifting the top of another trunk. "Sophia has some things at her house that she's going to loan them, too."

"What do you suppose the River Road ladies would say about this?"

Lizette peeked over his shoulder and whistled softly. "Every man's fantasy and every woman's nightmare."

Chris lifted out a black satin corset, heavily boned and stiffened. He held it up for Lizette to admire.

"See the way it's pinched in? This would have given the wearer a wasp waist," she explained, circling her own waist with her fingers to demonstrate.

"Show me."

She smiled. "Are you interested in fashion history?"

"I'm interested in seeing you in this."

She dug through the trunk until she came up with a delicate pink chemise adorned with thin satin ribbon and white lace. "A lady would have worn this next to her body, and then she would have put the corset over it, cinching it in the back. She probably would have tried for an eighteen-inch waist."

"I'm waiting."

Her eyes danced with laughter. "You're going to make me think you're serious."

"I am."

"Mardi Gras was months ago."

"I can be fooled. I'm from California."

"You really want to see me in this . . . this thing!"

"The corset and the chemise."

Lizette sensed that Chris's request was a dare. She was sure he didn't really expect her to undress right there and put on nineteenth-century underwear. The Lizette Stanhope who had been an avid high-school prankster came forward.

"All right." Before she could change her mind she stripped off her blouse and shorts. She stood in front of him in nothing more than a bra and panties, then lifted one hand in slow motion and reached around behind her. "They didn't wear bras." She unhooked hers and dropped it next to her shorts.

Chris marveled at the smooth, delicate lines of Lizette's body. If they were still together in twenty years and her body had changed through childbearing or through the gradual softening of age, he knew he would still want to look at her this way.

Desire under the eaves. He wondered if nineteenth-century men had worn anything to keep their bodies as tightly controlled as their women's. Before he could say or do a thing Lizette had wiggled into the chemise. She sneezed and realized she should have shaken the dust out of the garment first.

"You'll have to help me with the corset."

"Tell my shaking hands."

Lizette let her lips curve into a come-hither smile. "I'll hold it in the front and you cinch it, crisscross the laces and pull it tight. You'd better skip every other one or we might be here for days."

"How do you know all this?"

"I was in a historical pageant in high school." She took a deep breath, then let it out completely as Chris began to cinch the corset.

The corset just came to the tips of her breasts and the top of her hips. It was the type used in the 1890s and less restrictive than those used in previous decades. But for a twentieth-century woman used to nothing tighter than panty hose, it felt like a prison.

"What do you think?" She turned when he was finished with the laces and held out her arms.

"Can you breathe?" Chris realized he couldn't.

"It's not a turn-on?" she asked with a pretend pout.

For the first time Chris understood the male fascination with undergarments that restrained women's bodies so completely. Corsets and girdles had tremendous fantasy value. Not fantasies of a woman putting them on, but of a man taking them off. By the time a woman had been set free and her soft curves returned to their normal form, a man would be panting with lust.

"Let's just get this off you."

"I don't think so." Lizette sensed Chris's fascination. It excited her. She moved away. "Once started, I don't think I should stop. Do you?" She opened another chest and pulled out a pale yellow dress. "Just the thing. It's what they used to call a tea gown. My waist might just be small enough now to get into it."

Chris watched as she slipped the lightweight fabric over her head and straightened it as it fell into place. "Look at the leg-of-mutton sleeves and the lace on the front here. Of course, I need a ladies' maid to hook it for me," she told him, her eyes sparkling. She backed away a little as he moved toward her and grabbed one of the parasols they had taken out of the chest. She held him away with the end aimed at his navel.

"Then I'd need my hair up. Curls were in style during the Gay Nineties. I would have been fashionable." Lizette lifted her hair off her neck and piled it on her head, holding it in place with one hand. "What do you think? Would I have been a proper mistress for River Oaks?"

The desire that had heated Chris's blood suddenly began to cool, and not because her body was so well covered. She was lovely beyond imagining. Her cheeks were flushed and her eyes bright. But the woman standing in front of him in an ankle-length, lace-trimmed dress wasn't Lizette St. Hilaire anymore. She was the mistress of River Oaks. He had a sudden vision of generations of women who looked just like her wearing the same dress and smiling the same smile.

It suddenly seemed important to understand how much the same and how different she really was. "I know you said you leave all the papers up here to Barbara, but how much do you know about River Oaks' history?"

Lizette was surprised by Chris's question. She sobered a little. "The basics. Who was married to whom, that sort of thing."

"Did anyone ever leave?"

"Leave?"

"Did anyone ever turn their back on this place and go off to live a different kind of life?"

"I . . . I don't know. Not that I know of."

"I was afraid you'd say that."

"I'm sure some of them must have made compromises, though."

"Compromises?" Chris was sure Lizette knew they were no longer talking about her ancestors.

"Some of them must have found people from other places that they fell in love with and married."

"And brought to River Oaks to live?"

"Yes."

"I doubt it. I don't think it would have worked." He stepped close to her and smoothed her tumbled hair. "River Oaks is an all-or-nothing proposition. It doesn't allow for a different sort of person living a different sort of life here."

Lizette knew what Chris meant, and she knew he was right. Suddenly the attic heat was stifling, and the corset was making it difficult to breathe. "Would you help me out of this?"

"Yes." Chris gathered the fabric of her long skirt in his hands and helped her ease the tea gown over her head. Then he turned her and unlaced the corset as quickly as he could.

She sighed when it was off. Wearing only the thin chemise, she faced him, circling her arms around his waist. "I'm glad I don't live in the nineteenth century," she said, leaning against him.

Since Chris wasn't really sure that she didn't, he just pulled her closer and wondered what was going to happen to them.

Chapter Thirteen

Barbara knelt at her fireplace and fed sticks of kindling into a small flame. With careful nurturing she could have a fire that would burn brightly enough to warm the cabin before Paul woke up.

It was September, and although the days were still warm, it wasn't unusual for an occasional chilly morning like this one to come along as reassurance that the long, hot summer was going to end. The cool spell would help develop the sucrose content of the cane, too, so it was a double blessing.

"Didn't you ever hear of central heat and air?"

Barbara turned, resisting the temptation to crawl back into bed to warm Paul herself. The day was already late for a woman who usually rose before dawn, especially at planting season.

"If you want central heat and air, you'll have to spend all your nights in that cushy condo of yours back in New Orleans. Here you're going to get a fire in the winter and a breeze through the windows in the summer."

"What's that, then?" he asked, pointing to the air conditioner. "And that?" He pointed out a large electric space heater.

"That's cheating!"

"Seems to me I was in this cabin just last week and it was mighty cool for a hot August evening."

"I'm not above cheating." Barbara shot him a grin.

"Is that my T-shirt you've got on, woman?"

"Do you want me to run around this cold, cold cabin with nothing on?"

"This is your cabin. Your clothes live here."

"Your T-shirt was handier." Barbara stood and modeled it for him. It covered just enough of her to be provocative.

"Come on to bed and let me take back what's rightfully mine."

"I don't think so."

"The sun just came up. You don't have to be up with it."

"It's planting season. You've been hanging around here all summer watching me do a little of this, a little of that. Now the fun starts. This month we plant, and next month we harvest what we planted last year. This place'll be a circus."

"And I won't see you."

"You just try to disappear and see what happens," Barbara said, hands on her hips.

"My, my. What that does to my T-shirt."

She blew him a kiss before she grabbed a sweatshirt and jeans and took them into the bathroom. The rich smell of coffee brewing met her when she emerged from the shower. "Just coffee," she reminded him, pulling her sneakers on at the kitchen table. "We're supposed to have breakfast with Chris and Lizette at nine."

"And what am I supposed to do while you're off in the fields till then?"

"You can come with me." She laughed when he shook his head. "Or you can wait here and read one of those medical journals you always keep in your car in case you get a free minute."

"Know me pretty well, don't you?"

Barbara watched Paul pour her coffee. He knew how she liked it. Hot, strong, and black as the night. They had been lovers for a month, and there was no one who had ever known her as well as he did. And he was right; she knew him just as well. He was a confident man, a man who was used to going after what he wanted and winning. He wanted her, and Barbara was beginning to believe she might not be a passing fancy. He had told her as much, right from the beginning, but it had taken this long for her to believe him. Now she supposed she was falling in love.

"Yeah. I know you pretty well." Barbara reached for her coffee, but Paul held it firmly in his grasp.

"Shouldn't I at least get a good-morning kiss?"

Now that they were both fully dressed, or almost—Paul was still minus a shirt—Barbara agreed. The man was much too tempting otherwise, and these days she was easily tempted.

She leaned over the table and spent a long time apologizing nonverbally for not crawling back into bed with him.

"So, breakfast at the big house," he said when she was sipping her coffee.

"Chris is supposed to get there about nine. Lizette promised us a gourmet feast if we'd wait and eat with them."

"The River Oaks king and queen aren't going to be there, are they?"

Barbara chuckled over his titles for Jerome and Sophia. "No. They're out of town for a week, visiting family down in Mobile. Lizette gets a chance to act like a normal person for seven whole days. I'm hoping the freedom will put some sense into her head."

Paul just lifted an eyebrow.

"I know. I worry too much," Barbara said, so that he wouldn't have to.

"And what do you hope she'll decide?"

"To marry Chris and get out of this place! She's so head over heels in love with him it hurts to watch. But she's so tied to this two-bit piece of land that she doesn't know which end is up."

"Has Chris asked her to marry him?"

If he had, Lizette hadn't told her. Barbara had watched their relationship blossom all summer long. Lizette was ecstatic one moment and worried the next. She walked the razor's edge between her own happiness and her duties, and she rarely kept her balance, because it was an impossible feat. She couldn't please everyone, but she seemed determined to drive herself to the point of collapse trying.

Barbara shook her head. "Has Chris said anything to you?"

Paul smiled. "Why are we talking about Lizette and Chris?"

"Why not?"

"I think if you worry enough about Lizette, you don't have to worry about yourself. It's an old habit."

"I don't have any reason to worry about myself. I'm doing fine."

"What about me?"

"You're doing fine, too. Aren't you?"

Paul's smile widened. "Why aren't you worried about me in your life?"

She was trapped. "I don't have to worry. I don't have any old relatives breathing down my neck."

"That's true. In fact, you haven't even taken me home to meet your parents."

"When they left this place they went as far as they could go," she began.

"Monroe's not far."

Barbara was silent.

"When are you going to do what you keep telling Lizette she should do?"

She met his gaze. "What's that?"

"Admit you're in love and then go for it."

Paul had the deepest, most expressive eyes. Staring into them, she found it hard to keep the conversation light. "Would you really want a plantation manager messing around in your life?"

"I know one I might even want to mess around with for the rest of my life."

She swallowed. "That's a lot to think about."

"Then you'd better start on it as soon as possible."

She set down her coffee cup and looked at her watch. She could feel her heart pounding erratically in her throat. "I guess I'd better go."

"I love you."

Barbara looked up and saw that Paul wasn't smiling. In a second she was around the table and in his arms.

September's cooler weather had given new incentive to the rosebushes growing against the side pillars of the big house. Lizette thought of them as St. Hilaire roses. She had never seen their particular dark scarlet blossoms tipped with just a touch of ivory anywhere other than River Oaks. Sophia had told her once that she must care for them well, just as preceding generations had cared for them. The roses were part of J.J.'s heritage.

Years before, when the roses were in bloom, Julian had never come to see Lizette without the gift of one perfect bud. He had been a dashing figure, wonderfully handsome and always impeccably dressed, with one long-stemmed rosebud in his hand and the pride of possession in his eyes. She had been only seventeen when he had begun to court her, and Lizette imagined there were few seventeen-year-old girls in the world who could have resisted a man of Julian's charm, looks and social position.

Now, looking back on it, she wondered if she had resisted him anyway—at least at first. As impressed as she had been, Julian had always seemed like someone from her parents' generation. She had been fun-loving and popular, inclined to do tastefully zany things. She was always restrained by her upbringing, but it had been Lizette who had led the other girls at school in harmless pranks, Lizette who had challenged the status quo with her choice of friends and after-school activities. At first Julian's sense of dignity had been difficult to reconcile with her own free spirit.

Where had that spirited, adventurous girl gone? And when? Had it been after Julian's death, when the weight of single parenthood and River Oaks had dragged her into a life with no time for anything except endless duties? Or had it happened before that? Perhaps even before her marriage?

She had loved Julian. He had been a fantasy come true, a knight in shining armor. But perhaps she hadn't been a princess in need of rescuing.

Lizette realized that she had been staring at the St. Hilaire roses for a good five minutes, and she hadn't moved so much as an eyelid. She had become very good at staring off into space lately. There seemed to be so many answers out there, answers she wasn't able to grab and hold on to. They drifted just out of her reach, like the tiny specks of dust floating on the sunbeam striking one particularly perfect rose in front of her. If she reached out to grasp a dust speck it would disappear. Her answers seemed to disappear that way, too.

"I've never been jealous of a rose before, but I suppose there's a first time for everything."

"Chris!" Lizette whirled and threw her arms around Chris's neck.

"Hey, Lizzie-love, it's only been twenty-four hours since you saw me." Chris held her as tight as he could anyway. Despite his teasing, he had missed her enough to make him question his own sanity. Each day of the summer now past had made him realize more just how much she meant to him.

Lizette knew she had to get hold of herself. She was coming unglued over the silliest things these days. She pulled away, determined to be more nonchalant, but once out of his arms she felt so bereft that she threw herself back into them.

"Are we playing catch?"

"You're awful." She held on tighter, turning her face up to his for a lingering good-morning kiss.

"Awful hungry," he said when the kiss had turned into two and then, regretfully, ended. "I heard a rumor I was being served breakfast. At least, that's what I was told to lure me up here."

"Everything's ready. I just came out to get some roses for the table."

"Is staring at roses a secret way of getting them to leap into the basket?"

"While I cut some, remind me why I invited you to spend the day, would you?"

Chris watched Lizette stretch between the straggling canes to fill the basket at her feet with dew-moistened blossoms. The roses themselves were peculiar. He had never seen anything like them. They were blood-red, with just the faintest touch of white on the edges of their petals, almost too perfect to be real. Chris guessed that they had no scent. He stooped and brought one to his nose. He was right.

"That should do." Lizette lifted the basket and looped her arm through Chris's. "Did Paul come with you?" she asked as they started toward the house.

"He came up last night."

She was surprised. "Now how did I miss that?"

"Maybe Barbara didn't want you to know."

"Want me to know what? That they're crazy about each other? That more is going on than good-night kisses?"

"I think he's going to propose."

Lizette stopped. "You're kidding."

"Just call it male intuition."

They started toward the house once more. Lizette was so barraged by conflicting emotions that she couldn't sort them out as fast as they hit her. Happiness. She was definitely happy for Barbara and Paul. She knew the match was a good one, and they deserved each other. Concern. Barbara was the most independent woman Lizette had ever known. Would the idea of marriage to any man appeal to her? Fear. How was she going to manage without Barbara at River Oaks, both business-wise and personally? And last—though not last in power—jealousy. Lizette didn't begrudge Barbara her good fortune, but why couldn't life be that simple for her, too? What would it be like to have Chris propose and be able to consider the decision to marry him without having impossible obstacles in the way? She and Barbara were the same age. How had her own life become so unbearably complicated?

In the kitchen, Lizette put the roses in a vase while Chris stood at the sink and observed. There was an innate economy in the way Lizette moved. She did everything without fuss and without the useless flourishes some women believed made them more feminine. She did most things the way she ran, gracefully, cleanly and with wholehearted participation. He knew he would never want to stop watching her, not if they were together for a lifetime.

He wondered if the news about Barbara and Paul had sparked any feelings in Lizette about him and their situation. He couldn't tell by her expression, or by the way she went about placing the roses in water. She was a difficult woman to read, because she didn't want to admit to her feelings. She had trained herself not to show her responses—or perhaps she had been trained. Whichever it was, it was one of the few things about her he would like to change.

"Did I hear we were having breakfast sometime this morning?"

Lizette smiled her greeting to Paul, who had come in unannounced to stand next to Chris. "Where's Barbara?"

"She was out in the fields at dawn. She's back at the cabin taking a shower and changing."

"I'm here already." Barbara walked through the back doorway.

"How'd you get here so fast, woman?" Paul asked, holding out his hand.

Barbara let him pull her to rest against him. "I drove."

Paul hooted his disapproval, but he didn't let her go.

"What can I do?" Barbara offered.

"Get these men out of here for me, would you? And put these on the table." Lizette handed Barbara the roses. "Then I'll serve."

Breakfast was a pecan coffee cake and sausage soufflé with a fresh fruit salad that Barbara had contributed and Louisiana-style coffee with chicory.

The coffee cake was almost gone and everyone was on their second cup of coffee when Paul cleared his throat. "I've got something to say."

Lizette didn't know whether to clap her hands or cry. She was sure she knew what was coming.

"Barbara," Paul turned to look at her, "I don't want you to be mad about this, but I think if you keep waiting for the right time to tell Lizette your idea about opening up River Oaks, you're going to wait forever. I'd like to tell her myself."

Barbara's eyes gleamed with anger. "Drop it, Paul."

"That's what you've been doing, and it's too good an idea to drop."

"Barbara?" Lizette frowned at her friend. Apparently she had been wrong about Paul's announcement. "Is there really something you don't want to talk to me about?"

Barbara shot Paul an if-looks-could-kill glare. "It's an idea I had," she told Lizette. "It's not fleshed out yet."

Paul ignored the glare. "It's as thoroughly planned as anything I've ever seen. I've done major surgery with less attention to detail."

"Remind me to find a new doctor," Chris muttered.

"Sounds like you're going to have to tell me," Lizette told Barbara.

With an air of resignation Barbara launched into a description of the idea she had first shared with Paul. When she was finished everyone was silent while Lizette poured another round of coffee.

"I guess the thing that amazes me," Lizette said at last, "is that you've been thinking about this for some time, but you haven't told me about it before this. Why not?"

"You've had enough on your mind."

Lizette wondered if Barbara had tried to tell her and she had been so self-absorbed that she'd missed all the signals. "Have you considered the economics of it?"

Barbara explained her ideas on financing.

Lizette listened, nodding. "How about educational grants from the state? Surely they'd foot some of the bill, wouldn't they?"

The two women continued to bounce the idea back and forth while the men sat back and listened.

"We could do a quick tour," Barbara said at last. "I could show you exactly what I've been thinking about."

"Would you mind, Chris?" Lizette asked. "Would you come with us?"

Chris nodded.

"Paul?" Barbara reached for his hand.

"You're not too mad to invite me?"

"Infuriating man."

Forty-five minutes later they stood under the group of willows that had become a special place for Chris and Lizette.

Barbara began a nervous explanation of her idea for the area. "I think that for this to be really educational, we need to show the kids and the tourists how sugarcane was processed during the early part of the last century and before. I want to build a sugar mill, a very simple one, with nothing more than a frame and three grinders. We could use oxen or mules to power it—probably mules, since we'll be using them in the fields, too." Barbara walked a line about fifty feet long. "It would be about this diameter. We'd have to cut some of the trees, but not too many. The shade would be nice for people watching the mill in action."

"What would you do with the cane juice?" Lizette wanted to know. "If you build even a primitive sugarhouse, it's going to cost a fortune."

"I'm not sure we'd ever get to that point," Barbara agreed. "I thought maybe we'd just give demonstrations outside and boil the juice down in open kettles over a fire. If we can get someone really skilled to run this part of it, we might even be able to set it up to get it to granulate. If it didn't, though, that would be a lesson, too. And, of course, as part of the experience, we'll take the kids to one of the local mills and let them see how it's done today as a contrast."

"We've still got some of the equipment from the old sugarhouse in one of the barns." Lizette realized she was getting excited about the possibilities herself. Barbara's enthusiasm was catching. "Maybe we could include a walk-through display and lecture."

"Then you like the idea?"

"I do." Lizette was quiet for a moment. "The St. Hilaires won't," she added, having sobered quickly. "They pride themselves on the fact that River Oaks has never had to be opened to the public."

"They've gone through most of a considerable fortune to assure it, too."

"I know."

"I'm not saying that my idea would be the salvation of this place, but it would generate some income, especially if we open it to tour groups, too. As close as we are to Houmas House and Tezcuco, and as different an experience as this would be, we'd have busloads of people coming through. If you opened the big house for tours..."

"That's out of the question. Jerome and Sophia wouldn't allow it."

"They can't stand in your way."

Lizette knew that legally Barbara was right. But what about traditions? What about her duty to carry them on? "The big house would have to be off limits, but maybe the rest of it's possible."

"You're going to think about it, then?"

"I am."

"I'm going to pursue my ideas for financing some of the renovations and for building the grinding mill."

"Let me know what you find out."

Chris held Lizette back as Paul and Barbara started toward Barbara's truck. "Let's walk." Without waiting for an answer, he told the others to go on without them.

"What did you really think of Barbara's idea?" Chris asked as they cut through the fields to avoid the cloud of dust the truck had raised.

"It's going to take me some time to put it all together."

"What does that mean?"

Lizette heard the sharp tone of Chris's voice more clearly than she heard his question. "What's wrong?"

Chris ran his hand through his hair, and Lizette watched it fall back over his forehead. "Just once I'd like to see you think about something without considering how your in-laws will react."

"You're angry, aren't you?"

"Discouraged."

Strangely enough, discouraged was the word describing her own feelings. She was discouraged before she even had a chance to think about Barbara's plan. "It's not just Jerome and Sophia," she tried to explain. "It's everything. It's what River Oaks stands for."

"What does it stand for? Tell me, and then maybe I'll understand."

"River Oaks is a way of life. It's history. It's J.J.'s inheritance. If we open it to the public, it's not ours anymore, not really. It just becomes another house on River Road for strangers to stare at."

"What have you got if you don't? A huge old house that's falling down around your ears? A plantation that makes money one year and hovers on the brink of bankruptcy the next? A historic piece of property sandwiched in between the lush scenery of chemical plants and oil refineries?"

"I know it's hard for you to understand."

"Because I'm an outsider, you mean?"

"Chris, I don't want to fight with you."

Chris heard the plea in Lizette's voice. She didn't want a fight. He was her port in the storm, the one person who made no demands on her. He also knew that was about to change. It had to. "I'm going to tell you what I think about this place," he said quietly. "And if that turns into a fight, then maybe it has to."

She wanted to cover her ears. She wanted to run.

"River Oaks is a monument to a way of life that hasn't existed for a century. The equipment used out in these fields is different. You take your cane to a cooperative mill now instead of processing it right here on your property, but nothing else has changed. The St. Hilaires are caught in a time warp, but you're in an even worse position. You're caught with one foot in this century and one foot in the last.

Eventually you're going to have to choose which one you want to live in.''

"If all this is so ridiculous, why do you even bother to come here?"

"I don't come here to see River Oaks, that's for sure. I come here to see you. I love you." Chris grabbed Lizette's arm and forced her to stop. "I love you. You know I do. I have to grit my teeth to make myself set foot on this place, because when I do I see what it's doing to you. But I come anyway, because I can't stay away. And when I leave? Hell, when I leave, it's worse. I want to throw you over my shoulder and take you and J.J. with me. I want to get you away from this damned memorial to a way of life that was filled with inequities and heartbreak and despair!"

Lizette jerked her arm out of Chris's grasp. "Don't you dare talk about River Oaks as if it's nothing but a malicious waste of time!"

"It's worse than a waste of time. This place is destroying you. I watch you run, remember? What are you running from, Lizette? You run like you're pursued. And what's pursuing you? Maybe you need to turn around and look behind you to find out." He put his hands on her shoulders and forced her to turn. "That's what you'd see!"

River Oaks stood proudly in the background.

"Take your hands off me!" Lizette wrenched away from Chris's hold and started to run. She was halfway back to the house before Chris caught up with her.

"Slow down."

She continued to run, ignoring his command.

Chris put his hand on her arm. "Come on, Lizette."

She knew he could force her to stop. She slowed her pace and began a fast walk.

"Did you hear me tell you I love you?"

Tears sprang to her eyes, but she kept walking without a word to him.

Chris was silent until just before they turned onto the road leading up to the big house. "I think I fell in love with you when I saw you take off at the Classic. You were so determined to show me you weren't in the wrong category."

"I wasn't trying to show you anything!"

"I couldn't figure out why I kept after you the way I did. I had to move heaven and earth to get your address. Then I had to keep after you to see me."

"Maybe you should have put your energies into something more satisfying."

"Nothing could be more satisfying." His fingers brushed her arm, but it was enough to stop her.

"Well, which half do you love?" she asked, not quite meeting his eyes. "The half in this century or the half in the last?"

"I'm not going to apologize." Chris tipped her chin so she was looking right at him. "We've got a problem. And it's not just my imagination."

"You're the one with the problem."

"I don't think so." He framed her face with his hands. "You love me, too. As wrong as you believe it to be, as inconvenient as it is, you love me. You can keep pretending to yourself that it hasn't gone that far, but it will only be pretending. Eventually you're going to have to face the truth. And then you're going to have to make a decision."

She blinked back tears. "A decision?" Her voice cracked.

"Me or River Oaks. This century or the last."

"You take a lot for granted."

"I don't take anything for granted. Right now I wouldn't hedge my bets on which you're going to choose."

"There's so much you don't understand."

"And so much you don't see."

She smiled, because she knew that if she didn't, she'd cry. And she hadn't cried in front of anyone for more than a decade. "We're quite a pair, aren't we? Could we be any more different?"

Chris didn't smile back. He knew she was holding back tears, and he would have preferred them. He wondered if Julian St. Hilaire was responsible for her refusal to cry. "We're not so different. We want the same things. The difference is that you've been taught not to admit what you want. I haven't." He pulled her close to soften his words. "I don't want to ruin our day together. Let's go pick up J.J. at your parents' house and drive into town to a movie. We'll talk about this later.''

"I don't want to talk about it at all."

"I know."

They walked back toward the house in silence.

Chapter Fourteen

Her bedroom was enveloped in a white cloud.

For a moment Lizette wondered if she had mistakenly left the windows to the gallery open and the cloud was fog from the river. She opened her eyes wider, and then she remembered. The cloud was the Brussels-lace mosquito bar draped around her bed in a full circle from the tester overhead. She never used it herself, but Chris had pulled it around them last night when they climbed into the tall bed together. He had said it made their world more private.

Chris.

Lizette turned over and stared at the sleeping man next to her. Chris was here. At River Oaks. In her bed.

She knew she was smiling.

Lizette tried to remember the events of the evening. She, Chris and J.J. had returned from Baton Rouge about nine. It had turned chilly again after a reasonably warm day. She had promised Chris a hot toddy before his long, cold, lonely trip back to New Orleans. They had put J.J. to bed, then one hot toddy had turned into two. Two hot toddies had turned into a night of love.

And why not? The St. Hilaires were gone. J.J. could be told that Chris had slept in Lizette's office—if he even asked. No one else would know that the mistress of River Oaks plantation had spent one perfect night with her lover in her own bed.

It was Sunday. Chris would have to go back to New Orleans tonight after dinner, but in addition to one perfect night, they had another whole day to look forward to together. Almost like a family.

Lizette propped her head on one hand and watched Chris sleeping. She had done this before, but she never tired of it. Her eyes traced the firm, golden, stubble-roughened lines of his jaw to his lips, slightly parted in sleep. She examined his nose—his father's nose, he had once told her—and wondered in what other ways he resembled the man she had never met. She admired the golden brown of his lashes and brows, and the wide, smooth planes of his forehead—a forehead splashed with the silky gold of his hair. He was beautiful in sleep, but she found she missed not seeing his eyes, his laughter-filled, emerald eyes.

A sheet covered his body, except for his shoulders, which had the well-developed breadth of an athlete's. But then, she knew from experience that his whole body was well developed. There wasn't an ounce of fat anywhere on Chris. All of him was athletically trim and fit. And long. So long, in fact, that his feet had escaped the covers and now hung over the wooden footboard. So much for the delights of a modern man in an eighteenth-century bed.

"My feet are cold."

She giggled at his mumbled words. Tying back the mosquito bar on her side, she slipped down to the floor and around the bottom of the bed to shove his feet back onto the mattress and under the covers. She tucked the blanket and hand-crocheted spread under the mattress and crawled back into bed beside him.

"Better?"

"C'mere." Chris wrapped his arms around her and pulled her tightly against his chest. "Lemons. You always smell like lemons and roses. And fresh air." He yawned.

"Some wizened old perfume manufacturer in Paris is going to have a heart attack over that."

"Mmm . . . I like it. Tell him not to change a thing."

"Were you surprised to find out where you were sleeping?"

"After yesterday morning I thought I'd never wake up next to you again, anywhere."

Talking about their fight was the last thing Lizette wanted to do. "That just shows you how wrong you can be."

"I've never minded being wrong."

"Can you spend the day here, or do you have to get back to New Orleans?" She hurried on. "Before you answer, you should know that if you say you have to go back early, I'm going to get up and uncover your feet."

"I'll stay. I'll stay."

She turned over so they were face-to-face. "Do you have any plans for the day?"

As she watched, the clear green of his eyes seemed to darken. "How about plans for this morning—as in the next hour?"

"I believe that if he finds the door between our rooms locked, there might be a child standing at one of these windows watching us before too long."

"I knew there was something about the design of this house that I didn't like."

"I'm sorry," she said with real regret.

"Would you like me to get up and pretend I slept somewhere else?"

"Let's both get up and take a shower. J.J.'s not old enough to try to ferret out our sleeping arrangements."

"We can shower together."

She couldn't think of anything that was wrong with his plan.

Minutes later, with the warm water of the shower sluicing over her naked body and Chris's arms around her, she was even more convinced that his idea had been a good one.

The water turned cool before they finally got out. He dried her with such painstaking thoroughness that she threatened to make him get back in the shower, cool water and all. Then she turned around and paid the same amount of loving attention to him.

Finally, fully dressed, she left Chris to shave while she went down the backstairs to the kitchen to start breakfast. J.J., in his favorite red shirt and baseball cap, was sitting at the table munching a bowl of cereal without milk when she arrived.

Lizette got the milk out while she greeted him. "Sleep well last night?"

"Chris's car is still here."

"He stayed here last night. It was easier than going home and coming back again. He's going to spend today with us."

"Could Chris be my daddy?" J.J. put his hands over his bowl when Lizette tipped the carton over it. "I could ask him," he volunteered.

"I don't think that's a good idea. Do you want your milk in a glass?"

J.J. nodded. "A little glass. How come?"

"J.J., you had a daddy, but he died. You know that."

"Can't I have another one?"

How could she say that was impossible when they lived in a world where some kids had multiple fathers and mothers by the age of two? Lizette sat down in front of J.J. and propped her head on her folded hands. "Listen to me, sweetheart. Chris can't be your daddy because he's not married to me. We're just good friends."

"Good friends can be married," he pointed out stubbornly.

"We're not," she pointed out just as stubbornly.

"Can old people with kids get married?"

"Old people like me?" Lizette watched him nod and tried to hide her smile. "Yes, old people can get married."

"Then why don't you?"

She couldn't think of a single reason that would make sense to a six-year-old. "Drink your milk," she said at last.

"I'll ask Chris."

"Ask Chris what?" said a voice from the doorway.

J.J. gave Chris an ear-to-ear grin and jumped down from his chair for a hug. "Why don't you marry my mom?" he asked when Chris had put him down.

Chris saw the heightened color in Lizette's cheeks before he turned his attention back to J.J. "Your mom's just too pretty for an ugly slug like me." He made a face that had J.J. in hysterics in seconds. By the time the two had finished their roughhousing, Lizette had eggs and toast on the table and, to her profound relief, J.J.'s attention had turned elsewhere.

"Do you want some more batting practice today?" Chris asked the little boy when J.J. had finished his cereal.

"Yeah! Ricky too?"

"Ricky too."

"We should go to church." Lizette saw J.J.'s excitement fade. Now that he was back in school he had very little time to play with his friends. If he and Lizette went to church they would be expected to go to Lizette's parents' house for lunch, even though the rotating Sunday brunch had been canceled because the St. Hilaires were out of town. Chris could go with them, but the Stanhopes were as warmly welcoming to him as the St. Hilaires were. Lizette wouldn't ask Chris or J.J. to go through a day like that.

"Do we have to?" J.J. asked. "Couldn't I say my prayers after lunch or sumpthin'?"

"Just this once."

"I'm gonna go tell Ricky."

Lizette and Chris watched the little boy streak through the doorway. "He loves you," she said when J.J. was gone.

"It's mutual."

As they finished their meal Lizette wondered why something as special as the affection between Chris and J.J. could loom as a potential problem. What would J.J. do when Chris left?

Through the summer months, despite the heat, Chris had managed to teach J.J. and Ricky the rudiments of batting and catching. Thanks to Chris, each boy was the proud owner of a good glove and bat, and practicing their skills had almost taken the place of frog collecting. Now that the weather was cooler, their interest was even keener.

Chris spent most of the morning in a field behind the quarters teaching them to pitch the ball to each other so that they could each practice batting. Neither boy had much control over where the ball went, either when they pitched or when they batted it, but both were learning quickly.

"They're doing okay," Chris said proudly, flopping on the grass next to Lizette to watch the boys try to manage on their own.

"They were practicing this last week by themselves. J.J. missed more than he hit, but he hit one that landed on his grandmother's flower bed."

"And she wasn't amused."

"J.J. got a lecture on the damage a baseball could do to valuable property. That's why he's to come out here to practice from now on. Sophia's orders."

"It's not a bad idea."

"No. He won't forget it, either. She made him weed the flower bed."

Chris didn't laugh.

"He'll never like chrysanthemums again," Lizette added, hoping Chris would at least smile.

He didn't. "J.J.'s grandparents are too strict with him. He's a good kid. He doesn't need a heavy hand."

More than once she had had the same thought, but she told Chris what she had told herself. "They are his grandparents, and they love him."

"I'm not sure he knows it."

"We're getting dangerously close to another fight."

"We seem to have a growing list of things we can't talk about without fighting. River Oaks. J.J. The St. Hilaires." Chris stood to rejoin the boys. "If it gets any longer, neither one of us will be able to open our mouths."

Lizette watched Chris crouch behind Ricky and help him position his bat. He was right. If they continued to disagree on the most important issues in her life, there would be little they could talk about, and little reason to talk. And the thought of not being able to talk to Chris was like being told she couldn't breathe anymore. The problem was that she didn't know any way to change things without changing her whole life.

Lizette wandered back up to the big house to get soft drinks for everybody and to put a little distance between her and Chris. By the time she returned, baseball practice was over. J.J. requested hot dogs for lunch in between swallows of root beer.

"I don't think I have any." Lizette couldn't miss J.J.'s disappointment. Hot dogs were one of those treats she let him have when his grandparents weren't around to see. She imagined that when he had heard the St. Hilaires were going to be gone for a whole week, one of his first thoughts had been of hot dogs. Unfortunately, hers had not. "I'll tell you what. I'll run into Port A and get some. We need milk and bread anyway."

"I'll come with you." Chris crushed his can in one hand to the delight of the two boys, who immediately finished their drinks so that they could try. "Boys, are you coming?"

The boys elected to stay behind under Marydell's supervision. During the drive and once they reached Port Ascension, both Chris and Lizette made an effort to put their argument behind them. Chris teased her about buying hot dogs, then admitted that since they were sold at ball games, hot dogs had a special dispensation. At Mack's General Merchandise he stepped inside just long enough to buy her a red baseball cap like J.J.'s, then made her wear it backward over her dark curls in imitation of her son. On the way back to the van they both reminisced about the day Chris had stood in the post office waiting for her.

"You were by far the best thing I ever got with my mail," Lizette told him with a wink.

By the time they were almost back to River Oaks, they were able to sit in comfortable silence. As the levee-lined road curved and twisted along the river, Chris wondered if he and Lizette would continue their cycle of tension, intimacy, tension, intimacy, indefinitely, or if something was going to come along soon to make them confront the problems between them once and for all.

That thought was pushed aside by a glimpse of red behind a group of trees on the edge of the road. The finely honed reflexes of a third-baseman/surgeon took command, and before he was even sure what he'd seen, Chris was yelling, "Pull over!"

Startled, Lizette did as she'd been told. Slamming on the brakes, she parked the van on the shoulder of a sharp curve, just off the road. "What's wrong? This is a dangerous place to stop."

Chris was out of the van before she finished her sentence. He sprinted across the road and along the curve. He was out of sight in seconds. Lizette pulled the van back onto the road and around the corner to a safer spot. Then she got out, too, and began to jog along the shoulder in the direction Chris had taken.

He hadn't gone far. When she saw him, he was sitting on a slight rise above the road opposite the levee, with J.J. in his arms.

"J.J.!" Lizette joined them, trying to make sense of J.J.'s presence. "Chris?"

J.J. flung himself at her, and Lizette hugged him hard. "What on earth's the matter? What are you doing out here? You know you're never supposed to come out to the road. This is a great way to get hurt." Lizette realized she was babbling. She met Chris's eyes and saw they were blazing with anger. By now J.J. was sobbing too hard to tell her anything. "Chris?" she demanded. "What happened?"

"The St. Hilaires came back."

She frowned, rocking J.J. back and forth as she tried to figure out why Jerome and Sophia would be back and what that had to do with J.J. being on River Road by himself.

"J.J. and Ricky were up at the big house waiting for us to get back," Chris went on. "Apparently they were tossing the ball back and forth in front of the house—carefully, J.J. insists—when the St. Hilaires got there. Sophia got very angry and told Ricky to go home. Then she sent J.J. up to his room and told him not to come down until dinner. He's supposed to be there now.''

"I'm running away," J.J. said between sobs.

Lizette held him tighter. "You know you're not supposed to play with the ball by the house. What if you'd knocked out a window?"

"She told Ricky he couldn't play with me again! Never!"

Lizette stiffened.

"Grandfather St. Hilaire said Ricky was a bad infl'ence.''

Lizette wanted to cry, too.

"And he told me my daddy would be mad at me." The last precipitated a new round of sobs. "Would he?"

Lizette didn't want to believe it herself, but she was afraid Jerome was probably right. Julian would have been mad, but she just couldn't believe Jerome would have been cruel enough to say so. "Your daddy loved you," she assured J.J. "But that doesn't mean he would have liked it if you did things you weren't supposed to."

"We were practicing catching. Chris told us to, didn't you, Chris? We weren't throwing hard. We was being careful.''

"I'll explain to them, son." Chris stepped closer to stroke the little boy's hair. "We'll go back, and I'll tell them I asked you to practice."

"I don't think that would be a good idea." Lizette continued to sway from side to side to soothe the little boy, but her eyes sought Chris's. "I'd better handle it."

"Not this time."

Lizette had never heard Chris sound so cold. Or so firm. "I'm going to handle it," she repeated.

"No." Chris held out his hand. "Give me the keys. You can hold him on your lap while I drive."

"This isn't a good idea," she said, fishing for her keys in her pocket even as she said the words.

"It wasn't a good idea for two adults to browbeat two little boys, either, was it?"

Lizette felt her stomach knot with anxiety. She found her keys and handed them over. "Look, let's just sit on this a while. I'll make us lunch, and we can let the whole thing settle a little.''

"I'm not s'posed to have lunch," J.J. said tearfully.

"We're going to talk it out now!" Chris strode toward the van, and Lizette was left little choice except to follow with J.J.

"I wonder why they're back?" Lizette set J.J. down on the seat while she climbed up, then settled him on her lap.

"Maybe they didn't like the real world." Chris started the engine and pulled out on the road.

"You're in no shape to talk to anybody. Please wait, Chris."

He didn't answer.

At River Oaks, Chris pulled into the parking area and climbed down to come around and help Lizette with J.J. "Why don't you take him upstairs? I'll come and get you when I'm through talking to your in-laws."

"I'm going with you." Despite J.J.'s clinging body, Lizette grabbed Chris's arm. "Wait until I get J.J. settled."

They left J.J. in his room with a firm promise that he wouldn't run away again. Marydell was nowhere to be seen, and Lizette imagined that if she had heard Jerome's comments to Ricky, she was probably at home packing. Marydell and Tyrone were proud, capable people. Finding more amiable employment wouldn't be a strain.

Outside the big house, Lizette took Chris's arm to slow him down. "I know they were too tough on J.J., and much too tough on Ricky, but they're old and impatient. They just want J.J. to grow up with the right . . ." She fumbled for a word.

"Values? Values like things over people? Is that what you were striving for? River Oaks over everything else in the world?"

"You're just going to antagonize them further."

"Further? What have I ever done to antagonize them? I fell in love with their daughter-in-law. I made her think about something other than this . . . this shrine to the St. Hilaire family. Life antagonizes them, Lizette. Anyone who lives it antagonizes them."

"You're mad at me, too." She tried to hold him back.

"Yeah. I wish you'd open your eyes." He pulled his arm from her grasp and continued his purposeful stride toward the St. Hilaires' house.

They were waiting on the front porch. Jerome stepped forward. "I see you're back." His words were directed to Lizette. He ignored Chris.

Chris wouldn't be ignored. "We found J.J. on River Road. He was running away."

"I hope you intend to do something about his behavior, Lizette," Sophia said, joining her husband at the front of the porch. "He's getting out of hand." Her gaze settled on Chris. "It's the people he's around."

"Most of the people J.J.'s around remember he's just a little boy. Sometimes little boys make mistakes, but that doesn't mean they needed to be insulted or punished," Chris said.

"I don't see that this is any of your business." Jerome gave up the pretense of ignoring Chris. "This is my grandson we're discussing. He's nothing to you."

"I happen to love J.J. And I love his mother. If I have my way, J.J.'s going to be my son someday, and I don't want anybody abusing him."

"How dare you!" Sophia paled visibly. "Abuse?"

"There are lots of kinds of abuse, Mrs. St. Hilaire. Making a child feel that normal behavior is bad, and that he's bad because of it, is a form of abuse. I won't have J.J. abused by anyone."

Lizette was still in shock at Chris's announcement of his intentions. She only dimly heard the last exchange.

"What do you have to say, Lizette?"

Lizette looked up, startled. Jerome had been speaking to her. "I . . . I'd like to hear what happened. J.J. was so upset. . . ." Her voice trailed off.

"We drove in." Sophia backtracked. "Caroline caught a cold the first day we were in Mobile. We decided not to stay, so we left early this morning to come home."

Lizette wondered why they hadn't called. She didn't like her own suspicions, but she wondered if they had come home unannounced just so they could see what was happening in their absence. She pushed down the thought as Sophia continued.

"When we drove up, J.J. and Marydell's boy were right in front of the big house throwing a ball. I've told J.J. he's not to even have a ball near the house. What if he'd broken a window?"

"Glass can be replaced," Chris said, biting off the words. "A little boy's self-esteem can't."

"That glass can *not* be replaced. It's as old as this house."

Lizette cut in before Chris could say anything. "He shouldn't have had the ball so close to the house. But according to J.J., he and Ricky were just tossing it lightly back and forth. I'm not sure he understood that wasn't allowed. He knew he wasn't supposed to practice batting nearby."

"I told him no balls at all. When I took it away from him, Marydell's boy—"

"Ricky. The boy has a name. It's Ricky," Chris interrupted.

"Told me," Sophia went on, ignoring Chris, "that it was his ball and he wanted it back. When I told him no, he said he was going to tell his mother."

Chris didn't say anything, but Lizette saw his clenched jaw. Before she could try to defuse the situation, Sophia finished.

"That boy doesn't know his place. I don't want him playing with J.J. anymore. J.J. needs to learn who a friend is and who a friend isn't."

"Did you tell him that?" Chris asked.

"I told him the boy wasn't a good influence on him and that's why he had done such a bad thing. Then I sent him to his room to think."

"Did you know he hadn't eaten his lunch? Or did you think missing a meal would build his character?"

"I don't have to answer to you, Dr. Matthews. J.J. is a St. Hilaire. And he's my grandson."

Lizette fully expected Chris to launch into a tirade, but as she watched, he seemed to think better of it. When he turned to her, the fire in his eyes was banked. Barely. "All right,

Lizette," he said, his words icy cold in contrast to his eyes. "She has a point. I'm not the child's father. Not yet. But you're his mother."

He didn't have to add the rest. She was the child's mother, and it was up to her to take the St. Hilaires to task for their behavior.

And yet she couldn't. She understood them as no one else did. She had been married to their son; she had borne their grandson. There was no part of her that accepted their attitude toward Ricky and its inherent racism, just as there was no part of her that believed they had been just in dealing with J.J. But there was a part of her that understood. They were old, too old to change. River Oaks was their life, their whole world. When they felt a threat to it, they went a little crazy. But they weren't bad people. She couldn't believe that, and she couldn't believe they would hurt J.J., or even Ricky, intentionally.

"I'm sorry that J.J. disobeyed you," she said finally, not looking at Chris. "And I'm sorry if Ricky was rude to you. I think you were a little too harsh, though. Neither boy set out to cause trouble."

"We are J.J.'s grandparents," Jerome said, as if nothing else mattered.

"I know you are. I'll keep him in the house for the rest of the day. And I'll talk to both boys about an apology."

"An apology." Chris's words were said with no emotion, as if he were just underlining what Lizette had said.

"I expected you to understand." Sophia was triumphant.

Lizette didn't feel she had received a compliment.

"I don't understand," Chris said. "Neither of those boys has anything to apologize about."

"But then, you're not from here," Sophia reminded him. "We wouldn't expect you to understand our standards."

"We'll talk later." Lizette touched Chris's arm in an unspoken plea, then she turned and started toward the big house, hoping that Chris was behind her.

He caught up to her in a moment. "Well done, Lizette. You sold out with such grace."

"Look, I know you don't agree with me, but that was a compromise. J.J. can stay in the house, not his room, and he won't miss lunch. I'll talk to Marydell and calm her and Tyrone down if I can, and later, when everything is back to normal, I'll take Ricky and J.J. to apologize. Sophia and Jerome will be civil to them, and no one will say a word when they start playing together again."

"And you think that will take care of it? How about the next time? And the time after that? How about the day when Ricky gets old enough to really tell the St. Hilaires where they can get off, and J.J. has to choose between his best friend and the grandparents he's supposed to respect? What about the next time the St. Hilaires go too far and J.J. runs away again, only this time you don't find him right away? Whose side will you be on then?"

"I have to live at River Oaks!" Lizette stopped in the middle of the path between the two houses and faced him. "You don't! Sure, it's easy to just waltz in and see the problems here. But do you think you're going to solve them with a lecture or two? I have to do what's best. I have to live here with them!"

"No you don't!" Chris gripped her arms as if he wanted to shake her. "You don't have to live here, and neither does J.J. This isn't a prison, Lizette. You can leave anytime, and you can take your son with you. I meant what I said back there. Marry me and come with me away from River Oaks. There's a whole world out there, a world where people get to choose how they're going to be treated and what they're going to do with their lives. A world where people enjoy themselves. A world where some people even run because it's fun, not because they're so tied up in knots they're afraid they'll die if they don't!"

"How immensely flattering! You want to marry me to save me from something that doesn't even exist! I live here because I want to. This is my home. This is J.J.'s home. I don't need your help in escaping. I can walk out anytime I want!" She tried to pull away, but he wouldn't let her go.

"Then do it. Come with me. You know you love me, too. The three of us can be a family. A real family. Say goodbye to this place and leave Barbara in charge. Come with me."

Could it be that simple? Could she really walk away and just forget about River Oaks? Lizette's eyes filled with tears, and to her chagrin they overflowed and began to slide down her cheeks. "I can't." Her voice broke. "You don't understand. I belong here. J.J. belongs here. If there are problems, we have to deal with them here."

"And what about me?"

"You're going to California."

"And if I didn't? If I stayed in New Orleans, would you marry me and live there? You could come back to River Oaks whenever you wanted to check on things and bring J.J. to see his grandparents."

She was the world's expert on compromise, but she also knew when compromise was impossible. The situation Chris described would pull her to pieces in an emotional tug-of-war between River Oaks and her life with him. Eventually she would have to make the choice she was being called on to make now.

She wiped her cheek on her shoulder. "This is no time to ask me to marry you. Not when we're both angry and confused."

"I'm not confused." He lifted a hand and wiped her other cheek. He was silent a long time, searching her eyes. "And you're not either, are you?" he said sadly. "There's never even been a decision for you to make."

"I warned you right from the beginning that there was no place in my life for a relationship." Her voice broke as she said the words.

"And I didn't listen." He withdrew his hand and shoved it in the pocket of his jeans. The hand that had been holding her arm dropped to his side.

"You didn't listen."

"So tell me what our relationship has meant to you. What I've meant to you."

"It's meant everything," she said softly. "And so have you."

"Everything, but not enough."

"It's not you, Chris. You were right. I love you, more than I even knew I could love anybody. But my place is here. J.J.'s place is here. River Oaks is his inheritance. I can't take that away from him."

"It's a piece of land and some buildings. It will still be here in the years to come."

"It's more than land and buildings. That's what you'll never understand, because you really aren't one of us."

"For which I'm thankful." Chris stepped back as if to get a better look at her. A real look at her.

"I don't want us to part this way."

He nodded, but she knew it wasn't because he agreed with her. "Good luck, Lizette," he said finally. He turned and started toward his car.

"Chris?" She watched as he stopped, debating, she imagined, whether to turn around. He did. "Will you stay in touch?" Lizette knew her cheeks were wet again.

He shook his head. "I'll write to J.J. I don't want him to think any of this is his fault."

"He'll miss you."

His eyes held hers for a long moment, then he turned again and started walking. Lizette stood on the path and sobbed as he drove away.

Chapter Fifteen

The rain poured down in torrents, washing leaves from the roof across the rim of the gallery before draining off into puddles below. October was too late in the year for the heavenly fireworks display splitting the night sky, but it had been an unusual fall, alternately warm and cool, without any real hints of the winter just around the corner. Anything was to be expected.

In her bedroom, Lizette stood at the long window that overlooked the fields of sugarcane far beyond the house. Idly, she wondered how long this excessive rain could continue without damaging the crop that was soon to be harvested.

"Mommy!"

She crossed to the door separating her room from J.J.'s. In a minute she was at his bedside. "I'm here, sweetheart. Did the thunder scare you?" She sat on the edge of the four-poster bed and reached for his hand, clasping it firmly in her own.

"Grandfather St. Hilaire said I shouldn't be scared of nuthin'."

"Grandfather St. Hilaire doesn't always remember what it's like to be a little boy."

"Chris said when he was a little boy he used to sleep in the closet when there was lightning. I don't even have one." He giggled bravely.

Lizette smiled. River Oaks, like most plantation houses, had been built without closets. Early in Louisiana history closets had been considered rooms and were therefore taxable. Instead, beautifully crafted armoires like the rosewood one that matched J.J.'s bed had been used to store clothing.

"Once I crawled under my bed during a big storm," Lizette recalled. "And I fell asleep. When my mother came to get me up the next morning she couldn't find me."

"Was she mad?"

Lizette tried to remember. "I don't know."

"Grandma only gets mad when she thinks someone's watching," J.J. said with a child's innocent accuracy.

Lizette had never thought about it quite that way, but she imagined J.J. was right. Her mother had conformed to the Stanhope-St. Hilaire standards when she had to, but there had always been a wistful leniency that had softened the strict rules she had been called on to enforce. That's why she was J.J.'s favorite grandparent. When no one else was around to see, Mary Stanhope indulged him shamefully. Much like his mother.

"I think the storm is moving away," Lizette said, patting his hand before she stood. "Go back to sleep."

"I wish Chris was here."

It wasn't the first time J.J. had said those words, and Lizette knew it wouldn't be the last. The little boy missed Chris as he had never missed anyone before. Even Ricky, who had left with his parents a week after the St. Hilaires' abusive tirade, wasn't missed as much.

"You got another letter from him, didn't you?" Lizette asked.

"Letters aren't as good."

She couldn't tell him that letters were better than nothing. He was too young to understand just how empty "nothing" could be. "I'll help you write him back tomorrow," she promised. "Go to sleep now. I'll leave the door cracked in case you need me."

Lizette was slipping off her robe to return to bed when she heard tapping. With the next flash of lightning she could see Barbara on the gallery, silhouetted against the night sky. Quickly she unlocked a floor-to-ceiling window and slid it up to let Barbara through.

"Kind of a strange time to come visiting, wouldn't you say?" Lizette looked around for something to give her friend to dry off with, settling on a wool afghan draped across a rocking chair.

"I was just going to camp out downstairs when I saw your light." Barbara gratefully accepted the afghan.

"Why aren't you home in bed?"

"I've been at Paul's. The weather was fine down there, but it got worse as I got closer to home. I had to park my car next to the van. The road to the quarters and beyond is flooded."

"Let me get you something dry to put on. You can sleep in the bed in my office."

"Sounds better than the dining room."

"Marydell wouldn't be happy to find you on her..." Lizette stopped midsentence. "But then, Marydell's not here anymore."

"Nope." Barbara slipped off her clothes and finished drying herself before slipping on the flannel nightgown Lizette found for her. "Lots of people aren't here anymore," she pointed out. "And at least one isn't even going to be in the state before too long."

"Chris?"

"Yeah. He's found a practice to buy into near Santa Cruz. Just what he was looking for. He's leaving at the end of the month."

Lizette was surprised that she could still feel such pain. There was more pain in the world than she had ever imagined. "I thought he wasn't leaving until after Christmas."

"The woman he's been standing in for decided not to come back after her maternity leave's up. Paul's interviewing for a permanent replacement. He expects to find somebody soon, so he told Chris to go ahead and finalize his plans. He wanted Chris to stay for good," she added. "But Chris said he needed to go back home."

The end of the month. Three more weeks. It had only been three weeks since Lizette had seen Chris, three weeks since the fight that she replayed every day and every night. Three weeks of misery. Three more weeks.

"Why does it matter?" Barbara asked, watching Lizette's face carefully. "You already said goodbye to him."

"I guess it doesn't."

"I guess he's glad to be going, but he doesn't seem excited about it."

"You saw him? I thought you'd just heard about it from Paul."

"He was at Paul's when I got there."

"How did he look?"

Barbara heard the hunger for detail in Lizette's words. She ignored it. "About the same."

"Did he ask about me?"

"No."

"Oh."

"He asked about J.J."

"I'm beginning to think it was J.J. he loved, not me."

"J.J. didn't hurt him."

Lizette sat down on the bed and stared at the floor. "I didn't want to hurt him."

"I'll bet that makes it a whole lot better, doesn't it?"

"You always were fun to have around in a crisis."

Barbara sat down in the rocking chair. "Is this a crisis?" she asked with interest. "I thought the crisis was over. You threw the man out. Thump!"

"I didn't throw him out. He asked me to make a choice. I did."

"Chris or the St. Hilaires? I can see your problem."

"Not the St. Hilaires! River Oaks." Lizette raised her eyes to Barbara's. "You, of all people, should understand that. You've got River Oaks in your blood, too."

"You know, then."

Lizette frowned. "What do you mean, I know? Anybody could see this place is as much a part of you as it is of me. You grew up here."

"You said it was in my blood."

Now Lizette was truly puzzled. "It's just an expression."

"Not this time." Barbara rocked back and forth, but her eyes never left Lizette's.

"What's that supposed to mean?"

"Do you want to hear the truth? The St. Hilaires have known forever. It's one of the reasons they hate having me here as plantation manager, only I never understood."

Lizette shook her head, confused. "What are you talking about?"

"About my blood, about your blood. About a journal up in the attic buried so deep in a trunk that no one was ever supposed to find it."

"Journal?"

"We're cousins, Lizette. Distant, distant cousins. My great-great-grandfather is your great-great-grandfather. Only my great-great-grandmother was a slave and yours was the mistress of this place."

Lizette just stared at her.

"I just found out today. That's why I went into New Orleans to see Paul. I had to tell somebody."

"Cousins." Lizette tried out the word.

"Cousins way, way back."

"You told Paul before you told me."

"I wasn't sure how you'd feel."

"How could you doubt my reaction? You're my best friend."

"Sometimes I wonder if you're picking up Jerome and Sophia's prejudices."

"Never!"

Barbara nodded, pleased. "So River Oaks isn't just sweat and tears with me, it's blood, too. And you know what,

Cousin? River Oaks can be damned if it ever gets in the way of anything I really want in my life.''

"Cousins." Lizette laughed. "I'll be damned."

"Now, Miss Lizette, you know that's not a word for a lady to use!"

"Cut out the Mammy routine, will you?" Lizette rose and hugged Barbara. "Cousins!"

"Don't announce it to the world. I've got a reputation to maintain."

Lizette hugged her again. "Part of River Oaks should belong to you by right of inheritance."

"That's one legal mess I don't ever want to touch. Nope, by the blood of my slave-owning great-great, I don't want to own River Oaks or any part of it. Owning it seems to do strange things to people's heads. I just want to see it used constructively." She waited, but Lizette was silent. "Have you mentioned my idea to the St. Hilaires?"

Lizette sobered. "I've been waiting for the right moment."

"Like over their gravestones?"

"I'm sorry. I'll do it soon."

"Do something else, too."

"What?"

"Go see Chris. Say a real goodbye."

"I can't."

"For me? For your cousin Barbie?"

Despite herself, Lizette smiled. "You were hard to take before I knew we were related, but you're going to be a god-awful challenge now."

"Will you go?"

"I'll think about it."

"You do that."

Chris was surprised at how much there was to pack before a major move. But far worse was the job of deciding what not to pack. Looking around at the contents of his apartment, he thought he might need almost everything he owned before he left in two weeks. Kicking the box at his feet in frustration, he decided he was done. The day before the moving van arrived to take his furniture and put it in storage he'd pack all but the bare essentials. In the meantime, he pressed one more length of strapping tape across the box he had kicked before rising to stretch.

His body was kinked beyond recognition. He had gone weeks without any exercise, and he felt it in every stiff joint. Running didn't appeal to him anymore, but that wasn't surprising. Every time his feet hit the pavement he thought of Lizette. That had to stop. He was going to run that evening and every evening until he left New Orleans. He'd even signed up for a race on the Friday before Halloween just to spur himself to start training. The fact that the night of the race, October the thirtieth, was J.J.'s birthday hadn't influenced him at all. What was the point of grieving forever? So what if he couldn't spend it with J.J. and his mom?

Chris realized he wasn't very good at fooling himself. He supposed that would improve with time. Something in his life had to.

His hand was in the refrigerator reaching for a cold beer when the buzzer from downstairs sounded. He popped the top of his can while he waited for whoever it was to come upstairs. He hadn't even used the intercom to find out if it was someone he knew. If it was a burglar, maybe he'd help him pack. Burglars had to be good for something. There were enough of them around.

The knock, when it sounded, was tentative. Chris took another swallow of beer and opened the door.

"May I come in?" Lizette stood in the doorway, her hands clasped in front of her. It had taken her a week after her talk with Barbara to come. Now she realized that a week hadn't been long enough to straighten out her tangled emotions. A lifetime wouldn't have been enough.

Chris didn't smile. "Sure." He stepped aside and motioned her in. "Be my guest."

Lizette picked her way through the maze of boxes in the otherwise neat living room. "Barbara said you were moving. It looks like she knew what she was talking about."

"Yeah." Chris followed her to the sofa. "Have a seat, if you can find one."

Lizette perched on the sofa's edge. "When are you leaving?"

"Beginning of November sometime. It depends on the movers."

"And you have a house in California?"

Chris shook his head. "I'm going to wait and find something when I get there."

Lizette cast around for another polite topic of conversation. Chris still wasn't sitting. "Did I catch you at a bad time?"

There were no good times anymore. Chris just shrugged. "Can I get you something to drink? A beer? Juice?"

"I'll take some juice." She watched him disappear into the kitchen.

The apartment looked strangely bereft, like a fashion model caught in nothing more than a slip and stockings. Without any of Chris's personal touches, it was just an apartment, a nice apartment on one of New Orleans' most famous thoroughfares, but an apartment nonetheless. She scanned the room for the framed photograph of them crossing the finish line at the Crescent City Classic. It was nowhere in sight. He had packed it, undoubtedly certain he could well live without it for a while. Idly she picked up a flier advertising a Halloween race.

"All I had was apple." Chris came back and handed her a glass.

"Thanks." Lizette reached for the glass, and their hands touched momentarily. She looked up at him, but he had already turned to move to a nearby chair. He sat down, stretching his long legs in front of him.

"What's this?" She held up the flier. "Are you going to run in it?"

"Yeah. The Witch's Moonlight Run. The night before Halloween."

"That's J.J.'s birthday. He's going to be seven," she added unnecessarily.

"I know."

"Good luck."

"So why'd you come, Lizette?"

His tone was so brusque that she knew he was tired of small talk. "I brought a letter from J.J."

"I'm sure Miss Lucy Carroll would have been more than happy to send it for you."

"I wanted to say goodbye."

"You did that already."

Lizette set her glass on the coffee table next to a pile of books and leaned toward him. "I don't like the way we said goodbye. I never expected us to part that way. I knew you'd go, but I thought we'd stay friends. I want to be your friend, Chris."

"I don't want to be yours." He sipped his beer, but his eyes were a simmering green above the can.

"Then I shouldn't have come."

"What did you expect to accomplish?"

"I just told you."

He waved away her explanation. "You thought you could waltz in here, smile that endearingly sensual smile of yours and talk me into being your buddy? What did you want? To be on my Christmas card list? To get my home phone number in case you get to California on vacation someday? Come on, Lizette!"

Since she'd believed she had wanted just that, she couldn't think of anything to say.

"I'll tell you what you want," he continued. "You want to convince yourself you did the right thing. Having people angry at you makes you nervous. You want everybody to love you and love every decision you make."

"That's not true!"

"What other possible explanation is there for why you put up with what you do from your in-laws and parents? You want to be everybody's little darling. Well, you can't be mine."

Lizette leaned over and opened her purse. She took out J.J.'s letter and stood, purse in hand. "I'll find my own way to the door." She held out the letter to him.

Chris took it without standing. He ripped open the envelope and scanned the page. "Damn!"

Lizette knew what was in the letter. She had faithfully written every word J.J. had dictated, even though she hadn't wanted to. "I told J.J. you weren't angry at him, but he's having trouble believing it."

"He's a smart kid. He knows people don't just disappear for no reason."

"Would you write him again and try to convince him it's not his fault?"

"Whose fault do I convince him it is?"

Lizette saw the weariness in Chris's face, and she saw the sadness. Before she could think about what she was doing, she crouched at his feet so their eyes were on the same level. "It wasn't anybody's fault." She put one hand on his knee. "It wasn't. And it wasn't because I didn't love you. It's just that sometimes you can't have everything you want. Sometimes you have to do what's best for the biggest number of people."

"The greater good."

She tried to smile. "How is it that you always make me sound like the heroine in a piece of Communist propaganda?"

Chris's gaze locked with hers. He wished she would move her hand. "I'll write to J.J. again. I'll send *him* Christmas cards."

"I'm sorry, Chris. I really am."

"Yeah."

She knew that was her cue to stand, to turn and walk out his door for the last time, but her feet were strangely unwilling to move. She couldn't tear her gaze from his.

His hand crept to cover hers, but he encountered an obstacle. Chris looked down at the slender fingers lying open across his knee and saw her wedding ring. She had stopped wearing it in all their months together. Now it was firmly back in place. He turned it thoughtfully. "You're Julian's wife again. Or is it River Oaks you're married to?"

She had forgotten about the ring. It was a St. Hilaire heirloom, delicate and finely wrought. She loved it as she loved the St. Hilaire pearls and the antique hair-work brooch and mourning ring, fashioned from the hair of her great-great-grandmother after her death.

"Generations of St. Hilaire women have worn this ring," she tried to explain.

"Were they wed to River Oaks, too?"

"No."

Chris realized he was no longer angry at Lizette. He was just sad. And empty. "There are some things beyond my understanding."

Lizette slipped off the ring and dropped it in the pocket of her blouse. "Is that better?"

"It doesn't matter."

"It seemed to."

"It doesn't matter because when you leave here, you'll take it out of your pocket and put it on again. And that will be that."

There was really nothing left to say, but she still couldn't make herself leave. Like a British princess, she had been trained to make the proper responses and do the impeccably proper thing under any circumstances. Feelings had nothing to do with the correct course of action. And yet she couldn't make herself leave.

"You should go," Chris told her.

"I don't want to."

"Why not? You've gotten what you came for. We've said goodbye again."

She had come because she wanted him to make love to her. Lizette suddenly understood her motivation, and she was instantly ashamed. She needed him; she needed the solace of his arms, and she needed to know that when they parted he would still think of her, yearn for her, as she would always yearn for him. How cruel. How uncharacteristically cruel of her to want to punish them both.

She stood, turning toward the door, but her tears overwhelmed her before she could reach it.

"Lizette." Chris put his arms around her, but it was against his better judgment. He knew where this was going to lead. He turned her and pillowed her head against his chest. "Shh... Don't cry. No, go ahead and cry. Hell, I don't know what you should do." His arms tightened like a vise.

"I shouldn't have come. This was all wrong. But I needed to see you again, Chris. I couldn't . . . I couldn't let you go away without seeing you again."

"It's just making it worse." The words came out on a groan. His body had reacted instantly to hers. He could feel the softest parts of her pressing against him, arousing body parts that had been too long denied.

"I came to make it worse. I didn't even know it, but I did." She wiped her face against his shirt, but it didn't help. She was still crying.

"What are you saying?"

"I came hoping we'd make love." The words came out on another deluge of tears.

He was lost. How could she stand there, sweet and warm and achingly beautiful in his arms, and tell him something like that? Did she think he was so noble that he'd assure her it was better if they didn't and escort her to her car?

His hands moved up her back to her hair, tugging it gently until she turned her face up to his. "I'm afraid you're going to get your wish."

He saw her eyes widen, then close, as he bent his head the small distance to kiss her. Her lips softened and heated under his immediately. She gave a small sob, then opened her mouth for his pleasure. As the kiss finally ended, her arms came around him, and she held him as if she were afraid he would break away. "I've missed you so much," she said against his lips.

He didn't want to hope. Hope was painful and dangerous. She had made her decision, yet here she was in his arms. And she had missed him. "I've missed you, too. Every day. Every minute."

"Nights are the worst, because I have so much time to think."

He pulled away just far enough to unbutton the top three buttons of her blouse. He heard her soft gasp, and his gaze held hers as he continued undoing the row of buttons. "Stop me now," he whispered.

She shook her head. His fingers trembled, fumbling with the last button until she reached up to undo it herself. Then she tugged his shirt out of his pants, sliding her hands around to begin pulling it over his head.

In a moment their clothes were piled at their feet. In another they were on his bed together, locked in an embrace that seemed destined never to end. If they had been in a rush to be together, now neither of them was in a rush to culminate the act of love. With its end would come their final goodbye.

Chris smoothed his hands over Lizette's body, letting her moans guide him. His mouth found each sensitive area, dwelling everywhere he knew he was giving her pleasure. Attuned to each movement she made, he lingered at her breasts, shaping them with his hands, his mouth, his tongue, until she was writhing beneath him.

Lizette demanded and resisted release. She could think of nothing; she could feel everything. The room seemed ethereally bright. Her body felt as if it had wings. She was floating with only one reality, the man poised above her giving her such pleasure. Dazed, she rolled him over and began to take her pleasure of him. She had never been so bold, but she wanted to know all of him, each inch of skin each firmly padded muscle, each taste.

She discovered things she hadn't noticed before. A mole on his left arm, a tiny scar on his rib cage, the powerful muscles of his thighs. She wanted to discover everything. There was nothing she didn't want to know. When she remembered him, it would be the whole man she remembered, and the memory would be crystal clear. It had to be.

They held off their union as long as they could, but finally their need overcame their hesitation. Locked together in the most intimate of embraces, they reached their peak quickly and descended together.

Lizette lay in Chris's arms, fighting off the awareness of what had to come next. She didn't want to leave him. She belonged here with him. He was everything she'd ever wanted, and so much more than she'd ever expected to have. Why then must she leave him?

"Will you stay the night?" he asked at last. He could feel her body tensing. He, too, knew what was coming.

"I . . . I can't."

"Am I allowed to ask why not?"

"J.J. . . ." She couldn't lie. "It wouldn't be a good idea."

"I see. Well, why stop at one bad idea today, Lizette? Go for broke."

She wanted to cry again. "I didn't mean for this . . ."

"To happen? Sure you did. And so did I. And now it's over. Again." Chris pulled away from her and sat up. "Shall I get you your clothes?"

She had never felt so exposed. Right straight down to her soul. Lizette sat up, too, and swung her feet over the side of the bed. "I'll get them."

She changed in the living room, and Chris, ignoring the clothes he had taken off, put on fresh clothes in the bedroom. Lizette was just pulling a brush through her hair when he joined her. "I'll be leaving now," she said softly.

He nodded.

Her eyes filled with tears once more. She knew she would never again think of herself as a woman who never cried. "I . . . I don't know what to say."

"Don't say anything. Words never worked very well for us anyway."

She touched his shoulder, standing on tiptoe to kiss his cheek. "Goodbye."

"Yeah."

"I hope California is all you want it to be."

His eyes flashed. "And I hope River Oaks burns to the ground!"

She drew in a sharp breath.

"And when it does, I hope you realize you're still alive," he went on. "Still breathing, still thinking, still dreaming. Alive. Without River Oaks."

"It's not like you to be bitter!"

"I could wish nothing better for you." He touched her cheek, then let his hand fall to his side. "Go."

She was gone without another word.

Chapter Sixteen

I understand that Barbara's been talking to you."

Lizette was surprised to see her mother-in-law. Sophia had wasted no time coming up to the big house as soon as Lizette returned home from Chris's. Her timing was unfortunate. In fact, there was nothing in the world Lizette needed less than a conversation with either of the St. Hilaires.

"What are you referring to?" Lizette asked. Sophia was the picture of well-bred rage—seemingly unruffled, with only subtle signals to indicate what she was feeling. Lizette recognized those signals, however. Sophia's dark eyes were snapping, and her mouth was jerking in tiny, uncontrolled spasms.

"She told you that ridiculous story about her great-great-grandmother!"

Lizette couldn't imagine why Barbara had related their conversation to Sophia. "She told me," she admitted.

"It's nothing but a lie."

Lizette knew Barbara would have no reason to lie about her heritage. For that matter, Lizette knew Barbara didn't lie, period. Sophia, on the other hand, was perfectly capable of stretching the truth if it served her purpose. "Does it matter?" she asked gently.

"What else did she tell you?"

Now Lizette was truly in the dark. She was sure Barbara hadn't told Sophia about Chris leaving for California. It just wouldn't have come up. "I don't know what you're after," she admitted finally. "Why don't you tell me?"

"The grinding mill." Sophia waved her hand in exasperation. "That outrageous story about her great-great-grandmother being murdered at the grinding mill."

"She didn't say anything about the grinding mill."

"Well, at least she has some sense!"

"What's the story?"

Sophia seemed to realize she had overplayed her hand. "It's not worth repeating." She snapped her lips shut.

Lizette knew she would have to hear the details from Barbara. "Was there anything else?" she asked Sophia, hoping that the worst was over. She wanted to crawl into bed and cry until there wasn't a tear left anywhere inside her.

"There is." Sophia drew herself up until, even though she was Lizette's height, she seemed to tower over her. "River Oaks will never be opened to the public while Jerome and I are alive. And if you have any grasp of the responsibilities that have been handed down to you, you'll never allow it after we're gone, either!"

Lizette realized Sophia had saved the big guns for last. She wondered why Barbara had confronted the St. Hilaires by herself. But then, the answer was probably simple. Barbara knew Lizette for the coward she was. She had given up hope that Lizette would do it for her.

"I think Barbara's idea is a good one," Lizette said, feeling for the right mixture of strength and conciliation. "I'm going to explore it. I think we might be able to reach a compromise that satisfies everyone."

"Never."

"Sophia, you don't know that we can't. Don't close your mind before we have a chance to explore options."

"Never!" Sophia marched down the stairs. At the bottom she turned back to Lizette. "Don't make me sorry that our son chose you for his wife, Lizette!" She turned again and was gone.

"Sometimes I'm sorry enough for both of us, Sophia," Lizette whispered into the silence. "Sorry enough for you and me and everybody at River Oaks."

The sweetly acrid scent of burning leaves filled the air. The cane was being harvested. Piled in huge heaprows, it was torched by mechanical burner units on the plantation's tractors so that the leaves had been burned off the undamaged stalk when it was finally hoisted by loaders into cane carts and hauled to the mill.

The smoke stayed in the cool air, drifting above the fields like ghostly sentries guarding their sweet treasure. Grinding season was always Lizette's favorite time at River Oaks. The hot summer was past; the year's work was paying off; spirits were usually high.

Now, however, she sat listlessly on the front porch of Barbara's cabin and waited for her to come in from the fields. There was no time to mourn the end of her relationship with Chris. As always, River Oaks made its unceasing demands, and she was forced to meet them. She had to talk to Barbara and make sure Sophia hadn't alienated her the way Sophia and Jerome had alienated Ricky's family. She couldn't face Barbara leaving, too.

It was well past dinnertime, and J.J. was also out in the fields. Big Jake was showing the little boy the joys of harvesting cane. Lizette just hoped that Barbara appeared before J.J. did, so they would have a chance to talk.

The first stars were out when Lizette heard the rumble of Barbara's truck. Lizette watched as her friend pulled the old Ford next to the cabin. The battered door creaked, and Barbara stepped out. She was dressed in khaki work clothes, and her long braids were caught back in a green scarf. Before she could even get to the porch Lizette could tell she was exhausted. "J.J.'s at the tractor shed with Big Jake. He'll be here before long," Barbara told her as she climbed the stairs.

"I made you some soup." Lizette stood to follow Barbara inside. "I figured you'd be too tired to open a can yourself. There are hot rolls in the oven to go with it."

"Thanks. Sophia talked to you, huh?"

Lizette had known Barbara would understand why she was there. "Take a shower. I'll set the table for you."

Barbara sat down instead and started to pull off her work boots. "Better talk now before J.J. gets here."

"Why did you go to Sophia and Jerome about your idea for opening up River Oaks before I had a chance to talk to them myself?"

"I got tired of waiting."

There was little Lizette could say to that. "They're against the idea," she said, pushing on to the next unpleasant topic. "So what's new?"

"I've rarely seen Sophia so angry. Why on earth did you throw the story about us being related up to her at the same time? That didn't help."

"Story?" Barbara raised her eyebrows. "She knows it's not a story. Did she convince you it was?"

"Of course not! But she was going on about it as if there were more to it than I knew. She said something about the old grinding mill and your great-great-grandmother being murdered there."

"She's the ghost," Barbara said simply.

"Are you going to tell me what this is all about?"

"Not a pretty story, Lizette," Barbara said, shaking her head from side to side so that her braids slapped the back of the chair. "Not a pretty story for a well-bred young lady to hear."

"Cut it out!" Lizette was angry. "Don't give me a hard time like everybody else in the world. Just tell me the story!"

"Henri St. Hilaire, our mutual great-great, was in love with my great-great-grandmother, Ceile. Ceile was a slave he'd grown up with. When Henri inherited the plantation, he took Ceile to New Orleans as a servant in his house there. He kept her there so she'd be waiting for him when he went downriver to sell cane or buy supplies. But that couldn't last forever. Eventually Henri was married to your great-great-grandmother, Louise. He brought Ceile back to River Oaks as a house slave and gave her in marriage to one of his sugar makers, a free black man named Pierre Grafanier.

"Years later, Louise found out the whole story. Worst of all, she discovered that Ceile had given birth to Henri's baby in New Orleans and that the child was being raised on River Oaks as Pierre's daughter. Louise went crazy when she heard. She paid two men, River Oaks slaves, to kill Ceile. They caught her at the grinding mill, and they stabbed her. That night, in a fit of guilt, Louise told Henri what she had done. He rode to the grinding mill and found Ceile dying. She died in his arms before he could help her."

Lizette was stunned. "How do you know all this?"

"Louise and Henri had a daughter, Marie-Therese."

"My great-grandmother," Lizette said.

"Marie-Therese kept a series of journals. Sophia and Jerome have most of them, but I found this one when I was searching through some old papers in the attic last week to see if I could get the plans for the original grinding mill. She told the whole story in her journal. That's when I found out that we were related.

Lizette didn't know what to say. Nothing seemed appropriate. "It's so tragic," she said for lack of anything else.

"I think my parents have suspected for years that we were related to the St. Hilaires. It wasn't a connection they were particularly proud of."

"Louise St. Hilaire was a murderess."

"According to Marie-Therese, Louise walked the galleries of the big house every night after Ceile died until she would collapse from fatigue. Louise never recovered from what she had done."

"All because her husband had been unfaithful to her before he even married her."

"Evidently not only then. Henri St. Hilaire liked women. Ceile wasn't his only amour. Marie-Therese is quite frank about that."

Lizette tried to put all the revelations together in her head. The St. Hilaire family had practically been canonized in the stories she had been told. Now she was hearing a far different version. "A murderess. An adulterer."

"You find lots of things if you look hard enough, Lizette. Not just in the last century, either." Barbara stood. "I'll take that shower now."

"Barbara?"

Barbara didn't turn.

"I saw Chris today. I said goodbye."

"You're a fool."

Lizette flinched.

"Only a fool would give up a man like Chris for this place."

"You've given up a lot, too. River Oaks means—"

"I'm leaving myself."

Lizette felt herself go numb. "No!"

"Yeah." Barbara faced her. "I'm not going to let River Oaks kill my spirit the way it's killed yours. I'm leaving after grinding season. Paul and I are getting married, and I'll live in New Orleans with him."

"Stay here. Marry Paul, and both of you come to live here. He loves River Oaks. We can build a house. We can—"

"Come on, Lizette! I'm not going to watch River Oaks destroy you! You know, all those years I thought it was that bastard you were married to who was killing your spirit. But it wasn't. It's this place. It's filled with hatred and lies and secrets, and they're eating you alive."

Lizette shook her head. "No!"

"Secrets, Lizette!"

"What are you talking about?"

"Do you know that Julian, *St. Julian*, was the spitting image of Henri St. Hilaire?" Barbara laughed mirthlessly. "He was. In every way."

"I've seen Henri's portrait. There's a family resemblance to Julian, but what's that got to do with anything?"

"In *every* way. Julian had women all over this parish, just like Henri. Julian even hit up on me after you were married! Why do you think he didn't want me to spend any time with you? It wasn't just racism. Julian didn't want me to tell you about him, that's why! I wouldn't let him near me, but not everyone was as smart as I was. Julian St. Hilaire's life was exactly what this place stands for now. Lies and secrets! And you aren't going to change it. You were the hope of River Oaks, but that hope's gone."

Lizette felt her throat close, trapping a scream inside her. She felt as if she were going to explode. Fragments of incidents from the days when Julian had still been alive ran through her head. Nights he had been gone, unexplained phone calls, the expressions on the faces of friends who had seemed to pity her for more than a sick husband. She knew Barbara was right. How could she not have seen the truth herself?

Barbara turned and headed toward the bathroom. She stopped with one hand on the door. "Go on back to the big house, Lizette. You belong there, not here. There have been St. Hilaire women with strength and courage. There have been St. Hilaire women with vision. You're not one of them."

"Barbara..."

"Go on home. I don't want you here."

"Barbara!"

"Go on home." Wearily, Barbara closed the door behind her.

Lizette stood at the site of the old grinding mill and looked out at the fields of smoldering cane. Smoke hung over the horizon in wispy, fragmented clouds that changed with the whims of the chilling wind that had begun in the early afternoon. As she watched, one of the tractors lighting the cane made its way up a distant row toward her.

The tractor was far enough away that the mill site was still quiet. Today no woman wept, unless Lizette counted the tears inside her that just wouldn't be released. The tears had been frozen there for a week; she had wept in her heart every day, every night. Just like any good St. Hilaire woman.

She supposed that was exactly what she was. She had lost Chris; she had lost Barbara; and still she stayed at River Oaks, doing what needed to be done, carrying on the traditions, readying the next generation for the struggle to maintain a way of life that should have died out a century before.

She had lost Julian, too. The knight's armor was no longer shining, but tarnished beyond recognition. Strangely, she felt little sadness about that. She had never really had Julian, and on some level, although she hadn't understood why, she had always known it. He had been a man born to privilege in a century when privilege was less important than hard work. Julian hadn't managed River Oaks well; he hadn't managed his life well. Julian had been a failure, but he had given her the son she cherished. If for no other reason, she could thank him for that.

She still had J.J. Julian Jerome St. Hilaire, tree climber, frog catcher *extraordinaire*. Seven years old that day. Lizette remembered the night of J.J.'s birth. The St. Hilaires had been so happy; Julian had been so proud. And she had fallen in love, head over heels in love, with the tiny little boy in her arms. She could look back on mistakes she had made, paths where she had taken the wrong turn, places where she should have taken stands, but she knew there was one thing she had done right. She had given birth to J.J., and she was raising him to be the person his father hadn't been.

But it would have been easier with Chris by her side.

So why didn't she go to Chris and tell him she had made a terrible mistake? Why didn't she leave River Oaks behind forever? Duty? Tradition? Cowardice? Or did the plantation really have some evil hold on her?

"Hey, Mommy!"

Lizette waved, watching as J.J. bounded down from the tractor and ran toward her. The little boy loved the time he spent with Big Jake in the cane fields. Big Jake was the only man left in his life with the patience to treat him like the child he was. "Thank you," Lizette called, waving goodbye as Big Jake turned up the next row.

"Did you have fun, sweetheart?" She held out her arms for a hug, knowing she probably needed it more than J.J. did.

"Big Jake let me drive!"

"Big Jake is a sucker. We'd better get back to the house quick. Your grandparents are coming soon for your birthday party."

Although she'd said the words with all the enthusiasm she could muster, Lizette saw them fall flat. "Do I have to get dressed up?" J.J. asked.

Lizette nodded. "Suit and tie." She knew J.J. was old enough to remember his party of the previous year. A formal dinner wasn't an occasion any child looked forward to with delight. Unfortunately, the St. Hilaires and Stanhopes expected it. "Don't forget, though. If you behave yourself tonight, I'll take you and Billy into Baton Rouge tomorrow for lunch at McDonald's and a movie."

"You promise?"

"I sure do." Lizette draped her arm over her son's shoulders and escorted him to the car.

Back at the house, Lizette checked on dinner while J.J. took a bath. The new cook seemed to have everything under control, and the young woman who had been hired to serve for the occasion had set the table with the best china and silver—silver that had spent most of the Civil War buried in a sugarcane field. The only thing missing from the table was an arrangement of St. Hilaire roses, which was still in the kitchen waiting for finishing touches. They were the last roses of the season, and Sophia would want them shown off to their best advantage. Lizette patted them into place and set them on the table.

Back upstairs, she changed into a black silk dress and the River Oaks pearls. She only wore them on special occasions, and when she did, she usually felt a sense of pride in her heritage. Tonight she felt nothing except their unaccustomed weight around her neck. The birthday dinner, for her as well as for J.J., was something to be gotten through this year. Tomorrow would be his real celebration.

In J.J.'s room she laid out his clothes, then helped him dress. It wasn't yet dark when they went out on the front gallery to the dining room to greet the Stanhopes, who had just arrived.

"It's a little early for a dinner party, isn't it, dear?" Mary asked, kissing Lizette's cheek before she hugged her grandson.

"I didn't want J.J. falling asleep before dessert." Actually, Lizette wanted J.J. on his best behavior, and a tired J.J. was a rebellious J.J.

"Ah, yes, the birthday boy!" Mary tweaked J.J.'s cheek. "Do you deserve a present?"

"Yes!"

Lizette watched while J.J. opened the elaborate plastic construction set her parents had bought for him. It was a welcome contrast to the antique rosewood chest Sophia and Jerome had given him to match the bed in his room.

"Thanks!" J.J. gave his grandmother a hug and offered his hand to his grandfather.

The St. Hilaires arrived, and everyone chatted over drinks. Lizette tried to ignore the stultifying sameness of it all. She loved her parents, and if she didn't love the St. Hilaires, at least she understood what made them the way they were. She would get through this evening, and then she would get through the next. Now she concentrated on J.J., making sure he had enough ginger ale to drink and that he got a chance to talk, too.

At five-fifteen they went downstairs to begin dinner.

"Everything is lovely, dear," Mary complimented her daughter. "And look, there are still roses!"

Lizette straightened an errant bud. "It's been such a strange fall. I think these are the last of them, though."

"The year I came to River Oaks as a bride they bloomed until Christmas. I'll never forget it."

Lizette looked at her mother-in-law in surprise. Sophia had sounded young and wistful. She had never thought of Sophia as anything other than the stern matron whose job it was to preserve the heritage of the St. Hilaires. But Sophia had been young once, too. She had been a bride coming to River Oaks to begin a new life. Maybe she had even been in love. "I'll bet you appreciated them," Lizette said.

"I remember thinking they were so strange," Sophia went on, seeming to forget for a moment where she was and why she was there. "Blood-red roses tipped with ivory. I'd never seen any like them before. And it was my job to tend them. It frightened me. But I did it." Sophia pulled herself back from wherever she had been. "They're still blooming, and now it's your turn to make them grow."

Lizette felt a cold shiver run down her spine. "I do my best."

"You've done fine." Sophia sounded like herself again. "They're a credit to River Oaks."

Why did that sound so ominous? Lizette realized that she was staring at the roses and no one was moving. She lifted her gaze to her mother's. Mary seemed to understand. "Let's get seated," Mary said, taking charge. "Whatever's cooking in there smells wonderful."

Although Lizette had done her best to be sure the menu was one J.J. would approve of, the first course was met with a rumble in his throat that could only mean trouble.

"Soup?" The little boy looked at the seafood gumbo in the bowl in front of him. "I don't like soup."

"Don't eat it, then." Lizette said the words quietly, hoping no one else had heard.

"Your mother went to a lot of trouble to have this meal prepared for you," Jerome said sternly from the other side of the table.

J.J. looked down at his bowl. "There's shrimp in it. Marydell never put shrimp in her soup."

"It's gumbo," Lizette told him.

"Gumbo has chicken in it, not shrimp!"

"Marydell made a different kind, that's all. Just don't eat it if you don't want to."

"Why'd Marydell have to go?"

Lizette wondered why J.J. had chosen this moment for petulance. Apparently a day at school and an afternoon out in the cane had tired him more than she'd thought. And it was his birthday. "We'll talk about that later."

"J.J., you're the master of River Oaks now, and the master of River Oaks never complains about his dinner." Sophia delivered her words with a stern expression.

"What's a master?"

"The boss," Lizette explained.

"Barbara's the boss, not me. She's the one that tells everybody what to do. Let's give her my soup." He giggled.

Lizette smiled, but before she could say anything, Jerome cut in. "You're the master," he told the little boy. "River Oaks is going to be yours someday, and you must be polite. Now sit up and eat your gumbo."

J.J. sat up, but his eyes were rebellious. "I can't eat it. I'll be sick!"

"He really doesn't like shrimp," Lizette apologized. "I should have foreseen this and specified chicken gumbo."

"Do as your grandfather St. Hilaire says," Stephen told his grandson. "Mind your manners."

"No." J.J. stuck out his bottom lip in the pout Lizette knew so well. "I can't."

"Please, just let it go," she pleaded. "I promise he'll eat everything else. Right, J.J.?"

The little boy's eyes were filling with tears. "It's my birthday. I oughta get to do what I want."

"You're spoiling him." Sophia tapped her plate to get Lizette's attention. "He's got to learn."

To Lizette's utter relief, the young woman serving them came into the room and began to collect the bowls. The next course was salad, but Lizette had made sure that there were mandarin orange sections and almonds in with the salad greens. She knew J.J. would at least eat that much. She watched him pick silently at his portion. Obviously whatever fun there had been in his birthday dinner in the first place was spoiled. Her heart went out to him.

"Eat the lettuce," Jerome told him when everyone else was done and they were waiting for the next course.

"That's what Chris told me, too," J.J. said grudgingly. He speared a lettuce leaf. "He said I wouldn't get strong if I didn't. I told Barbara to ask him to come tonight, but he said he couldn't 'cause he was in a race."

Everyone was silent, but Lizette could feel the tension building.

Disaster struck with the main course. J.J. took one look at the chicken smothered in a heavy orange sauce and pushed his plate away. It skidded across the lace tablecloth, knocking over the arrangement of St. Hilaire roses. They fell against Jerome's plate, splashing water and sauce from his serving of chicken against his dinner jacket.

"Look what you've done!" Jerome stood up, his face contorted with anger. "What would your father say!"

Lizette watched J.J.'s expression turn to one of pure horror. "I'm sorry, Grandfather!"

"Sorry? Do you think that helps?"

"I didn't mean to."

"That doesn't matter. You've ruined dinner, and you've ruined my coat!"

"Coats can be cleaned." J.J. stood up and moved behind his chair as if to shield himself. "Chris said they can!"

Lizette remembered the day at the Riverwalk and Chris's reaction to the little boy's clumsiness. She wanted to weep, but her tears were still frozen inside. She stood, too, and began gathering up the roses, strewn now over the middle of the table. "I'm sorry," she soothed Jerome. "I'm sure J.J. didn't mean for this to happen."

"Go up to your room," Sophia commanded. She stood and pointed a finger at the little boy. "You can go to bed without dinner if that's the way you're going to act. Your father never would have done such a thing. Never!"

"Go up to your room," Jerome repeated, sponging off his coat with a napkin.

"Chris said little boys make mistakes. Didn't he, Mommy? You don't hate me, do you?" J.J. was pleading. Lizette could hear what he was really asking. *I'm all right, aren't I, Mommy? I'm still all right even if I did something bad?*

You don't hate me?

She dropped the roses in the middle of the table and they lay across the lace tablecloth, petals scattered like drops of blood. How could she have denied the truth for so long?

River Oaks was going to destroy J.J., just as it had almost destroyed her. She had nearly sacrificed herself, but was she willing to sacrifice her son?

You don't hate me?

What had ever possessed her to believe she was staying here for J.J.'s good? What was River Oaks giving the little boy except heartache? And what had it ever given her except the same? Yet she had stayed on. She had lost everything that gave her life meaning, but she had clung to the one thing that made her life hell. River Oaks.

You don't hate me?

"Never!" Lizette pushed her chair in so hard the table slid an inch across the floor. "I'm not even mad at you, sweetheart. Now you go upstairs like your grandmother said. I'll be up in just a few minutes myself. Change your clothes. We're going somewhere."

J.J. took one frightened look around the room and then scurried out. Lizette heard the sound of his footsteps running up the front stairs.

"What do you mean, you're going somewhere?" Sophia demanded.

"I'm leaving this place. And I'm taking my son!" Lizette began to pace. She could hardly get the words out fast enough. "I've been crazy to stay this long. I thought I had to for J.J.'s sake. I thought this was his inheritance!"

"It is his inheritance." Jerome came around the table to block her way. "River Oaks is his."

"No. J.J.'s inheritance is freedom! J.J.'s inheritance is self-respect. J.J.'s inheritance is whatever love I have to give him and whatever love you find in your hearts! But every one of us lost sight of that."

"You're overwrought!" Jerome put his hand on Lizette's arm. "You're tired. J.J.'s tired. This has been a difficult fall. Grinding season is always a difficult time."

"Grinding season?" She laughed, and she was surprised at how natural, how free, the sound was. "There are no good seasons here, Jerome. Don't you know that? There's nothing here except lies and secrets and a way of life that's got to die!"

"How dare you say that! Our son left you River Oaks. It was his most precious possession."

"Your son was a fraud!" Lizette looked straight into Jerome's eyes and saw that he knew where she was leading. He had known about Julian. Everyone had known about him except her.

"The only thing your son left me that I want is his son," she said more calmly. "I don't want River Oaks. I give it back to you and Sophia, Jerome. When you die, you can pass it on to J.J., but I can assure you that he's not going to live here a day longer while he's growing up. Maybe by the time he inherits this place he'll be strong enough to know what to do with it."

"I . . . I can't take care of it. I'm too old."

"Then you'll have to see if Barbara will do it for you." Lizette lifted her chin. "She will, I think, if you raise her salary and let her open River Oaks to the public. If you don't, then you can try to hire somebody else, but eventually you're probably going to lose it. Barbara's the only person who knows River Oaks well enough to pull it out of the hole Julian left it in."

"Barbara's not one of us!"

"Yes she is!"

"How can you do this!" Sophia asked from the other side of the table. She banged on it for emphasis. "How can you?"

The question was how could she not have done it years before? Lizette wondered if she would ever understand the powerful hold River Oaks had had over her.

"I can do it because I'm strong," Lizette said, facing her mother-in-law. "I'm stronger than I knew. And smarter."

She caught a glimpse of her mother's face. Mary Stanhope understood. It was there in the curve of her mouth and the expression in her eyes. Someday they would talk about it. But not now.

Lizette turned and started for the door, but Jerome was still in front of her. "Excuse me, Jerome. I'm leaving now." She emphasized the last word. "My son needs me."

"Where will you go?" Stephen came around the table and took Lizette's arm, as if to keep her in the room.

Lizette hadn't thought that far ahead, but the answer was easy. "New Orleans," she said, pulling her arm from her father's grasp.

"Dr. Matthews?"

"That's right." She stepped around Jerome and out of the room. The door banged shut behind her.

Chapter Seventeen

Lizette knew her decision to leave River Oaks had come too late. Barbara had told her she was a fool, but if she was, she wasn't a big enough one to believe that Chris was going to be waiting for her with open arms. Knowing that didn't seem to have much effect on her right foot, however. It was lying heavily on the gas pedal of the van. Any minute she expected to hear the whine of a state police siren.

No, Chris wasn't going to welcome her with open arms, but he was going to be happy to hear she had come to her senses and left River Oaks behind. Perhaps he could comfort J.J., too. The little boy's face was still streaked with tears, although he was sound asleep in the back seat. Lizette knew J.J. would recover. Right now it might seem like the worst birthday ever, but someday he would understand. In the meantime, they would start a new life together somewhere, and J.J. would have the chance to grow up like the normal little boy he was.

Somewhere. Anywhere away from River Oaks.

Anywhere? No, she might as well be honest with herself. There was only one place that sounded right. California. Wherever Chris was. Even before she'd made the decision to leave River Oaks, she'd thought about nothing else. Why had it taken her so long to see that she could just walk out on her life at the plantation and be with him? All it had taken was opening a door and shutting it behind her.

There would never be another Chris. He had come into her life before she was ready for him. But maybe she never would have been ready if he hadn't come. It was a paradox.

Whatever the answer, she had to see him, had to tell him what had happened. Because deep down inside, deep, deep down, she still hoped. One miracle had occurred that evening. She had seen the truth about her life. Another one could happen.

"Where're we going?"

Lizette smiled at J.J. in the rearview mirror. "To see if Chris is home."

J.J. came up to sit in the seat beside his mother's, buckling his seat belt before he spoke. "He's not. He's at a race."

Lizette hit the steering wheel in frustration. "Darn. You're right. He'll probably be out all evening."

"I was cryin'."

"Yes, you were. Do you feel better now?"

"Everybody's mad at me."

After leaving the dining room Lizette had gone upstairs to find the little boy lying on his bed sobbing his heart out. She had scooped him up and carried him out to the van without changing so much as his shoes or hers. J.J. had fallen asleep almost as soon as she had started the engine. They hadn't had a chance to talk.

"Grown-ups do get mad," she tried to explain. "But it really wasn't your fault. You were tired, and I know that's not the way you wanted to spend your birthday. You shouldn't have made such a fuss, but I know you didn't really mean to. Your grandparents know it, too."

"Will Chris be mad?"

Lizette tried to imagine Chris getting mad at J.J. about anything. The image wouldn't come. "Not at all. He's going to be happy to see you.'' She was suddenly inspired. ''We'll find him at his race.''

''We can go?''

''We can. We will.''

They talked for the rest of the trip. By the time they turned off the interstate into the central business district of New Orleans, Lizette was feeling confident that J.J. would eventually put the incident at his birthday party behind him. She was also feeling anxious about seeing Chris.

It was quarter past seven by the time she found a parking space near where she thought the race was scheduled to begin. The Witch's Moonlight Run was an annual event and an excuse for New Orleans' runners to have some good-natured Halloween fun. Costumed runners milling nearby pointed to the intersection where race registration was being held for latecomers. With J.J. in tow, Lizette hurried to the area to see if she could find Chris.

Her heart sank. The race was well attended. Very well attended. And ninety percent of the runners were in costume. She would never find Chris in this crowd. She grabbed a Tweetie Bird clothed in a yellow plush sweatshirt teamed with yellow tights and running shorts. ''Where does the race end?''

By the time she finished handling Tweetie Bird's very polite pass, Lizette had discovered that there was a party after the race, and she had to be registered for the race to go, even if she didn't run.

She dug through her purse and paid the registration fees for both J.J. and herself. J.J. promptly pinned his number on his suit coat and announced he was going to run.

''You can't, sweetheart. I can't run with you. I'm still wearing heels.'' She pointed to her feet.

''Maybe Barbara will run with me!''

''Barbara?''

J.J. pointed into the crowd. Barbara and Paul were standing at the starting line. Apparently Paul had been tapped to be medic again. ''Hey, Barbara!'' J.J. yelled.

Barbara turned and saw them. She pushed her way through the crowd. ''What are you doing here?''

"I want to run!" J.J. answered before Lizette could. "Will you run with me?"

"I'm not running, but I know some people who are, and they have kids just about your age." She looked at Lizette, and her eyes were filled with questions.

"Go ahead." Lizette smiled her answers. "I may not be here when you get back, Barbara. I'm going to find Chris."

"Chris?"

"I'll tell you later." She kissed J.J. and watched him skip off with Barbara at his side. She was just glad his shoes had rubber soles.

Without J.J. to impede her progress she searched through the crowd gathering at the starting line. Chris was nowhere in sight, and minutes later, when the starting gun sounded, he still wasn't there.

Lizette was disconsolate. J.J. flashed by, talking as fast as he was running. She wondered if he would make the whole three miles. It would be a contest between his short legs and his boundless energy. She searched the faces of every man about Chris's height and weight. Many were disguised. There were Draculas and devils, animals and vegetables. A redhead was costumed as a giant New Orleans-style roach; a brunette sped by in an orange-and-black tutu. There was no sign of Chris. At least, not a Chris she could recognize.

She was about to give up and walk back to find Barbara when she saw him. He was dressed in green surgical clothes, but he'd made no other attempt to enter into the spirit of the race. As costumes went, it was a dud, but he was gorgeous anyway. Completely masculine and gorgeous and running right toward her.

"Chris!" Lizette bounced up and down and waved, but he ran past. The race official at the starting line was calling out times, and Lizette knew Chris hadn't heard her. She ran a few paces down the sidewalk and tried again. "Chris!"

By now he was yards ahead of her. She ran a little farther, her black alligator pumps hitting the pavement with a sharp click. "Chris!"

She saw his head swivel briefly over his shoulder. In the glow of the streetlights she could see his puzzled expression. He had heard something, but he hadn't seen her. Lizette knew the smart thing to do was slow down, stop and look for Barbara. She knew what Chris was wearing now; she wasn't going to lose him. For that matter even if she did lose him, she knew where he lived. It wasn't as if he were going to disappear from the face of the earth.

Why then was she suddenly in the middle of the street, kicking expensive high heels into the gutter?

"Lizette! You can't race barefooted!" Barbara materialized from the sidelines to stop her.

"Will you hold my purse?" Lizette didn't wait for an answer. She thrust the alligator bag that matched her shoes at an astounded Barbara and took off down the street.

She was one of the last runners to cross the starting line. A police car tooted at her, and the policeman waved. His job was to motivate the stragglers to do their best so the street could be opened for traffic flow as quickly as possible. Lizette wished she could tell him that he had nothing to worry about from her.

The asphalt was rough under the soles of her now-shredded stockings. Her feet weren't as tough as they'd been before Chris insisted she wear running shoes, but they were tough enough. The wind was chilly against her face, but she knew that wouldn't last. Soon she would be overheated, exhausted and footsore. She had to catch up with Chris before that happened.

Cautiously, she sped up a little. Her dress whipped around her legs, then clung. The River Oaks pearls bounced against her throat in rhythm with her feet slapping the pavement. Tendrils of hair that had been gathered in a loose knot on top of her head slipped out of their restraining pins to dance in front of her eyes.

She had never felt freer. She had never been happier, although she imagined that if the impossible happened and Chris still wanted her, what she was feeling now would be considered nothing more than a prelude to real happiness. For the first time she was running toward something instead of running away. She ran a little faster and found she felt even better.

She was passing people as she picked up speed. Two here, three there. The race was a rollicking Halloween parade. The costumes were delightful. In her growing euphoria she wanted to tell everyone how clever they were. Instead she pushed on. Past Goldilocks and the three bears, past Mr. Spock, past a spryly running cluster of grapes. On she ran, searching for Chris.

He was so far ahead of her that at first, when she caught the glimpse of green, she wasn't sure it was him. Apparently he had been warming up at the beginning of the race and now he had hit his stride. She wondered what he would say when he passed J.J.

"Mommy!"

She looked in the direction of the voice. J.J. and his companions were coming down the home strip on the other side of the neutral ground. Apparently they had tired, cut across and begun the run back without going all the way to the halfway point. She locked her hands over her head like a proud boxing champion to show him she was all right. Then she picked up speed.

She could do what J.J. had done. There was no shame in it. When she saw Chris coming up the other side of the road she could cut over, catch up and stay with him for the duration. There was only one problem with that. By now it was a matter of honor. She wanted to finish the race. Fair and square.

"Nice duds." A dragon or a lizard—Lizette wasn't sure which—saluted her as she ran past. "Hey, you've got no shoes!"

"I never learned to tie a bow," she called back to him, speeding onward.

She was approaching the bulk of the racers now. It was a sea of costumes, and since she had temporarily lost sight of Chris, she imagined he might be at the front of it. She concentrated on dodging runners, looking for holes and corridors to help her weave through the crowd. Her feet were beginning to ache. She wondered if she would be able to walk tomorrow. She envisioned herself in a hotel room with

J.J., her feet propped up on two pillows while they ate room-service hamburgers and planned the rest of their lives.

The rest of her life. She might go back to school. Marrying Julian had cut her education short. Hadn't Chris gone to a university in Santa Cruz? Maybe she'd go there, even if Chris didn't invite her to come to California. After this race she'd need a good orthopedic surgeon. And a podiatrist. And a psychiatrist...

"You forgot your shoes," Bugs Bunny reminded her as she surged ahead of a group of six cartoon characters running side by side.

"They give me blisters," she yelled over her shoulder.

It wasn't until the one-mile mark was far behind that Lizette realized she had taken her eyes off the runners rounding the bend to begin the trip back to the finish line. To her dismay she saw that Chris had made the turn and was well beyond her.

She had planned to let him know she was in the race when he passed her on the other side of the neutral ground. Now he might finish and head home before he even knew she'd been running behind him. That possibility gave her a new surge of energy. She rounded the corner and increased her speed. She had passed the largest block of runners and the way was fairly clear.

"Feet, do your thing," she muttered. She felt as if she were flying. The wind whistled through the folds of black silk whipping around her legs, and she imagined herself as a primitive parachute. Any minute she would rise above the crowd and go sailing backward, right into the Mississippi. At least the river ran toward the Gulf, away from River Oaks.

She wiped a hand across her forehead, trying to forget about the pain in her feet. Running on asphalt was not the same as running through a cane field. She was beginning to wonder if she would make the end of the race at all when she saw Chris in the distance. She was gaining on him. He was keeping a good steady pace, but he didn't seem to be in any hurry.

That was Chris, all right. He didn't want to win. He just wanted to run. No pretenses, no goals to meet, no jealousy of the winners. He'd overcome a lot to become that kind of person. She'd had a lot to overcome, too. Maybe he would understand.

She ran faster and passed the two-mile marker.

She wondered if she called to him whether he would hear her. It seemed worth a try. "Chris! Chris Matthews!" He didn't turn. She summoned up every bit of oxygen left in her body. "Hey, Doc!"

Other runners in front of her turned curiously to see who was yelling like a madwoman, but Chris didn't. Just when she thought she was going to have to give up, slow down and hope he'd stay around for a while at the end of the race, he turned.

He had the expression of a man who's been deep in thought and has just realized someone's been speaking to him. His gaze passed over her at first and then returned. His expression changed into the classic picture of a man in shock. She saw his lips form her name.

He slowed down so drastically that she caught up to him in a minute. "Hi," she said, breathing hard. "Remember me?"

He stared at her as if she'd just come back from the dead. Lizette was afraid she might just look like someone who had, too. The black silk dress was damp and clinging to her breasts and back; her hair was in complete disarray, half up, half down; her feet were bare. She hoped he didn't notice the last right away.

"Are the pearls real?" he asked finally, turning his attention in front of him again.

Under the circumstances, the question seemed strange, but she answered it as if it weren't. "They're the St. Hilaire pearls, so you never know. They could be plastic."

"Did you get lost on your way to a wake?"

"To a birthday party. J.J.'s."

"A black cocktail dress for a seven-year-old's birthday party?"

"He's a pretty special seven-year-old."

"Black silk and running sh—" Chris looked down at her feet for the first time. "Where in the hell are your shoes?"

"I hope they're at the finish line."

"You can't run on this road without your shoes." Chris reached out as if to grab her, but Lizette evaded him.

"Sure I can, Doc. I've just done about two and a half miles this way."

"Your feet will be ruined for life."

"I know this great doctor."

"He doesn't treat patients from Port Ascension!"

"Well, I'm not from Port Ascension anymore, so that won't matter." She stumbled over a crack in the road and winced as her toe struck a ridge.

"You've lost your mind."

"From what I hear, it runs in my family." She danced away from him as he made an attempt to grab her again.

"Stop fooling around, Lizette. You're going to get hurt!"

"Remember the Classic? You were sure I was going to get trampled. I ended up crossing the finish line at your side. And I was wearing flimsy little tennis shoes that day. I've got great feet. You ought to do research on my feet and use them as models for your patients."

He lunged for her again, succeeding this time in grasping her arm. "Slow down!"

"You're afraid I'm going to beat you!"

"I'm afraid the little men in straitjackets are going to come and get you."

"Don't you want to know why I'm here?"

"Not now I don't. Be quiet and watch where you're stepping."

Chris seemed so stern, so unreachable. Lizette realized that the events of the past hours had her wired for sound. She was running on adrenaline, and adrenaline could disappear at any moment. She wondered if she was going to crash. She wondered if J.J. was going to be cooped up in a hotel room with a crippled, despondent woman. Apparently the adrenaline—if that was what it was—hadn't disappeared yet; she smiled at the imaginary picture.

"I've left River Oaks for good," she said in a conversational tone punctuated by pants. She ended the sentence by stumbling again. Pain shot up her leg as it twisted under her.

Chris felt Lizette stumble and pulled her over to the side, as if to get her out of the way. "You'll walk the rest."

"I'm going to finish this race!" She jerked her arm from his hand and began to half hobble, half jog toward the huge digital clock marking the race's finish.

"Why?"

She wasn't sure why. Somehow the race marked the beginning of her life as a free woman. Maybe it was superstition, but she felt compelled to cross the finish line. Each step she took seemed to clear away some of the cobwebs of twenty-five years of training to be the perfect plantation belle. When she crossed the finish line she knew the real Lizette Stanhope St. Hilaire was going to emerge on the other side. And that Lizette could make Chris Matthews realize he couldn't live without her.

"You don't have to prove anything, Lizette. For God's sake, get out of this race!"

She stumbled again. Something sharp stung her foot. She had a feeling that if she looked down she'd discover it was bleeding. She looked straight ahead at the road instead, watching out for more booby traps.

Chris looked down at her feet and saw blood. She had cut her foot, yet she was still running. "Lizette, stop!"

"I'm going to run across that finish line," she declared. "You just watch me!"

She would, too. He knew from experience that her mind was very hard to change. "All right, Lizzie-love," he yelled, putting on a little speed to move ahead of her. "You can cross the finish line at a run." He stopped, grabbed her as she hobble-jogged by and scooped her off the road before she could say a word. "My run. We'll do it together!"

Lizette wove her arms around his neck and laid her head against his shoulder. "Put me down," she said, with no force.

Despite himself, Chris smiled. "Next time you get to carry me across."

The best part of his statement was the "next time." The tears that had been frozen for so long seemed to melt and drain away. She cleared her throat once, then twice. "Is there going to be a next time?" she asked huskily.

He didn't answer, but then, she couldn't blame him. He'd already run almost three miles, and now he had one hundred and ten pounds of woman in his arms. She wondered if Paul was going to have to treat them both.

They crossed the finish line amid cheers. Apparently no one thought too much about a doctor in surgical clothes carrying a barefoot woman in a black silk dress, not when Mary Poppins with an open umbrella and a human pop-corn popper throwing samples to the crowd crossing with them.

Chris slowed to a walk, veering off to an empty spot on the sidewalk before he stopped and set Lizette down.

"How'd we do?" she asked.

Chris ignored her question. "Sit down and let me take a look at that foot."

Meekly she did as she was told.

"This is a mess. When was your last tetanus shot?"

"About three months ago." She winced as Chris probed the cut.

"Whatever cut it—glass probably—is out."

"Does it need stitches?"

"I doubt it. Your feet are so tough they'd have to use a darning needle, anyway."

"I think I feel faint."

Chris stood. "Paul's here. I'll get him to clean it out for you and bandage it. When you get back to River Oaks, stay off it as much as you can for a few days. Then, if it gets swollen or feels hot, you'll need to see your doctor for treatment."

"I'm not going back to River Oaks."

"Where are you going?"

"That depends on Barbara, I guess."

"What are you talking about?"

Lizette pulled the remaining pins out of her hair and let it fall to her shoulders. "Well, if I can find Barbara in this crowd, I'll still have the keys to my van, my credit cards...and a hairbrush," she added, raking her fingers through her curls to try to restore some order. "Then I can go to a Holiday Inn or something. Otherwise it's the Salvation Army for J.J. and me. Does New Orleans have a Salvation Army?"

"There she is!" J.J. materialized out of the crowd with Barbara at his side. "Hey, Mom! Did you see me run?"

"You were great, sweetheart." Lizette opened her arms for J.J.'s hug.

"Great!" He stepped away from her and looked at Chris. Lizette expected J.J. to throw himself at Chris, but J.J. held himself back. "Hello, Chris," he said politely.

"Happy birthday, J.J."

"Thanks."

"Have you lost your mind?" Barbara sat down on the curb at Lizette's side. "What are you doing here?"

Paul came and stood behind Barbara, his hands on her shoulders.

"What's the fuss? I just thought I'd go for a run."

"In pearls and a cocktail dress?"

"I ran in a suit," J.J. said proudly.

"Lizette cut her foot," Chris told Paul. "She's going to need some medical attention."

Barbara put her arm around Lizette's shoulders, and the two women exchanged long looks. "You've left River Oaks for good?" Barbara asked softly.

Lizette nodded. "I suspect Jerome's going to make you an offer. If he does, make sure you ask for everything you want. I think he'll give it to you."

"What about you?"

"I've got what I want. My freedom, and J.J.'s, too."

Barbara looked up at Chris, then back down at Lizette. "Everything you want?"

Lizette shrugged. "I don't know."

Barbara stood up. "You don't have the right stuff to treat Lizette here, do you, Paul? She's got to soak that foot."

"That's what I was thinking, too," Paul said smoothly. "Chris, you'd better take her back to your apartment. You're closer than I am."

"J.J., Paul and I are going out for a pizza. Why don't you come with us, and then we'll drop you off at Chris's afterward?" Barbara suggested.

"Pizza?" J.J.'s eyes lit up. "Could I?" he asked Lizette.

Lizette looked at Chris for confirmation. Although she had seen him smile when he was carrying her, now his face was somber and unwelcoming. She felt suddenly weary, and her foot began to throb. Worse yet, the frozen tears that had melted so naturally during the race were threatening to overflow. Her adrenaline was all used up. She turned to Barbara. "I can take care of my foot without bothering Chris. Why don't you take J.J. over to Paul's when you're done eating, and I'll come and get him. I should be settled somewhere by then."

"Bring him to my house," Chris told Paul, ignoring Lizette's statement. "For birthday cake."

J.J. threw himself at Chris, and Chris's arms closed around him in a bear hug. "I'll see you later, son."

Barbara and Paul wasted no time spiriting J.J. through the crowd. Lizette stood, putting her weight on her uninjured foot and her toes. "You didn't have to do that."

"Let's go."

"I'm not going anywhere with you." Lizette lifted her chin. "I'm going to find a good hotel, and then Barbara and Paul can bring J.J. to me after your little birthday party. I'll let you know where I am." She started to limp in the direction of her van.

Chris scooped her up from behind and turned in the other direction. "My car's this way."

"Put me down." She threaded her arms around his neck and laid her head against his shoulder. She squeezed her eyes shut to seal in the tears.

They were almost at Chris's car before he said anything. "Why did you come here tonight, Lizette?"

"To tell you I've left River Oaks for good."

"Why?"

"I finally saw what *it* was and what I *wasn't*."

"And you wanted me to know?"

"Yes."

"So what are you going to do now?"

"Plan the rest of my life, I guess."

He shifted her so she rested more comfortably against his hip. "Did you think I might want to be included?"

"If I did, I've seen how crazy it was."

Chris carried her the rest of the way in silence. At his car, he set her on her feet and reached for his keys to unlock the door. "Did you think I was going to propose again?" he asked when they were driving toward his apartment.

"I don't know."

"I have a very firm rule about proposals. I only propose once, twice max, to the same woman. You've had your two chances."

She searched his profile and tried to figure out if the humor in his voice had been her imagination. She sniffed back tears. "Then I guess I wasted my time and ruined my feet for nothing."

"Maybe."

Chris left her in the car while he ran into a deli near his apartment, returning in minutes with a bakery box. At his apartment he picked her up once more for the climb up the stairs, leaving the cake in the car.

"Rhett Butler did this for Scarlett." Lizette snuggled as close as she could, wondering if this would be the last time Chris's arms were around her.

"I'm no Rhett Butler."

"And I'm no plantation belle. Not anymore."

"Who are you, then?"

"The woman who loves you." She felt him release a long breath.

He set her down at the door to his apartment and unlocked it, stepping aside so she could hobble across on her own. Chris passed her and went straight to the bathroom. She could hear him running water in the bathtub, and she hobbled after him.

"Sit here on the edge and soak your foot," he commanded.

"I have this hypothetical question."

Chris turned off the faucets and watched as she wiggled out of her panty hose. "What?"

"Suppose a man proposed to a woman twice, and suppose that woman said no, not because she didn't adore him, but because something stood in the way."

"That's not a question. He helped her settle on the bathtub's edge.

Lizette winced as she lowered her foot into the water. 'I'm not done yet. Suppose this woman finally realized that nothing had to stand in the way of her love for this man, so she fixed it so they could be together."

"That's still not a question." Chris leaned against the doorjamb and folded his arms.

"Then the woman went to the man to tell him, but he was still angry. He refused to propose again because she'd hurt him twice and he's not a masochist."

"I'm waiting."

"What should she do?"

"I'd say it depends."

"On what?"

"If she's still a nineteenth-century maiden at heart, she should go home and forget the man. If she's a twentieth-century, red-blooded woman, the answer is simple."

"Suppose you tell her the simple answer."

"She proposes to him." Chris pushed himself away from the doorjamb. In a moment he was gone, shutting the door behind him.

When Lizette finally emerged from the bathroom, the lights were off in Chris's apartment. She found him in his bedroom, lying on his bed with his hands folded under his head and moonlight playing across his face. He wore sweatpants and no shirt. She knew he had washed in the little bathroom off his bedroom, because she had heard the water running while she had stripped to soak in the bathtub.

She unwrapped her towel and watched his eyes roam her naked body. "This is the body of a twentieth-century woman," she said proudly.

"Looks can be deceiving." He turned on his side to watch her more closely.

"This time what you see is what you get."

"What do I get?"

"Me, if you'll have me. Forever. And I get you, if you'll give yourself to me. Forever."

"And do I get J.J., too?"

"Your son," she said with a nod.

"I'm going to California. Are you coming, too?"

"Try and stop me."

He held out his arms, and she was in them immediately. "Then you'll marry me?" she asked, wanting to be sure.

"Try and stop me."

"As soon as possible?"

"J.J. can give you away"

"I give myself away. All of me."

He kissed her then, and there were no more doubts. Later there would be time to talk, time to tell each other what they had learned. But for now, there was only time for love.

Epilogue

"Hey, lady, you all right?"

Barbara lifted her head and gave a reassuring smile to the sixth grader with the wrinkled brow. "I'm fine, honey. Just resting for a minute before we take the mules back to the barn."

"I can do it for you!"

"Well, now, that's just exactly what I had planned." Barbara watched the boy's face relax into a smile.

"Neat!"

"Choose a couple of friends who'd like to help, and then see if Big Jake will show you what to do." She coughed as the boy's quick departure raised a cloud of dust under the conical wooden roof of the grinding mill.

"Every sixth-grade boy in the river parishes is in love with you."

Barbara hadn't realized that Paul had come up behind her. She rose slowly and faced him. "I've noticed a sixth-grade girl or two trying to impress a certain orthopedic surgeon."

He put his arms around her, laughing in frustration as her well-rounded belly kept them farther apart than he wanted to be. He rubbed it. "How's my kid?"

"Champing at the bit, and so am I."

"You've got no business being out here doing this. You know that, don't you?"

"I'd go crazy waiting around to have this baby. I'm just supervising. The rest of the staff and the kids are taking care of all the work."

"Sophia asked me to try to make you rest. She says she's worried about you."

Barbara snorted, then burst into laughter at her husband's disapproving expression. "Okay, okay. Old habits die hard. Maybe she is worried."

"She's trying, Barbara, and so is Jerome. I even heard her telling some of the kids that were here last week about the St. Hilaire roses. And she was cutting one for each of them as she talked."

"You know, it's funny. As hard as the St. Hilaires fight every change we make, I think they're actually learning to like some of them. They can talk about River Oaks now to their hearts' content and there's always somebody to listen. The school kids eat up the stories about the Civil War."

"And I think they're glad to have the big house finally undergoing the restoration it deserves." Paul put his arm around Barbara's shoulders and began to steer her toward his car. They walked along the path in silence, content just to have a few quiet moments together.

Paul had driven the short trip home and parked beside Barbara's truck before he spoke again. "What would make your life perfect?"

For a moment she couldn't think of anything. She had the man she loved, and she was carrying his child. Her dream for opening River Oaks to the public had been fulfilled, and although the work was hard, she knew it was work she would always want to do. The house in front of her was a dream come true, too. It was a seven-room overseer's cottage moved from another plantation on the river, and she and Paul were restoring it to its former glory. She had everything she could ever have wanted. Almost.

"Lizette," she said finally. "I wish I could see Lizette more often. With the baby coming and all the work here..." Her voice trailed off. Both of them knew it would be a long time before they got to California to see Lizette, Chris and J.J. again. In the two years since Lizette and Chris had been married, Barbara and Paul had only found time for one short trip to Santa Cruz.

Paul nodded. "Well, Lizette could visit us here. Maybe it's time for her to come back for a while. Time to make peace."

Barbara turned to tell him he was wrong, to tell him that Lizette would never set foot on River Oaks again, not even for a visit, when a movement on the front porch caught her eye. Then she was out of the car running up the path, her arms open wide.

Paul slipped out of the car and watched Lizette and Barbara embrace, then he raised a hand in salute to Chris, who stood watching from the porch, his arm resting on J.J.'s shoulders.

The boy turned his face to Chris's. "Dad, can I go look around now?" he asked, unmoved by the tearful display of the two women.

"Just don't get too dirty. Your grandparents are expecting us to have dinner with them."

"I'll remember." J.J. gave Barbara and Paul a quick hug as he loped past them.

When he was almost to the grove of trees that separated the house from the cabin where Barbara used to live, J.J. stopped and stared at the grown-ups on the porch. The pristine white of Barbara and Paul's house sparkled brightly enough in the light of the late afternoon to hurt his eyes. He was too far away to hear what anyone was saying, but he knew enough about grown-ups to imagine that it was silly stuff.

They would talk about babies. First Barbara would talk about hers, and then his mom would tell Barbara she was going to have one, too. Barbara would ask why they had decided to come, and his mom would get that funny faraway look in her eyes. She'd say something like "I needed to come back more than I needed to stay away." He'd heard her tell his dad that last night. Then, if today was anything like last night, his dad would put his arms around his mom and hold her close, and they'd look at each other like they were in some kissy movie.

J.J. shrugged and started through the trees. For his part, he was glad to be back at River Oaks. Santa Cruz was neat, and he'd be glad to get home to his friends at the end of the week, but right now there were frogs to catch. And his grandmother St. Hilaire had promised him he could have anything he wanted for dinner. Maybe he'd ask for tacos.

* * * * *

TALES OF THE RISING MOON
A Desire trilogy by Joyce Thies

MOON OF THE RAVEN—June

Conlan Fox was part American Indian and as tough as the Montana land he rode, but it took fragile yet strong-willed Kerry Armstrong to make his dreams come true.

REACH FOR THE MOON—August

It would take a heart of stone for Steven Armstrong to evict the woman and children living on his land. But when Steven met Samantha, eviction was the last thing on his mind!

GYPSY MOON—October

Robert Armstrong met Serena when he returned to his ancestral estate in Connecticut. Their fiery temperaments clashed from the start, but despite himself, Rob was falling under the Gypsy's spell.

Don't miss any of Joyce Thies's enchanting
TALES OF THE RISING MOON,
coming to you from Silhouette Desire.

SD 432

WHITE LIES*
by
Linda Howard

Bestselling author Linda Howard is back with a story that is
exciting, enticing and—most of all—compellingly romantic.

Heroine Jay Granger's life was turned upside down when she was
called to her ex-husband's side. Now, injured and unconscious,
he needed her more than he ever had during their brief marriage.
Finally he awoke, and Jay found him stronger and more
fascinating than before. Was she asking too much, or could they
have a chance to recapture the past and learn the value of love the
second time around?

Find out the answer this month, only in
SILHOUETTE SPECIAL EDITION.

*Previously advertised as MIRRORS.

SSE452-R

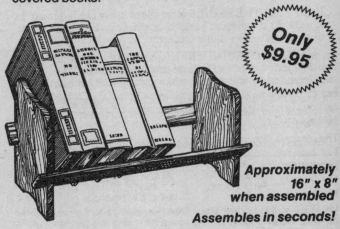

Silhouette Intimate Moments

Rx: One Dose of

```
┌─────────────────────────┐
│                         │
│         DODD            │
│      MEMORIAL           │
│      HOSPITAL           │
│                         │
└─────────────────────────┘
```

In sickness and in health the employees of Dodd Memorial Hospital stick together, sharing triumphs and defeats, and sometimes their hearts as well. Revisit these special people this month in the newest book in Lucy Hamilton's Dodd Memorial Hospital Trilogy, *After Midnight*—IM #237, the time when romance begins.

Thea Stevens knew there was no room for a man in her life—she had a young daughter to care for and a demanding new job as the hospital's media coordinator. But then Luke Adams walked through the door, and everything changed. She had never met a man like him before—handsome enough to be the movie star he was, yet thoughtful, considerate and absolutely determined to get the one thing he wanted—Thea.

Finish the trilogy in July with *Heartbeats*—IM #245.

Silhouette Special Edition

**In May, Silhouette SPECIAL EDITION
shoots for the stars with six heavenly romances
by a stellar cast of Silhouette favorites. . . .**

Nora Roberts
celebrates a golden anniversary—her 50th Silhouette
novel—and launches a delightful new family series, THE
O'HURLEYS! with *THE LAST HONEST WOMAN* (#451)

Linda Howard
weaves a delicious web of FBI deceit—and slightly embellished
"home truths"—in *WHITE LIES** (#452)

Tracy Sinclair
whisks us to Rome, where the jet set is rocked by a cat
burglar—and a woman is shocked by a thief of hearts—in
MORE PRECIOUS THAN JEWELS (#453)

Curtiss Ann Matlock
plumbs the very depths of love as an errant husband attempts
to mend his tattered marriage, in *WELLSPRING* (#454)

Jo Ann Algermissen
gives new meaning to "labor of love" and "Special Delivery"
in her modern medical marvel *BLUE EMERALDS* (#455)

Emilie Richards
sets pulses racing as a traditional Southern widow tries to run
from romance California-style, in *A CLASSIC ENCOUNTER*
(#456)

**Don't miss this dazzling constellation of romance stars in
May—Only in Silhouette SPECIAL EDITION!**

*previously advertised as *MIRRORS*   SSE05-1